T0167318

# OF POPES
AND KINGS

# OF POPES AND KINGS

JOE LE BLANC

# OF POPES AND KINGS

*This is a work of fiction. All of the characters, names, incidents, organizations, and dialogue in this novel are either the products of the author's imagination or are used fictitiously.*

*iUniverse books may be ordered through booksellers or by contacting:*

*iUniverse*
*1663 Liberty Drive*
*Bloomington, IN 47403*
*www.iuniverse.com*
*1-800-Authors (1-800-288-4677)*

*Because of the dynamic nature of the Internet, any web addresses or links contained in this book may have changed since publication and may no longer be valid. The views expressed in this work are solely those of the author and do not necessarily reflect the views of the publisher, and the publisher hereby disclaims any responsibility for them.*

*Any people depicted in stock imagery provided by Thinkstock are models, and such images are being used for illustrative purposes only. Certain stock imagery © Thinkstock.*

*ISBN: 978-1-4917-6483-1 (sc)*
*ISBN: 978-1-4917-6485-5 (hc)*
*ISBN: 978-1-4917-6484-8 (e)*

*Library of Congress Control Number: 2015905483*

*Print information available on the last page.*

*iUniverse rev. date: 04/06/2015*

# Acknowledgements

I wish to thank my wife, Midge for her patience and understanding. My thanks also go to the Acadians who gave me my birthright which I will proudly carry to my grave.

# Introduction

I was born in a time that may seem strange to most people who read this but I feel I should tell you how it was like at that time. I will limit my story of what happened during a brief time when the village I was born I and lived in went through a series of disturbing events that led to my realization that not all the people in the world are to be trusted.

My name is Danny and I was 14 years old in 1938 when these events happened. I am now retired after a fairly productive and enjoyable life.

I feel compelled to tell about the events that I'm certain have been incompletely and inaccurately recorded in history including a way of life and several murders that happened.

The following is a description of the place I lived in and the people who shared my lifestyle.

The small village of Seal Lake is located in the south west part of the province of Nova Scotia, Canada and the time is in the middle of the great depression.

The name of the village was derived from the beautiful lake upon whose shores it was located. This lake was in a way unique with its waters directly connected to the Atlantic Ocean via the Bay of Fundy. Twice a day the salt water flowed into the lake through a twenty foot wide inlet as the tide rose and reversed its flow outwards as the tide ebbed.

With an abundance of fresh water flowing in from the surrounding area, the lake with an area of approximately five square miles acquired a balanced brackish water quality that was favorable to many unusual life forms. One of these was the namesake of the lake, the seals.

The shores were abundantly forested by a mixture of evergreen and hardwood trees and it was unusual to see a building near the water.

The inhabitants were practical people who built their houses for convenience rather than for pleasurable views.

As one followed the dirt road, the trees obstructed any sign of the lake and the homes were all built very close to the roadside. Most of the homes were accompanied by barns and the fields that surrounded these buildings contained a few milking cows and in some cases an ox or two. Horses were a rarity and only the more affluent farmers had them. When an ox wasn't fit to work any longer, it could be fattened and used for food, a horse, on the other hand was only good for mink food.

If you wanted to eat in those days, you had to work. The farmland, although productive, was limited in available space and very rocky. Years of labor were invested in each tillable acre and each year produced a new array of rocks that had to be removed.

There was another source of food within reachable distance, the ocean. The men that pursued this means of livelihoods were individuals with courage and endurance. The fish were plentiful but the ocean was frequently unforgiving. The methods used to harvest the ocean were primitive but it was also non destructive to the environment or to the creatures of the sea. Each year produced a predictable catch and also a predictable loss of fishermen.

For those who chose not to farm, fish or work in the forests there remained one source of income, leaving home to work in the cities. Most of these workers were carpenters or laborers. Their families were left to fend for themselves with the help of the small amount of money sent home by the absent provider. The outside work required on the premises was done by the older boys.

Our education was provided in the immediate area in a one-room school house. To progress beyond the eight grades was extremely difficult for several reasons. The main reason was that most of the teachers didn't have the knowledge to teach above that level and the other reason was the need for the student to help at home. For those of you who complain about long school bus rides imagine walking a mile in a winter blizzard to a school heated by a potbellied stove. The school system was set up to accommodate the needs of the students to function in both English and French with equal time devoted to each. One teacher with as many as thirty-five students was hard pressed to keep all eight grades occupied

I must give credit to the fact that education alone was not an assurance of success. Intelligence is probably of equal, if not greater importance for gaining ones goals in any society and these people had their fair share of that ingredient.

The language spoken in the village was French with modifications acquired through the years. Even adjacent villages had acquired differences in their accents and word usage. The differences were not significant but served to reveal the village that an individual came from. Most of the residents were bilingual with English as the second language.

Seal Lake was only one of several villages that made up Saint Madeline Parish. There were no clear lines of demarcation between the villages except for arbitrary lines established by the school tax districts. Based on a power play by one district to gain more tax money for their school the Seal Lake school was located right on the district line.

Surrounding the parish were other villages that were of English origin. There was always a definite gap between the last French home and the first adjoining English village home. Religion, language and a mistrust of each other were some of the underlying causes of this segregation but a certain degree of discrimination was imposed by the English majority. This had prevailed since the French expulsion made famous by Longfellow's poem, Tale of Evangeline.

One of the two major authorities that controlled the lives of the community was the Roman Catholic Pope. Of course the Pope was not able to be present in all of the vast empire he ruled but he was represented by his underling, the parish priest. The priest didn't rule by an authority granted to him by any government but he ruled by the fear he imposed from the pulpit. When you live in a society where certain religious beliefs were ground into people's minds for many preceding generations it is not surprising that the person who has been appointed to guide you in such matters had power.

The pulpit was his main tool for intimidation. Imagine being told by this figure of immense standing that if you failed to follow Gods commandments and the rules of Church and died without absolution, which only he could grant, you would go straight to hell. This rhetoric was indeed frightening to most but particularly to the young.

The church was the most elaborate building in the parish. In this one area the French outdid the English whose houses of worship were pale in comparison to the elaborate churches these poor people erected.

The other entity that ruled was the King of England. The group that represented him in the minds of the people was the Royal Canadian Mounted Police. Most of the residents were law abiding and visits to the village and surrounding area by the RCMP were infrequent. The laws most often broken had to do with fish and game laws. When you live off the land a good feed of deer meat, in season or out, were a welcome treat.

The residents of Seal Lake were, for the most part, denied the luxury of electricity and telephone service. Only those who lived on the main road that skirted the village had access to these amenities and in any case most couldn't afford it. Mail was delivered once a day to the post office in Seal Lake, which was a house whose owner had a contract to receive and sort the items delivered by a mail man. Usually the mail room was in the kitchen. The mail deliverer would pick up the mail at the train station and distribute it to the several villages within his jurisdiction. Each household was responsible for picking up its own letters and parcels from the post office which for some was as far as a mile away.

The home I lived in was two storey's high with a full dirt floored cellar set on a rock foundation. The upstairs was devoted to bedrooms while the main floor had a kitchen, living room and a parlor. It was shingled by spruce shingles, including the roof that remained unpainted. The more fortunate people had a hand pump in the kitchen but most had to bring in their water by buckets full from the well. Bath rooms were nonexistent and outhouses were a necessity.

Heating, hot water and cooking were derived from a wood burning stove located in the kitchen. In the winter the fire would extinguish itself from lack of fuel at night and someone, usually one of the elders, would get up early to restart it. Without fire everyone would have to miss their breakfast of hot oatmeal. On a hot summer day the person cooking the meals was forced to sweat in an uncomfortable environment

Lighting was provided by kerosene lamps and in the early winter darkness I had to squint hard to do my homework.

The cellar was important as a freeze proof storage for farm produce.

Wood for the year was cut during the fall and winter and hauled out over snow–covered woodland roads on bobsleds pulled by oxen. A typical household burned ten to twelve cords of wood that, once delivered, had to be cut to length and split. Most of these tasks were accomplished by the male members of the household. The one item that reduced this effort was a device that blocked the wood by use of a circular saw powered by an automobile engine. The splitting was all manual labor done by swinging an ax. Chainsaws and other tools that make cutting wood easy weren't even known.

Entertainment was usually provided by residents who had self-developed talents. The main musical instruments played were fiddles and guitars. Pianos were the prize possession of the few who could afford them. In spite of the poverty that existed each of the larger villages or, in some cases, several smaller villages joined to build their own meeting halls. These were constructed by a joint effort of the villagers on a voluntary basis. An occasional traveling show would stop and for a nominal fee one could watch a magician or a silent film. The halls always had a large dance floor where the people could dance to the music of the local fiddle player. These dances were infrequent because according to the priest they were tools of the Devil. Without the Holy Father's permission one would risk his soul to everlasting hell by attending an unapproved dance.

With many families having carpentry tools available the boys were very adept at building replicas of almost anything for use as playthings. Sleds and skates were favorites made from old files and wood. Girls, sometimes with their mother's help, made rag dolls and outfits to dress them.

There was one modern source of entertainment which drew large crowds on Saturday night, the movies in town. For a bus fare of twenty-five cents and another quarter for the theater ticket one could watch Roy Rogers or Gene Autry save the west.

Sports were as important an item for the young as any other. Baseball was at the forefront in the boys' fun. Not being able to afford store—bought equipment they developed ingenious ways of making what they needed themselves. A ball, for instance, was created using a rag core placed in a discarded silk stocking, Tied repeatedly as it was inverted onto itself until the desired size was obtained. Of course the game had to be adjusted to accommodate the ball's lack of bounce and weight but it was baseball. Winter brought out the skates and sleds and if it was storming too hard there was always the radio, for those who were lucky enough to have one

The Nova Scotia Acadian lived a hard but satisfying life.

# 1

I was sitting on the deck of our home that faced the Seal Lake shore. My wife, Sandra and I had returned to the place of our birth after a fairly successful life away from our Acadian heritage and we were enjoying our retirement.

My thoughts wandered to a part of my life that had left a lasting mark on my personality. It's remarkable how the details of a way of life long gone by remain imbedded in ones mind.

The thing that came back to me in vivid detail was when, at the age of 14 I walked into the kitchen of the widow I did chores for and found her sprawled on the floor, dead. The horror that engulfed me was enough to last a lifetime.

My thoughts were interrupted by the sound of footsteps coming up the stairs that led from the yard to the raised deck. Distracted from my deep thoughts I looked up to see my friend, Bob. He walked to the chair next to mine and sat down. He was no longer the slim and trim Bob of long ago but except for being overweight he had maintained his keen mind and good health.

We have known each other since childhood and went our separate ways during World War 2.

He was a significant partner in the events that happened in 1938 which was the time when the memories I had been exploring occurred.

"I hope I didn't wake you up." He said as soon as he had made himself comfortable.

"I wasn't asleep but my mind was far away reminiscing about the adventure we shared years ago."

"That is certainly something that has remained in my thoughts although the years have dimmed some of the details."

While I listened to Bob a part of my mind had shifted to the reality of the changes that had taken place since 1938. At that time we were no longer thought of as children at the age of fourteen but rather we were accepted as young adults. Today I wonder if children are ever allowed to reach adulthood.

We began our voyage into the past by reconstructing the village and the surrounding area in our minds. Some of these details came to us in the aftermath of the tragic events that we encountered later.

The town of Rivemouth was a busy transportation center that handled the bulk of the goods coming in and going out of Southwest Nova Scotia. The town had once been one of the busiest ports on the Atlantic side of the continent and although it had lost much of its past activity it still was a vital link in the local economy. The harbor was long and narrow and protected in all directions from the fierce wind that frequently plagued the area. The port had been ideal for the shallow draft sailing ships of the past and was still adequate for the medium sized steamships of the day.

As one looked at the harbor activities from the vantage point of the top of a sloping hill, it was obvious that the main exports were lumber and fish.

Imports were a mixture of items that could not be produced in the relatively harsh environment of the area. The unloading of ships filled with flour, sugar and salt were amongst the frequently seen activities.

By far the most action was from the fishing vessels moving in and out of the sheltered area as the fishermen braved the rough Atlantic to gather the fish that was their livelihood.

The town itself was shaped like the harbor, long and narrow. Only the West side of the harbor was incorporated into the town leaving the East side in the county's domain.

The entire business district was located on the west side of the harbor and mostly on Main Street which ran parallel to the ship docking area.

There was an area close to Main Street that had been built during the town's prosperous era that was occupied by large very ornate, Victorian mansions.

These homes for the most part were lived in by the richer residents of the town although some of these beautiful homes were being converted into apartments and a few were being used as places of business.

It was in one of these buildings that the Royal Canadian Mounted Police detachment for the county was located.

Although situated in the town proper the RCMP had no jurisdiction in the town itself except when a federal crime was committed within its boundaries. Its authority extended to the remainder of the county.

The town itself was policed by a local force that had been in place since the town was incorporated.

There was no love lost between the two enforcement groups.

The house occupied by the RCMP detachment was one of the largest in the town. The grounds had been modified to provide parking for the mixture of Ford and Chevrolet unmarked automobiles that had one thing in common, they were all painted black. Included with the 5 motorcars was a powerful Indian motorcycle.

The building itself was three stories high and was arranged to provide living quarters for the unmarried officers and office space for the detachment personnel. An addition had been built onto the back main floor to provide for cooking, dining and entertaining.

Only detachment members except for the maid were allowed above the main level. The large elaborate front entrance had been converted into a reception area with a desk located next to the large staircase which was the main entrance to the two top floors. This desk was manned by a civilian secretary during normal work hours and by an assigned officer the rest of the time. A collapsible cot was kept in a closet for the late night duty officer to sleep behind a locked front door. The remainder of the main floor was divided into an Inspector's office, three Sergeants' offices, an interrogation room and a large room where the lower—ranking police had their desks.

Communication was provided by telephone, personal contact and mail. The Inspector had a direct line to his office and all other calls were received at the front desk and directed via a switch board to the desired recipient. Actually the incoming calls to report law violations were infrequent as most of the people didn't thrust the police and phones in the rural areas were few and far between. Of course serious crimes were reported promptly but these were not frequent occurrences and the more minor offences were revealed to the police by people motivated by some personal quirk.

It was therefore unusual to find many of the 11 assigned officers, one Inspector, three Sergeants, two Corporals and five Constables present when the detachment was fully manned. One constable was scheduled for transfer and this created a position to be filled after he left.

The officer in charge, Inspector James Connally was the only one who, along with the secretary, Alice White, was readily available in the office during standard hours. The rest were out in their automobiles enforcing the law or in and out of the office recording their efforts or getting instructions on where to go on their next assignment.

Although Inspector Connally was in charge of the detachment, his efforts were mostly dedicated to the administrative operations of the unit. Paul Naples was the senior operations officer and he had control of all outside assignments. The two remaining Sergeants were assigned areas of approximately the same size that covered the entire county and each had a Corporal as an assistant. The Constables were used by either group on an as needed basis. Sgt. Naples, hands on type, who was known to get involved in many of the investigations and at times, would overrule his subordinates. He was not well liked.

There were four Constables and the two Corporals who lived in the headquarters building as they were single. Some of the disadvantages of serving in the RCMP were the policy of frequent transfers and the tendency of not allowing assignments close to a person's hometown. The three sergeants and the Inspector lived in single family homes. Inspector Connally and Sgt. Naples owned their homes and the other two leased theirs.

4

Inspector Connally's home was located a few blocks from headquarters and was a modest one storey building. He and his wife lived alone and were not known to be great entertainers. John was a tall man with a gaunt build, steel blue penetrating eyes and thinning light brown hair. At 51 years he was still a man to be reckoned with. His background belied the position he held but even the most able sometimes get caught in a situation that cuts short a rise to the top. He had adjusted to the role of detachment leader and was looking forward to retirement. He still maintained ties to his former colleagues who had continued up the ladder and was a particularly good friend of Senior Inspector Maurice Levesque who was stationed in Ottawa and was part of an undercover group that investigated RCMP oversights. One of John's peculiarities was that he never drove an official auto while on duty. He was always chauffeured by one of his subordinates.

Sgt. Naples was in his twenty fifth year in the force. He was tall, had a muscular body that didn't show his 46 years except for a slight bulge at his waist and a tinge of gray in his jet black hair. His jovial face hid his tendency to lose his temper when countered by anyone he considered his inferior. He was a strict boss who allowed little room for error from his crew. He lived in a home that rivaled the best in Rivemouth. It was built in the same time frame as the RCMP headquarters but was much more elaborate. The Sgt. and his wife Mary were frequent entertainers and their home's interior decor was well suited for that purpose. If one happened to wonder how Paul Naples could afford such lavish surroundings it was only necessary to ask. The people in the know said his wife had inherited a large sum and his RCMP salary was insignificant in comparison.

Rivemouth was proud of their police force which was completely separate from the RCMP. The lines of jurisdiction were clearly defined and although there was no need for confrontation between them they also had no great respect for each other. Police Chief Ronald White headed up the town police that consisted of Assistant Chief Richard Beacon, Detective Sam Gleason and seven constables.

The town only provided three automobiles for the police unit so most of the policing was done on foot. Chief White had insisted on having a small powered boat to assist in harbor law enforcement and the town had reluctantly agreed. The building from which they operated was close to the main commercial dock. It was a single story turn of the century structure that had once been a warehouse. In its converted form it contained four offices and a makeshift jail in the back. Major Law violations were few and far between and Chief White was comfortable with his troop. Only Detective Gleason had any law enforcement training from a recognized source. He had served for a few years with the RCMP and had chosen to return to Rivemouth to be close to his ageing mother. The rest of the force had been chosen by either a political or family connection and there was a degree of corruption in how the law was enforced.

Main Street was the location of all the major stores. The three clothes' stores were owned by Jewish proprietors and one of them, Marty Cohen, had equipped a truck to vend in the rural areas. There were two Department stores that included food as part of their inventory and one store that sold groceries exclusively. This grocery store, run by Jack Lacy, also delivered goods to the many rural stores that resold to the local residents

The busiest store in town was the government liquor outlet. It was the only place where one could legally buy alcoholic beverages. There were no taverns or bars and even the restaurants were dry. Of course there were other ways to obtain liquor but they were all illegal. One could brew his own beer or distill his own moonshine but the most popular method was by buying from the local bootlegger. His supply was from the government store to which he added a reasonable increase in price and which he sold at his back door or in a room where his patrons could sit, argue, and drink. The bootlegger's only risk was an unexpected raid by the police which would cost him his liquor supply, a few days in jail and the loss of business until he could reorganize.

Access to Rivemouth by people without their own automobiles was provided by a one vehicle bus line that was located in the rural area and made one round trip a day except on Sunday and the Canadian National Railway that passed through Seal Lake at approximately 5:00 P.M., Monday thru Friday.

Saturday included an additional bus night run and Sunday was of course a day of rest. With money in short supply the bus was seldom overloaded except for the Saturday night trip when the younger crowd went to the movies. The few people fortunate enough to own their vehicles would supplement their income by taking passengers to town for twenty-five cents round trip.

The rural area surrounding Rivemouth was sparsely populated except along the shore line. There were several inland villages that were located alongside rivers. Most of the best land was occupied by people of British ancestry. The French Acadians had been deported in the eighteenth century and those who managed to regain a foothold in the province had to take what was available. This resulted in an unusual distribution of segregated villages. These were made up of English-speaking Protestants and French-speaking Roman Catholics. The villages were not only separated by language and religion but also by distance. There were very seldom next-door neighbors with different ethnic origins. The only interchange between the two was the occasional exchange of goods such as farm produce.

The town was less segregated than the rural areas but the Acadians were on the low end of the economy and tended to associate with their own kind. An area where the Acadians excelled was in the churches they worshiped in. These were generally elaborate in both their architecture and decor. Outside the town limits the protestant houses of worship were more practical but the French churches were marvels to behold. Certainly for poor people they didn't economize when it came to creating a path to heaven

"Although the town didn't seem important to us during our initial involvement in the events that shook our village, it and its occupants certainly contributed to the ultimate conclusion." Bob said.

"I feel that the affair in town would never have been solved if it hadn't been intertwined with what happened here. Let's look at the areas involved beyond the town proper and see if my observations fit."

With both of us in agreement we proceeded in our memories along the road that led from Rivemouth to the village where we lived.

We traveled south west from town on the main road, Route 5 that meandered along the ocean shoreline; the first villages encountered were occupied by the English. The initial indication that one was about to enter the French village of St. Agnes Bay was by going through an uninhabited section followed by the beginning of a new village with houses that were basically the same as the ones previously encountered. The final clue that you had arrived was the diminished distance between homes followed by the appearance of a spectacular church that was identified by a large sign, Saint Agnes Catholic Church. The church had two tall steeples that overlooked the area. The peaks reached at least sixty feet above ground and a huge bell was mounted in the right tower. Branching out from the main road were roads that led to other villages that formed part of the Parish. Some went inland while others connected to settlements located on points that jutted out into the Bay of Fundy. The church was located in St. Agnes Bay which was considered the elite part of the Parish.

Continuing southerly was the reverse of the approach with the gradual thinning out of residences until an unoccupied area was reached. If one kept going the start of an English village would soon become evident.

Saint Agnes Parish was made up of six communities. St. Agnes Bay was the largest and most sophisticated of the group with the Doctor and Priest living close to the church. The school, also close to the church, was taught by Catholic Nuns and was the only one in the Parish that consisted of more than one room and offered a high school diploma. First thru eight grades were taught in one room and ninth to twelfth in the second room. There were two stores that served the area with groceries, hardware and some clothing. One store also sold automotive necessities such as gasoline, lube oil and limited repair services. Each of the remaining five villages had their own schools, small private home grocery outlets and meeting halls that were used for entertainment and village meetings. Needless to say, St. Agnes Bay residents considered themselves the cream of the crop.

Stretching along the East side of St. Agnes Bay village was a long lake named Seal Lake. Changes had been made that had converted it from a fresh water body into a brackish water lake. The lakeside farmers had deepened the river that emptied into the ocean so that at high tide a rowboat loaded with salt hay could be floated into the lake. With the adding of ocean water twice a day the lake acquired a new equilibrium through the years that became the preferred swimming place for the youngsters of the area.

On the east side of the lake that was four miles long stood two of the villages that formed part of the Parish. Access to these villages, North Seal Lake and South Seal Lake, was by Seal Lake Road that veered off the main road north of the church, looped around the lake and rejoined the main road at the lake's south end. At this southern intersection the side road crossed and became Belle Pointe Road that led to the village of Belle Pointe. This road looped along the shoreline and rejoined itself a short distance before returning to Route 5.

The two remaining parts of the Parish were located north of the church and were both on the ocean side. Marsh Road, which cut Westerly from Route 5, was appropriately named. It began in a gentle rise which ran for about one mile where it crested and then went downhill to a large salt hay marsh. Hay Marsh village occupied the area from Route 5 up to the marsh crossing. Spread out in a panoramic view from the hill crest was a vast marsh of salt water hay with a road crossing it and disappearing into a crevice that had been cut into a cliff.

The island was called Isle a Joe and the village located on it was Le Village a Joe. The island had a secure harbor and was the fishing center of the Parish. It also was the richest part of the parish although not on the same social level as St. Agnes Bay.

Belle Pointe was on the lowest scale both economically and socially but the residents managed to keep their heads held high when they went to church on Sunday.

The population of the parish was approximately 1000.

"I used to think that it was a long way from here to town but with the new highway its only minutes away."

"The passage of time has resulted in a lot of changes, that's for sure." Bob answered.

# 2

I was named Daniel Adolph Pottier when I was born on April fifteenth, 1924 and soon acquired the nickname Danny. I was the oldest son in a family of two boys and two girls, a small family for that era.

My oldest sister, Maggie, was serving as an all-around helper for Mrs. Muise who was about to give birth to her eighth child. Although my mother, Mary, wished that Maggie was home on laundry and floor scrubbing days she was pleased that there was one mouth less to feed.

Boys were not expected to do the chores traditionally done by women so Betty, my youngest sister was force to pitch in at the tender age of twelve. The only help available to me was my brother Richard who, at ten-years of age was the baby. Richard, or Dick, which is the name he went by was in general a hindrance rather than a help.

My father, Louis, was working in Halifax on a new school project. The family got to see him once a month if he could afford travel fees and during his short stays he gave us advise on what had to be done before his next visit. My dad was missed a lot, both for the loving care he provided to the entire family and especially when major farm tasks came up.

He had taught me that there were rewards, however sparse, in doing what was expected and punishment if I erred. In spite of only completing the fifth grade, Louis was very knowledgeable in world affairs. He sometimes startled me with his keen observations about the possible war in Europe. On his last trip home he had made sure that our potato field, that normally yielded one hundred bushels, was free of bugs and properly cultivated. He must have been pleased with Dick and my efforts because he took us to the local store and bought us each a Pepsi, something that rarely happened.

My mother was a saint in disguise. She had a frail build, stood five feet six inches tall, and had dark hair that was beginning to turn gray and soft brown eyes. There wasn't an ounce of fat on her body. Her harshest dealing with any of the children was to make us ashamed of not having done our best. The only thing that I found questionable about her behavior was her inordinate belief in the church. To her, the catholic religion was a guarantee of an everlasting life in heaven and the priest was, like the pope, infallible.

We all had to attend mass on Sunday and were never excused from the periodic lessons given by the priest for boys and by the nuns for girls. I understood my mother's efforts to have us become true believers like she was but I could never accept the dictatorial position of the priest and the religion he represented. Having my ear grasped by the parish priest as leverage to strike my head against an oak bench because I failed to answer a question correctly during catechism lessons didn't help my beliefs.

The house we lived in stood on a rock foundation which was riddled with holes. It had a full basement with a dirt floor. For summer living this was fine and even helped cool the house on hot days and prevented rotting of the main floor but with the cold days of winter the cellar was needed to store crops. In the fall we banked the foundation with either dry seaweed or sawdust that was held in place with boards. The dirt floor provided enough heat and moisture to maintain an ideal storage space for root crops and apples.

It was June 29, 1938 and I was graduating from the eight grades. Today was the last day of school in all the parish schools and for some, like me it was the last school day that we expected to attend in our lifetime.

The school district adjacent to our school district was in Belle Point. Two girls who had completed grade eight and would now become full time house keepers, either for their mothers or in another home where help was needed. Other students who had been held back for low grades but had reached the mandatory age of 14required by law before they could quit were happy to leave. In their minds education was a waste of time.

The younger children would spend the two summer months enjoying their favorite pursuits while those old enough to help at home had to split their effort between fun and work.

The teacher, Mrs. Edna D'Eon, had turned in her resignation to the village elders. She could no longer keep up with the twenty-plus students that she had taught for years and was reluctantly leaving her position to younger more capable hands.

James Babin, the unelected leader of Belle Pointe, was faced with the task of finding a new educator for the school. With a budget that only allowed $250 a year for the teacher's salary he knew that he would have to settle for someone who didn't have the best qualifications. He had pleaded with Mrs. D'Eon to stay another year but that plea had been rejected. At the next village meeting a maximum of six dollars was allocated to advertise for Mrs. D'Eon's replacement.

On that same date the school I attended, South Seal Lake School was also ending its school year. The school was typical of the Acadian village schools of the era. It was a one story building that consisted of a single room with two separate front entrances, one was for girls and the other was for boys. Both doors led to enclosed hallways equipped with wall hooks for the students to hang their excess clothes. At the far end of each hall was a door that entered into the main room that was furnished with four rows of seats with attached desks. The two entrance walls formed a narrow space in which an elevated platform contained the teacher's chair and desk at the front of the class. There was a large window that overlooked the front school yard and gave the teacher ability to monitor her students during recess.

In the center of the room, with two rows of desks on each side, was a pot bellied stove which was the sole source of heat. Water was supplied by a bucket mounted on a stool with a tin dipper hanging on a hook nearby.

Selected students were assigned to keep the stove heating and the water bucket full. Toilet facilities were provided by two

13

separate outhouses, one for girls and one for boys. The school yard was graveled in front with the back left in its normal state. The subjects taught were split into two categorize, some taught in French and some taught in English. This was the environment in which Mrs. Vacon was dismissing her class.

The morning had been spent doing normal school activities and after lunch the teacher, Mrs. Amy Vacon, proceeded to give out certificates to the individual students starting with the first grade. By the time she reached the eight grade students, the highest grade she could teach, there were only two students left, Bob Muise and me. We were both fourteen—year-old and were destined to follow in our father's footsteps. With our formal education over we would spend a few years at home until we found an occupation that suited our abilities and desires.

Mrs. Vacon addressed us with a certain degree of sadness. She told us that we had shown above average learning ability and she felt it was unfair that our minds would be wasted on the vocations that were available. I had an opposite view from hers, I was finally free of the burden of school homework and would have more time to do my chores and pursue the pleasures of youth.

"I'm proud of your accomplishments and wish you had the opportunity of continuing on to a higher level of schooling." She said, as she looked directly at us. "I'll miss you both but I'm sure you feel you've had your share of this part of your young lives. I have enclosed a note to your parents in these envelopes in which I encourage them to seek ways to have you enhance your formal knowledge." A broad smile spread over her face as she added. "I'm especially going to miss that warm, sizzling fire you have kept us warm with through the heating season, Bob." As she handed us our envelopes, she felt that her hopes would not be realized but then she thought, "I could be wrong this time."

Bob and I left the school and headed towards Bob's home which was only a short distance from the school. As we walked I said. "Bob, I'm going to look for a part time job now that I'm done with school. There's always someone looking for help around their farm but I hope to find something that is regular. It's nice to have money every week to pay for going to town."

Bob thought for a moment and replied. "I just heard that the widow Le Have lost her helper, Tom, who was doing her chores. Maybe you could apply to take his place. She pays well and on schedule and according to Tom she's easy to work for."

"You know", I said, "that's a good idea, I'll stop by tomorrow and ask if she still needs help. The way she looks I'd almost work for her for nothing."

We walked slowly towards Bob's and took in the sights. It was a sunny day and the nature of how the people lived was visible in all directions. The road was graveled and hardly wide enough for two vehicles to pass without one taking the ditch. The houses were mostly built close to the road and they were basically all the same design. They were all made out of wood and shingled with spruce shingles including the roof and very few were painted. Each had a front door which was seldom used and a back or side door that opened into the kitchen. Most homes were accompanied by a barn setting to one side and behind the house.

The property lines were clearly marked by stone walls or barbed wire fences. Cleared fields surrounded the living areas and these were divided into gardens and pastures. The animals in the pastures were either cows or oxen with a few horses.

We arrived at Bob's home and entered the pathway that led past the back door of the house to the barn. The path was wide enough to take an ox wagon and could accommodate an automobile if the surface was dry. We walked past the house and entered the barn where we had spent many hours discussing our many common interests

The barn layout was typical of the ones in use in the area. It was three stories high and approximately 26 x 30 feet at the main floor. These barns were built with a cellar accessible from the outside so that the material used to fertilize the crops was easily removed by oxen or horse cart. The source of the fertilizer was the milk cows, oxen and horses manure and any other biodegradable ingredients that would feed the crops during the short growing season. One of the standards was the carcasses of surplus alewives fish caught in the spring.

The hay mow was located above the main floor and the hay could be piled up to the peaked ceiling as there was no floor separating the top two stories. Salt marsh hay and field hay were stored separately and these would be mixed in proper proportions at feeding time. The front had two doors, one large enough to allow a loaded hay cart to enter for unloading and the other for frequent access by both humans and farm animals.

The stall area took up about one forth of the main floor and the remaining area was used to keep tools out of the weather. Bob and I had created a small private sitting area in a rear corner where one of the two windows was located

We had found an old table and three chairs that had been discarded and with a little rearranging our hideaway was created. Seated at our table by the window we could see the hay field grass that was waving in the soft June wind.

Bob said. "School just let out in time for the first cutting. Are we going to share our hay harvest like we did last year, Danny?"

"Yes," I replied, "and it looks like we'd better get started on yours soon. Let's start tomorrow after I see the widow about working for her."

Bob agreed and as I left he said. "Don't get lost over there because I'm going to need your help." be harvested

On my way home I reviewed the things that I had to do from now until winter set in. My responsibilities in addition to doing daily chores included harvesting the crops, getting the wood for the following year and generally preparing the house for the coming winter. The rest of the family would help when they could. Equipped with no more than hand tools and a wheelbarrow I would dig up and cart the entire crop to the proper bins in the basement. The hard work ahead was not pleasant to look forward to but how could I resent doing what must be done?

The following morning I did my chores, ate breakfast, cleaned up and headed for Diane Le Have residence. The air was crisp and clear and showed every indication of being a perfect haying day. The distance from home to the widow's house was approximately one mile so I had plenty of time to think over what I would ask as pay if she hire

# 3

Diane was cleaning her kitchen where she lived alone since her husband Jacque had been lost at sea 18 months ago.

As she worked, she remembered vividly the cold winter morning when the owner of the Jolie Marie, the boat that Jacque fished from, came to her door accompanied by the parish priest, Father Frotten. Both men had grim looks fixed on their faces and Remi, the owner tearfully blurted out, "We lost them all," as he relinquished all control over his emotions and did what few men of that day did, he cried like a baby.

As the impact of what she had been told sank in she went into a state of shock and as she started to crumple to the floor Father Frotten grabbed her and gently guided her to a chair. Her thoughts were interrupted by a timid knock on the back door. Thankful for any interruption that broke up those painful memories she walked to the door and opened it.

Standing there was a teenage boy of medium height and muscular build; her first thoughts were about how innocent he looked with his shy almost embarrassed expression. Realizing that some-one had to speak first she asked. "What can I do for you?"

Before he had time to answer she added. "Aren't you Danny Pottier?"

I hadn't expected to be recognized and was momentarily dumfounded. Bob and I had admired the widow from a distance but I didn't expect that she would have the faintest idea I existed. Quickly gathering my thoughts I answered in as polite a voice as I could muster. "Yes, Mrs. Le Have, I'm Danny Pottier and I came to see if you needed some work done around the house on a regular basis?"

Diane took an immediate liking to Danny. Wanting to make him more at ease she invited him into the kitchen and had him sit at the table. "I'm making myself a cup of tea, would you like one with me?"

I nodded in agreement and at that instant I lost my heart to the beautiful, young widow. A pot of water was boiling on the stove and Diane was soon making the tea.

Tea in these days was made strong by simply placing the leaves in the water and waiting until the right strength was reached.

As we waited, she continued our conversation. "First, if you're going to work for me I want you to call me Diane, just as if you were my younger brother. My second requirement is that you be very punctual in the time you arrive and leave. I would expect you to begin at 9AM on Monday and finish at 12:00 noon and follow the same schedule on Thursday. The work will consist of keeping me supplied with firewood and a supply of water fetched from the well and stored in the barrels in the porch. There'll also be yard work and snow shoveling but only during the time you are scheduled to work. As I will be paying you for those specific hours I will expect you to be here for the entire period even if all the work is done. Do you think $1.00 a week will be a fair wage?"

As she waited for my answer she went to the stove and took the pot with the brewed tea to the table where she placed it on an iron trivet. She brought two large mugs, a can of evaporated milk and a bowl of sugar from the pantry and told me to help myself.

I sat as if in a dream but my mind was really in overtime. Not only had I found a job that would give me spending money but I would be working for the most beautiful woman in the village. "Diane," I said hesitatingly, "I'll be happy to work for that amount. When do you want me to start?"

"Monday will be fine, now let's relax and enjoy our tea."

We sat and talked about what was happening in the village and how the crops were fairing. When my cup was empty I excused myself and left. If I had a pair of wings, I would have been flying. The dollar a week would be more than enough to pay for a Saturday night in town for a movie with plenty to spare. A thought occurred as I walked towards Bob's where we were scheduled to cut hay. "Why was Diane so exact in the schedule I was to work?"

Bob spotted me as I turned towards the house and greeted me. "Why are you so late? We should have been in the field cutting a half hour ago."

I was almost ready to fall apart in my haste to tell my friend the good news about my new job. "Bob, Diane—I mean Mrs. Le Have, hired me and she's going to pay me $1 a week and all I have to do is perform chores two mornings a week." Bob said. "Lucky you, don't forget who gave you the idea. Well, let's get started."

The reason these two young men had to cut the hay as well as do many other tasks that were normally done by adults was because their fathers were in Halifax working as carpenters on a new school. This was common practice during this time period and the youngsters didn't resent the need to help their families live in comfort, however marginal that comfort was.

The scythe blades were already sharpened and mounted on their wooden curved frames. I loosened the handles on mine and adjusted their positions to give the scythe the optimum shape for my build. Using a scythe was a tiresome task and every trick of the trade was utilized to lighten the load. Keeping the blade sharp was of utmost importance and each mower carried his own sharpening stone to ensure this was the case.

Bob started off the first cut at the corner of the field following the edge until a complete circuit of the field was completed. I followed 10 feet behind cutting my own row that commenced where Bob's row ended and the combined width was about 8 feet. We would continue to circle in a diminishing diameter until the entire crop was lying in the sun to dry.

The next day would be spent turning the hay to ensure complete drying but on the following day, Sunday, no work would be done regardless of the weather predictions.

Working on that Holy day was equivalent to digging oneself deeper into the fires of hell according to Father Frotten. The earliest the hay could be raked into piles and carried into the barn on poles designed to slip under each pile was Monday afternoon.

I was scheduled to start work for Diane that morning.

# 4

After Diane's talk with Danny on Friday her thoughts wandered back to the past. She remembered meeting her husband to be, Jacque, because her mother insisted she continue her education at the St. Agnes Bay School. She had completed the eight grades at North Seal Lake School at the age of thirteen and her only option to continue her education was to attend the school taught by the Nuns in St. Agnes Bay. Jacque was starting the tenth grade and as luck would have it; his seat was right behind hers. Their friendship developed slowly during the 10 months they were seated close together and it had developed into a love affair that peaked when they were married in St. Agnes church by Father Frotten.

One instance that helped cement their relationship was when Jacque challenged the teacher, Sister Greta, for slapping Diane across the face when she answered a mathematic problem incorrectly. They had both been expelled but were allowed to return to class after apologizing to the teacher. That instance was also the key factor in both Diane and Jacque ending their formal education at the end of the school year. It also was instrumental in Diane beginning to doubt her deeply ingrained belief in the religion she was brought up in.

Diane started her teen years as a short and skinny girl who always seemed ill at ease amongst her peers. As she grew older, she blossomed out into a petite, very beautiful young woman and along with her improved looks she attained the self—assurance she had lacked. Her long black hair along with her sparkling dark-brown eyes would captivate you with a single look. Her bond with Jacque was never broken. Most of the single men in the Parish and even those from other areas tried to lure her away but all their efforts failed.

At the age of 18 she married Jacque and they moved in with an old widow named Gloria Surette. In those days elderly people with no close relatives would offer their property to couples in return for in home care until the god took them away. Gloria only survived for one year and the house and land became Jacque's. As Diane continued tidying up she thought of the old furnishings they had inherited with the house and how they compared with the items she had acquired in the interim. Jacque hadn't contributed greatly to these improvements as his salary in his chosen trade, a fisherman, was meager during the 30's. They had managed to live comfortably until that cold wintry day when she learned of Jacque's untimely death in January, 1937,

Now on her own she was at her wit's end on how she would survive. At least she had no children to feed and the boat owners had provided a small insurance policy for each crew member.

The villagers collected donations and the church donated the Sunday collection on the week after the disaster. Equipped with this she started to gather herself to start a new life. "If only I was 14 again." She thought as she began to return to reality. She realized she had completed all the things she had set out to do while she daydreamed and it was time to reenter the new world she had created for herself.

# 5

Monday morning arrived with the sun shining brightly in the cloudless eastern sky. I had risen early so that I could be finished with my chores in time to start my new job at Diane's. My first thoughts were on how the weather had co-operated in giving Bob a good crop of preserved hay.

With breakfast eaten and the cow, Molly, fed and milked, I set out to start my new venture. I had never owned a watch so I had to guess my arrival time by the interval I knew it would take to walk from home to Diane's. Arriving a few minutes early I knocked at her kitchen door and was immediately let in.

"We will always start the morning's work by having tea or milk, whichever you prefer." Diane said as she set the teapot on the table. She was dressed in a loose-fitting cotton dress covered with a brightly colored flower pattern. As she leaned over to fill her cup with tea my mind turned somersaults. I imagined the dress dissolving into invisibility and Diane standing there naked. I blushed and quickly turned my thoughts to a less intriguing thing. Diane pretended not to notice my obvious reaction and took her seat.

"You were three minutes early," she said as she stirred her tea, "and although that's only a short time I wouldn't want you to vary your arrival and departure times significantly. The solution is contained in this box. It contains a Dollar watch that belonged to Jacque and it still keeps good time as long as you wind it once a day. Consider it a starting day bonus."

I was overcome with gratitude. None of my friends had one and the one my father had was broken. I suddenly felt like I had reached adulthood. "Thank you very much Mrs. Le Have— I mean Diane I'll take good care of it."

We drank our tea slowly and I began to wonder when my work would start. As if she had read my mind Diane said "Danny, I want you to know that part of your job is to keep me company. I have several friends but none of them are aware of what goes on in the village like you. Bear with me and you will soon understand the full meaning of what I need from you."

I had listened attentively but to my mind there was much that was unclear.

Diane rose from her chair and put on a light sweater. "Come with me and I'll give you an idea of what your main duties will be." I got up from my seat and followed Diane out the back door. She led me to the road which in this case was at least 100 feet from the house." I'll expect you to keep the brush on each side of the entrance cut back to allow an automobile to enter without getting scratched." She said. She then followed the path to an old barn located behind the house that had a large swinging door that was secured by a padlock. Removing a key from her sweater pocket she unlocked the door and it slid quietly open. Immediately behind the door was a space large enough to park a large motor vehicle. "This space must always be kept open except when you are here using it as part of your work. As you can see I keep my fire wood stored in here and also all the tools required to support any outside tasks that might come up. I expect you to keep the door locked when the building's not in use and to give me the key when you leave." As an after thought she added, "Never open the shades on the two windows."

She closed and locked the door and then went to the stone lined well that was accessed by a footpath. "This is where you will get the water to fill the barrels. The well has a secret dweller that Jacque placed here when we moved into our house. It's Billy and he's a brook trout. He doesn't need any attention and he keeps the well clear of unwanted insects. Don't forget he's there and you should be careful not to hit him with the water bucket." Danny peered into the well and was able to see a dark shadow moving around in the clear water. "I use Billy as a memory jogger and when

I try to remember something that has slipped my mind I find it helps. You might want to try that trick yourself."

Retracing her steps back to the barn, she proudly showed me her small garden of flowers and salad items. The main garden had been neglected for years and was overgrown with weeds. "I won't expect you to do any gardening but you will have to store the winter vegetables I buy into the cellar".

I glanced over the landscape. The road was not visible from any part of the yard and the land in the back was occupied by the untended garden and an orchard that contained at least 15 apple and pear trees. The house was on the east side of Seal Lake Road and with the exception of a side road called Mill Road one could walk for miles without encountering human habitations.

Mill Road branched off of Seal Lake north of Diane's home and angled to the South East for about one mile where it ended at a water powered saw mill. There was a foot path that led from Mill Road through the rear of Diane's property to the one room store operated by Mrs. Sandra Benoit. The house could only be seen from a very small part of the path because of the land being reclaimed by nature. I knew this path well as it was a shortcut to use when I went to my favorite fishing-hole. As I surveyed the area I could make out a faint line of different vegetation from where I stood that revealed its location.

Diane brought me back to the present by saying. "There are two tasks that I haven't mentioned yet. One will be a one time affair and the other will be required every year. The first of these tasks that should be finished by fall is to have a trench dug from the well to the basement. When it's ready Mr. Pierre promised he would install a lead pipe and a hand pump so I can have all the water I need right in the kitchen. I won't expect you to work at that regularly but the digging should be done before the cold weather sets in. The other task is one you're familiar with, banking the house. The material needed is stored in the barn and I will have the sawdust delivered in the fall. Enough instructions for one day, why don't you bring in my cooking wood and water and when you're done, come into the kitchen?" She reached into her sweater pocket and handed him the barn key.

I unlocked the barn door and noticed it swung open with ease as you would expect a frequently used door would. I carried enough wood into the entry hall to fill the wood box and after several trips to the well had filled the two storage barrels.

Diane reminded me to rinse the two buckets setting by the sink and refill them with clean water from the well. When this was done, she invited me to sit down at the table where a steaming cup of tea was setting. I handed her the barn key and she went to a wall cabinet and opened its door. Inside were five pegs on which four identical padlocks hung with a key hanging above each lock. She placed the key on the hook with its mate above the empty peg and quickly closed the door.

"What do you think of your first day, Danny?" She asked. "Do you think you'll be able to handle the job?"

I was still excited about the watch she had given me and was momentarily at a loss for words. After a moment's hesitation I replied. "Diane, I'll do the work with ease and I want to thank you again for the watch."

She gave Danny a faint smile but said nothing. They spent the remaining time till noon talking about mundane things and as the wall clock struck twelve Diane said. "Its time for you to go, I'll see you Thursday."

# 6

I arrived home in time to eat a late noon meal and then hurried to Bob's to help with the hay harvest. The weekend had stayed dry and Bob should have the hay neatly raked in piles ready to carry into the barn using a rake that was completely home made out of wood. Its handle was six feet long and made from a pole that had been whittled to a uniform diameter of 3/4 inch and it was attached to the head cross member through a drilled hole. The rake's head was 24 inches wide with 12 teeth evenly spaced. The teeth were made of 4 inches long pegs that had been driven securely into holes in the head cross member and the entire assembly was made secure by three semicircular supports that keep the head rigidly at its proper angle.

The hay carrying poles were laying by the first hay pile ready for use.

As I approached Bob I pulled out my new watch and slowly swung it on the end of its short chain.

Bob's eyes lit up in surprise and he asked. "Where'd you get that?"

Without replying I handed it over for Bob to examine. After admiring the watch he remarked that it seemed to be keeping the correct time and handed it back to me.

I then explained that it was a present from Diane. "She seems to want every thing done right on time and she gave me the watch to keep me on schedule." I explained.

"Well we'd better get started on this hay or we won't get it in the barn before dark." Bob said as he inserted a pole under the hay. With both poles in place parallel to each other we lifted the hay and headed for the barn. Many loads later we finally pitched the last fork full into the mow and relaxed at their table.

We had just begun to settle down when a voice interrupted us.

"Would you like a glass of lemonade to help you relax?" It asked, as a tall light haired girl came through the door with a pitcher and two glasses. "Mom said you guys deserved this after all that hard work." She said to Bob.

"Thanks Nellie," Bob said as he replied to his sister, "and please thank Mom when you go back in."

We quickly emptied the pitcher of its delicious fluid and now rested; we discussed the next pressing task we had to do. "We should mow my field next and then we'll have a few days of leisure." I said. "If we start tomorrow morning, we can be finished by Saturday morning and then we can get ready to go to town."

"That's fine for you to say with that dollar you'll get from Mrs. Le Have but what will I use for money?" Bob asked.

"If we get my hay into the barn in time, I'll split the dollar with you and we'll both be able to enjoy that Gene Autry movie that's playing at the Capitol. How's that sound?" There was no disagreement from Bob.

I looked at my watch and said. "It's only half past four and this is the best time for the white perch to be biting at the mill dam. Let's go give it a try before milking time."

Bob answered with enthusiasm. "I'm game; I hope the mill isn't running because otherwise we'll be wasting our time."

We grabbed two alder poles with lines and hooks already attached and went under the barn to dig a few worms. Fully prepared we headed north towards the shortcut to Mill Road.

On the way we crossed the bridge over Smelt Creek and in doing so Bob said. "It's too bad we can't just follow the creek to the mill. It would be a lot closer."

The creek that discharged the mill water into Seal Lake passed through a large swamp, making its banks inhospitable to foot travel.

When we reached Mrs. Benoit's store we turned left onto the path that would take us to Mill Road.

Whenever a fence or rock wall intersected the path, a set of three posts was implanted to allow a person to twist past without providing room for the domestic animals to go through.

We reached a spot where Bob stopped and said. "Danny, I can see your new boss' house from here."

We stopped and examined the landscape. Only part of Diane's house was clearly shown through the overgrowth but the entrance from the road alongside her home was in plain sight.

"There seems to be an old unused path that goes straight towards her place over here." I said "I'll bet it goes to her well. I noticed that there was a path that went beyond the well when I was there today." We continued to the end of the path and turned right towards the mill.

As we approached, we heard noises that told us that the mill was operating.

"Oh well," Bob said, "at least we can watch them saw some boards."

We watched as the mill-hands dragged individual logs from the large raft into the mill opening facing the water. The water turbine was turning and its power was transferred through pulleys and wide leather belts to the cutting mechanisms.

With all this commotion going on it was unrealistic to expect any fish to remain in the area. After seeing a few logs turned into planks we started our journey back the way we had come.

When we arrived at the path, we saw Leo Petite was at his wood pile splitting wood. Leo's house was located on the opposite side of the road from the path's end. It was a one storey structure in need of repair.

I turned to Bob and said. "Let's stop and talk to Leo."

Bob nodded in agreement and we crossed the yard to the wood pile. Without any thing more than a nod of recognition Bob and I laid down our fishing gear and began stacking the wood Leo had already split.

When we caught up to Leo's splitting all three of us stopped and sat down on blocks that were large enough to make conformable seats.

Leo was a tall, lean, bearded man in his late forties. He was obviously single and could have been mistaken for a hobo if one didn't know him. In fact, he was, to the male residents, a very important member of North Seal Lake. He was the local bootlegger.

Leo had started off life as a law-abiding citizen. Following in his father's footsteps he had become a lumberjack and in pursuit of his trade had lost his left leg.

Fitted with a peg leg of his own design he was able to provide for himself as long as he had a small income. Work for a one legged man was hard to come by in the 30's so Leo started his own bootlegging business and before long he was in great demand.

His rules were simple and fair; he didn't sell to the underage, insisted on cash sales and didn't tolerate any fighting in his establishment. His merchandise came from the liquor store in town which he acquired by using several friends as procurers. Unlike some of the others who sold illegally brewed beverages Leo only sold liquor that originated at the Nova Scotia liquor store.

Police raids were rare and the price paid when caught wasn't too severe. He had only been raided once and his loss was his supply of merchandise and the money that was lying on the table in plain sight. The RCMP Corporal who had made the raid had warned him that the next time the penalty would be more severe.

One of Leo's peculiarities, in spite of his refusal to serve them, was that he didn't object to being visited by the younger males during his open hours and he enjoyed the witty inputs they contributed to the conversations. That's how Bob and I had become friendly with him.

"Thanks for the help." Leo said. "I haven't seen you two in a while. What have you been up to?" We explained that we were done with school and were now involved in doing the required work in preparation for the coming winter. Bob mentioned that I was working part time for Mrs. Le Have and this brought an immediate reaction from Leo.

"She's the best looking woman around here and I'm sure she is pleasant to work for but don't get in over your head with her."

Leo had a habit of offering advice at times without any further explanation and this was one of those times.

We spent 15 minutes talking about the weather and the village in general. Leo told us about the near fight that had started over who had caught the largest cod and how he had to bring out his axe handle to quiet things down.

That brought an end to the visit and as we left I promise to drop off a few perch the next time I caught a batch.

Walking along the path towards home we startled a half—grown snowshoe hare that bounded off through the brush without making a sound. "There goes a good meal if it was October." Said Bob, "As he pretended he had a gun and had shot it."

When we reached the spot where Diane's house became visible we stopped and examined the scene with renewed interest.

"This would be a good spot to spy on Diane if the need arose." Bob said.

"Why would anyone want to do that?" I asked.

"I don't know, it was just a passing thought but I wonder what Leo meant when he told you not to get in over your head with Diane."

I started walking onward and mulled over what Bob had said. "I've only just started so there'll be plenty of time to find out what Leo was implying."

A sudden thunderous noise erupted in front of us and Bob said. "There goes another meal." A grouse flew across their path as a second explosion erupted and another bird left the area twisting and turning to avoid obstructions in its path.

We finally came out at Mrs. Benoit's store, followed the road over the bridge until we arrived at the front of my home which was approximately five minutes walk North of Bobs.

We reaffirmed that except for Thursday morning we would devote our time to making and storing my hay and with that understanding we parted.

# 7

Located in a dingy building on an obscure street in Ottawa was Chief Inspector Maurice Levesque's RCMP headquarters. His operation was unknown except for a few superior officers and the people who worked for him. Wearing any part of their RCMP uniforms was strictly forbidden by all members of his group for fear of revealing the nature of their task, the undercover investigation of possibly errant police officers.

Inspector John Connally of the Rivemouth detachment had once worked with Maurice in this pursuit and was aware that he was still involved at a higher level.

Maurice and his wife, Susan, had only had one child. A daughter named Julie. To them she was the child every parent wished for. She was pretty, intelligent and obedient up to a point. After competing high school in Ottawa she showed her stubborn streak for the first time. Her mother had planned to have her attend a finishing school where she would become acquainted with people of high social and political standing. Julie, however, had two goals that she had nurtured through her school years and she was determined to pursue them at all costs.

First, although unheard of at the time for women, she wanted to learn more about the art of catching criminals. Her father's work had always fascinated her and he had kept the fascination alive by telling her stories about the many crimes he had helped solve and some of the ones where the criminal got away. She would undoubtedly have become a member of the RCMP if she had been born a male.

Her second goal was to become familiar with the history and present day living conditions of the French Acadians. She had read Longfellow's poem, Evangeline, where he fictionalized their expulsion from Canada and this had opened a curiosity that she intended to satisfy.

Having established her goals, she had then set out to find the best method available to her in pursuing them. It was obvious that she had to find a college where she could study the subjects but it soon became clear that there was no institution that satisfied all her needs. She finally settled on attending an obscure school in Quebec City that offered both criminology and teaching degrees. Unfortunately the criminology degree was only offered to males but after a lot of negotiations she was allowed to take some of the classes as alternates.

She graduated with a bachelor's degree in teaching in June, 1938 and returned to her parents' home in Ottawa.

Julie was unwilling to accept the history she had learned concerning the Acadians from the text books and she was trying to find alternate ways of increasing her knowledge about the subject. She was fluent in both French and English and could have found work in several fields in Ottawa but her need to follow the path of Evangeline could not be denied.

She discussed the situation with her father hoping that he might help. Inspector Levesque had hoped that his daughter would do what most girls her age did find an acceptable young man and get married. However it was obvious to him that for the time being it was best to help her in hopes she would reconsider her goals with time.

One evening, as they sat in the parlor while Mrs. Levesque cleaned the dining room table, Maurice spoke to his daughter. "Julie, I have an idea that might help. Do your remember corporal Connally? You used to sit on his lap when you were a little girl." Julie face lit up in a happy smile as she answered. "Of course I remember him. He used to bring candy every time he came. He was one of my favorite people." "Well Julie, he's now an Inspector and in charge of the Rivemouth, Nova Scotia detachment. As you know, Rivemouth is in the center of Acadian country and I thought he might be convinced to help you find a job in a library where you could satisfy your search for accurate history. I personally agree that the information in the history books is tainted. I'll call John and ask him what he thinks of the idea."

# 8

On Thursday I was up earlier then usual.. I started the fire in the wood stove and when I was positive my mother was awake I went to the barn to milk the cow and after milking her I turned her loose in the pasture. By the time I had completed my morning chores my mother had my two younger siblings ready for breakfast. A large pot of oatmeal was boiling on the stove and as soon as I had washed my hands in the wash pan on the sink everyone took a bowl and helped them—selves to the hot cereal. With the four of us seated in our designated places, my mother, Mary, said grace. Milk and sugar were added to the oatmeal and everyone ate in silence.

As she ate Mary's thoughts wondered back to the time when she married Louis. They had been going together for a year and Louis, like all young males had wanted to make love to his girlfriend. She had resisted, not because of her lack of desire but because of the teachings of the Church. Louis, in one last desperate effort told Mary he was leaving her unless she changed her mind. As he walked away, she called out to him with tears running down her cheeks. "Louis, I love you too much to let you go this way, please come back." That evening her oldest child was conceived.

They were married three months later and by the time Maggie arrived they were settled down in the old Benoit farm. Her remaining three children, Daniel, Betty and Richard were born at two year intervals.

Maggie was working for Mrs. Muise, Bob's mother; who was expecting her eighth child in the fall. Danny was his mother's favorite and she felt that he would excel in any pursuit in spite of having to take on the job of providing for the household while his father was away. She had proudly shown the note the teacher had sent her about his potential to her closest friends. Her other two were still in need of parental care and Betty, at twelve, was beginning to help her in keeping the house in order. Richard, or Dick as he was called, was of little help and he seemed to be always getting in the way.

A clatter of dishes being stacked together brought Mary out of her deep thoughts and she took her last bite of oatmeal and started to clear the table.

My family had a battery powered radio, a luxury at that time, so we were able to listen to our favorite programs. This morning I turned it on to make certain my watch was set at the right time.

I then started off for Diane's with the intention of arriving at precisely 9 A M. The three hours passed quickly with the actual work taking less than two hours and the remaining time spent at the kitchen table talking about what was going on in the Parish.

Diane seemed to need companionship as much as she needed help with her chores. "I think things are going to work out well between us." She told me as she handed me my dollar. On my way to the road I noticed tire marks in the entrance way. "I wonder who was here." I asked myself.

I erased part of the marks with my foot, a trick frequently used in the woods while hunting to keep tabs on the wildlife movements. "I'll see if there are new tracks on Monday."

Bob was waiting for me when I got home and after a late meal we walked to the hay field to turn the cut hay. "It looks like we'll be done by Friday evening so you're going to owe me that trip to the movies." Bob said.

Let's reserve a ride with Larry Landry for both of us. Riding in the back of his pickup is a little rough but we'll get more time in town going with him."

# 9

The hay had been safely stored in the barn in time to avoid a rain storm that was expected Saturday morning. Both of us had finished our work for the day and decided to make sure we had a ride into town the following evening. We walked to Larry's home that was located on the South bank of Smelt Creek.

When we arrived Larry was in the midst of putting his homemade passenger cap on the back of his pickup truck.

Greetings were exchanged and Larry said. "I'm glad you're here. Sam was supposed to help me but he never showed up. I'll bet he went to Leo's and forgot all about me but you two will do just as well."

With a little guidance the cap was raised unto the back of the truck and clamped in place. It was designed to hold 10 people on wooden benches and Larry would usually stuff in a few extras on the pickup floor. The ride wasn't comfortable but it better than walking.

With the cap in place I asked Larry if he had room for us and he assured us that he had. "Just be here by 6 P M with your 25 cents." He said.

A very important part of Saturday was that it was bath day. The younger children would bathe in the morning and the adults and teenagers in the afternoon.

The hot water was obtained from the stove hot water tank that was built into the stove and from pots heated on top.

The bath tub was a large galvanized container that was also use as a clothing wash tub. The kitchen became the bath room and was closed off to all except the bather.

The bather would stand in a half-filled tub of warm water and scrub to his heart's content. Rinsing was done with a cloth that was periodically dipped into a smaller pot of warm water setting on top of the stove to remove the soap suds.

A bath towel that hung on the back of a chair near the stove provided the last touch to a pleasant experience. Of course the youngsters had to be helped by their mother or older sister to ensure they didn't skip any of the necessary steps.

The traditional Saturday supper amongst the Acadian was baked beans with corn meal bread. Baking the beans in the wood stove oven was an all day affair and this fit in well with heating the several gallons of hot bath water needed for the baths. The leftover beans were kept to provide the Sunday breakfast.

At 5:30 P M I was ready to go. I felt good in my clean Sunday clothes which were reserved for very special occasion wear. Bob arrived and we headed for Larry's. On the way I handed Bob two quarters so no one would know that he wasn't paying with his own money.

We left at 6:00 p.m. on the dot. The trip took about 30 minutes including the time Larry needed to find a parking spot close to Charlie's pool hall. Departure time was always 10:30 p.m. and Larry had a reputation of not waiting for anyone. His routine was to take in the movie and then play a few games of pool before leaving. Both Bob and I liked this schedule as it gave us time to spend in the pool hall eavesdropping on the local rumor mongers.

We hurried to the theater to make sure we could get in before the place was filled up. Tonight's feature was "The Roping of the Rustlers." staring Roy Rogers. The program started at 7 with the news followed by the 11th chapter of "The Shadow becomes Visible."

We were out of the theater by nine and were soon at Charlie's. Walking through the door exposed us to the familiar odor of stale beer and old urine.

Charlie, the owner, was a huge man with a pot belly that hung over his belt In spite of his apparent lack of physical fortitude no one had ever been known to violate his pool hall rules except one and he had lived, but just barely, to regret it.

The rules were really quite simple, no fighting and wait for your number to come up before taking a cue in your hands. Drinking alcoholic beverages was forbidden by Provincial law except in private homes but here, like in a lot of other places, no one bothered to notice. I had taken my first drink of beer in the toilet in the back of the hall.

When we entered, I noticed a group gathered in a corner and it appeared that a lively discussion was in progress. The center of attention was Jules Green, one of the town constables. He was telling the pool hall patrons about a robbery that had taken place the night before that had the town police baffled. The talk continued until Bob and I had to leave for the truck.

On the way home the only thing that was talked about was the robbery. By 11:30 P.M. I was in bed and soon fast asleep.

# 10

The Sunday morning routine was much like the rest of the week except for beans instead of oatmeal for breakfast. After that came preparations for attending Mass. For Mary Sunday Mass attendance was a must. The distance to church by road was 3 ½ miles but depending on the season this was cut down to two miles by crossing the lake by row-boat or on the ice.

St. Agnes church was an architectural marvel. It had been copied from a church in France and built by the many talented men of the area. The main features from the outside were the two towers, one containing the bell, and the stained—glass windows that were made up of all the colors of the rainbow. The inside was large enough to seat at least 800 people in 4 rows of oak benches in the center section with additional seating in two wings and a balcony located in the rear. Looking up from the center aisle it was apparent that the center and wings were joined to form a cross. The highest parts of the ceiling were 25 feet from the main floor. The arms and body of the cross they formed were made up of inverted half cylinders. All of this was held up by artistically formed pillars and religious-based paintings decorated the entire overhead. The altar was isolated from the pew area by an elaborate railing that was where the recipients would kneel to receive Holy Communion. The front and side walls were decorated with statues and the Way of the Cross, a series of plaques depicting Christ's journey to his crucifixion. Each plaque had an inscription below it giving the name of its donor.

The church bell was located in the north tower and was a wonder to observe. It was 4 feet tall and 4 feet in diameter at its base and made of solid cast bronze. It was hung on a pivot that allowed it to swing in an arc sufficient to have the striker hit its side. As the bell was used to signal the parish about special events, a method was required to control its peal rate. This was done by a lever attached at the top of the bell with a rope connected to the free end. The rope hung down to the floor of the bell compartment and had knots tied in it along its length. Adjacent to the rope was a 3-foot high platform for the ringer to mount in preparation for ringing the bell. By grasping the rope and jumping off the platform his weight swung the bell and it rang. A second peal was followed when the ringer jumped upward and he could continue the ringing at a steady rate indefinitely. To stop the bell from ringing he had simply to land on the platform on his way down. Properly done any desire interval between rings was obtained.

The bell served as a message carrier to the parish residents. Its main function was to remind the devout that at 9:00 A.M. the Sunday Mass would start in one hour and at 10:00 A.M. it would signal the start of the ceremony. It was also rung at noon each day, whenever a person died and as a signal of a major emergency in progress.

The pulpit from which the priest, Father Frotten, would present his condemnation of the sinners in the congregation was set on a track which allowed it to be rolled into the background during the saying of Mass. It was a sight to see with its intricate woodwork and awesome size. It was brought to the front where he stood looking down at his flock and instilled the fear of hell into their hearts.

Belonging to the church's congregation was not free. The church had several methods of extracting money from its members. The seat that one occupied had to be purchase for a one year period and that seat was reserved for the purchaser's use. Danny's family always paid for a 5-seat bench in the left wing, where the price was less than the center isle seats. The basket was passed every Sunday to add to the income, each ceremony performed had a fee attached, Masses said for the dead had to be bought and the priest made the rounds of his parish each year to beg what he could from his flock.

There was a certain amount of entertainment just prior to the start of Mass. The most affluent members would strut up the center isle in their splendor to take their places at the front. Madame Poisson, the doctor's wife, was always the star of that show arriving just seconds before the priest started Mass.

Father Frotten's sermon on this particular Sunday was about the Seventh Commandment. He was able to word it in such a way that the adults understood the full meaning and the youngsters were left with a warped view of something that only their parents could do without going to hell. At 11:30 a.m. the people were released and they found their way to their separate goals.

# 11

Sunday was the ideal day to fish the mill dam waters as the mill was guaranteed to be dormant. Doing any work except the daily chores was not allowed by church rules and my mother made sure her children obeyed them but recreation was allowed. Bob and I were about to leave when Dick asked if he could come along. He promised to mind and wouldn't scare the fish with unnecessary noise. Against our better judgment we agreed to take him with the threat to send him home if he misbehaved.

When we arrived at the mill, the conditions were favorable and we had our bait in the water in no time. The fish must have been hungry as we started getting bites right away. In 15 minutes the three of us had caught about 20 big white perch. As quickly as they had started biting, they stopped. Wanting to catch enough to feed both families Bob and I keep fishing but Dick had decided that skipping rocks on the water was more fun. After a few warnings Dick was reminded of his promise and sent home.

Bob and I managed to catch several more fish and departed for home after gutting our catch. When we reached Leo's, we stopped to give him enough for a meal and continued on.

Arriving at the Smelt Creek Bridge, we found Dick throwing rocks into the running water. We paused and Danny asked Dick what had taken him so long to get this far. Dick replied that he had played on the short cut and had stopped to observe Mrs. Le Have's house for a while. "You know what," he said, "she had a visitor while I was watching. A dark car came down her drive and disappeared behind the trees in back. I left as soon as I saw the car. I didn't want to be seen spying." After arriving at my home we split the fish with Bob taking the biggest share to feed his larger family.

# 12

A fisherman returning to his wharf in Rivemouth Harbor had spotted a body floating face down at approximately 10:00A.M. The man was obviously dead so he continued to his dock and notified the town police. By the time the police got their boat in the water and running 2 hours had gone by. They finally located the corpse on Heron Island at 12:30 P.M. with his body lying against a post that was part of the surveyed line that separated the town from the county. After documenting their find the body was taken to Gordon's mortuary for examination.

There was unusual activity at the Rivemouth police station. Chief Roland White and Detective Sam Gleason were having a discussion with Sgt. Naples. The subject was about the body found in the harbor on Saturday. He had been identified as Joel Batist who lived in a small house close to the harbor's edge just outside town limits. He had a record of minor offences and had spent a few nights in jail. No one came forward to claim him as a relative. The police had heard rumors that he had been bootlegging for a long time but so far nothing official had done in that area..

Dr. Fred Donnelly had examined the body and concluded that Joel had fallen into the harbor, struck his head and drowned. The damage to Joel's head was behind his left ear and looked serious enough to have killed him outright but to Dr. Donnelly an accurate cause of death in this matter wasn't worth the extra work he would have to go through on a Sunday. Regardless of the cause it was purely accidental and Sgt. Naples supported this theory.

Sgt. Naples and Detective Gleason were involved in an argument about who had jurisdiction in the case. Joel lived outside of town but his body was originally spotted in what was thought to be town water. On the other hand he was found in a place that could be claimed by both. Detective Gleason wanted a full autopsy performed and a search made to determine where the body had entered the water. Sam knew that the way the tides flowed Joel could not have entered the harbor close to his home as his body would have ended out to sea. In his mind there were a lot of unanswered questions that needed looking into.

Unfortunately Sam was overruled when Sgt. Naples went to Mayor Simms and convinced him that the effort of doing a complete investigation would be costly and the results wouldn't alter the final determination of accidental death. With the RCMP in charge Sgt. Naples explained that a simple accidental death report would be filed and the mater would be put to rest. The Mayor applied pressure on the chief to withdraw the town from the case and Joel Batist was scheduled to be buried as an accident victim. At the next Naples's party the Mayor was the guest of honor.

Detective Gleason prepared his own report that was critical of the decisions made by his superiors and filed it into his private locked desk. He also told himself that this case was not closed.

# 13

James Babin had just left a meeting of the six men who controlled the Belle Pointe school finances. Concern had been expressed about the slow process of hiring a new teacher. He had advertised in the Rivemouth News, a weekly newspaper, for two weeks without any results. He decided to try once more before asking for an increase in advertising funds. Chief Inspector Levesque had called his friend Inspector Connally and apprised him of his daughter's desire to gain more knowledge in Acadian history and John promised Maurice that he would inquire about employment possibilities but cautioned his friend that positions for college graduates in Rivemouth were scarce.

By chance he noticed James Babin's ad and although he knew the wages, $250 for the full school year, were ridiculous for a college-educated teacher he passed the information on to Maurice. Julie convinced her father to pay for her trip to Nova Scotia so she could evaluate the situation and she was met at the bus station in Rivemouth by Mrs. Connally who greeted her like a long lost child.

Her first impression of Julie was to marvel at how the little girl she had known years ago had blossomed out into this beautiful lady that stood before her. They embraced, exchanged greetings and drove to the Connally home in a taxi. "You must be tired after your two-day trip from Ottawa. Follow me and I'll show you the room where you'll be staying. The bath room is located next to your room and there are clean towels hanging on the holder. I'll see you when you've had time to relax." "Thank you, Mrs. Connally." Julie said as she laid her suit cases on the bed and opened the smaller one.

The room she found herself in was medium sized, with a single bed and a small desk and one chair in a corner. An armoire took up space along the back wall and one had to turn sideways to pass between it and the bed. Having changed into her bathrobe, she went to the bathroom to freshen up. Unlike the facilities available in Seal Lake everything required for proper body care, including hot water was included. A long hot bath which almost lulled her to sleep resulted in her feeling like a new woman. She finished her toiletries and returned to her room were she donned a skirt and blouse and low heeled shoes prior to going into the parlor where Mrs. Connally was waiting.

Julie was 5 feet tall and had long, black curly hair and blue eyes that created an unexpected contrast. Her peachy cream complexion and bright red lips completed a picture seldom seen in this small town. When Inspector Connally came home, his first comment was. "I'll have to assign a constable full time to protect you from our local young men." Julie blushed at the complement but soon recovered her composure.

Arrangements had been made with Mr. Babin to meet at his home the following evening. The Inspector had the constable on duty drive Julie to the meeting and he waited for her until it was over. She was met at the door by both Mr. and Mrs. Babin and all three went into the kitchen and sat at the table. James looked at Julie as thoughts passed through his head. He was certain that there was no chance that this sophisticated lady was going to be willing to bury herself in this village for the money they were offering but he was willing to try and negotiate.

His house had the luxury of electric power and as they sat in the brightly lit room, no one seemed to want to begin the conversation. Mrs. Babin rose from her chair with the comment. "I'll make some tea while you two talk over the situation."

With the ice broken James explained the duties a teacher had to fulfill and the disadvantages she would face. The conversation had started in English but suddenly Julie began to speak in French. "I know all about teaching in a multi-grade classroom. Quebec, where I went to school, has them as their main source of education and I practice taught in several as I studied for my degree."

James' face lit up as he realized that the main obstacle he thought would block Julie from taking the position was understood by her and seemed to be acceptable. Julie continued. "The salary is very small but if you meet certain conditions I will be your teacher for one year. What I need is a place to stay that has electricity and phone service and a private room which includes meals. I will pay for my phone calls, of course.

There is another thing I need but this is not part of the requirements for me taking the job. I need access to older Acadians who can tell me about the real history of their people."

Mrs. Babin, Nancy, had been listening attentively and blurted out. "James, we have the perfect place for her right here, I don't mind cooking for one more person, we have a spare room and everything she needs is available." She looked at Julie and realizing she had left her out of the conversation she apologized. James was pleased with the way things were progressing except his share of the teachers salary had just jumped up by several Dollars. Perhaps they could edge up the tax rate a bit to cover the increase.

Nancy suggested that Mrs. Belle Muise who was in her 90's and seemed to remember everything that had happened during her lifetime and also everything that she had been told by her grandmother would be a perfect source for Julie's data on the Acadians. "She lives near here and enjoys talking about her memories." She said.

"I'd like to have a look at the school as soon as possible. I'm going back to my parents place for the rest of the summer and that will give me time to plan the arrangement of the students' placement. If the school is what I expect Belle Pointe has a new teacher." She extended her hand to James and they shook. James' face revealed the lifting of a burden that had plagued him since Mrs. D'Eon had announced her retirement. Not only had he hired a new teacher but he had acquired one with an excellent education. What he didn't realize was she had talents that went beyond teaching. "I'll show you the school tomorrow morning at 10:00 A.M. By then the sun will have the room lit up and the morning chill will be moderated." He said. Julie agreed

Julie returned to the Connally home and spent a pleasant evening with the occupants. The Inspector made the same arrangements he had made for Julie the previous evening and at 10 she was in front of Belle Pointe School waiting for James. He arrived on foot a few minutes later and unlocked the front door. They spent an hour going over the inside and James observed that the roof was leaking in one area. "I'll have that repaired before school is scheduled to open." He told Julie.

The yard needed cleaning and James promised to have the students who were coming back in the fall take care of that. The one remaining task that Julie commented on was the state of disrepair that the two outhouses had fallen into. "I would expect that these items should be repaired or replaced by the time I come back to teach." She said. James had agreed with every thing Julie had asked for but the outhouse replacement came as a shock. This would surely break his school budget.

He examined the structures and realized that they had been neglected too long and something had to be done. He threw caution to the wind and said. "I'm glad you brought this to my attention. We'll do what you ask." He was already formulating a way to raise money without antagonizing the village residents. They would have a school repair dance. The priest could not refuse permission for such a noble cause and the people would have fun while contributing to a needed function.

Having completed their business Julie got into the auto while James locked up the school. Through the car's open window Julie called out she would be back the last week in August. As the car headed for town, James waved.

A few days later Julie took the bus and returned to her parents' home.

# 14

I had fallen into a routine while working for Diane. One of the items I observed carefully was the tire tracks in her driveway. I had determined that at least 4 automobiles were regularly coming to her house although I had yet to see any of them.

As time passed Diane and I became friends and I was exposed to a female point of view that most boys my age never had a chance to observe. There were always sisters, mothers and girlfriends that a young man associated with but in all those relationships there was never a situation that didn't include adverse desires.

With the passage of time, I began to see her as an equal. My puppy love stage had passed and our discussions at the kitchen table became more at ease. Her requirement to have a confidant she could trust and talk openly to had almost broken though a few times but at the last moment she had changed the subject. "What is she holding back?" I asked myself but I never tried to pry.

The ditch from the well to the house had been dug and was waiting for the plumbing to be installed. As the summer passed, I gathered the material needed to winterize the house. Needing a tool from the barn, I had asked Diane for the key and when I tried to unlock the door the key didn't fit.

I went back to the house and told her about the problem and handed her the key. She thought for a moment, went back to the kitchen and returned with a different key and a lock in which a key was inserted. "The lock with the key is the one that belongs on the door. Please switch it with the other lock and bring the replaced lock and the two keys to me."

I heard her mutter that she had to be more careful as the wrong person might have discovered her mistake. She never mentioned the switched locks again.

# 15

With summer coming to an end the berry season was over and the jams and preserves prepared by the women were stored in the basement. The next big harvests were the root crops. The potatoes would require the biggest effort as they had to be dug out with hand hoes, dried, bagged and stored in bins in the cellar. This was a time when I wished my father was home.

There was a rumor that the job in Halifax was to be shut down for a week to accomplish blasting and that workers would be going home for a short break. That was to happen in the last week in August, the week the Belle Pointe school benefit dance was scheduled.

James Babin had convinced Father Frotten that money was needed to update the school and the good father had agreed as long as the church got its cut. Father Frotten had resisted initially, only giving his permission weeks after he was asked. James had taken it on himself to do all repairs to the school rather than to take a chance of losing his new teacher. The positive side of all this was that Julie would be able to attend an Acadian dance that had changed very little since the expulsion.

# 16

The Halifax school construction had been halted and three workers who resided in Seal Lake arrived during the weekend. One of them, Jules Comeau, was not going back as soon as the others because of a minor injury but the other two, Louis Pottier [my father] and Simon Muise [Bob's dad] were to return in ten days. Jules had driven down in his Model T Ford so the others planned to take a bus back.

The magic of coincidence had struck for both of us. With our fathers home the harvesting had become one of joy instead of pure labor. With the dance coming up Friday night it looked like a fun week was in the offing.

My father, after having been away for so long, spent most of his time looking over his farm with me by his side and complemented me on my accomplishments. With the exception of assisting me with the potato harvest Louis did very little else to help.

"You've done such a good job I don't want to upset your operation." He told me. "I heard that you are working for the widow Le Have. How did that come about?" He asked.

After explaining that her former helper had quit and I had applied to replace him my father said. "You're a lucky young man to be able to earn money while working for such a pretty woman. I wish I had been that fortunate when I was your age." That ended the conversation about Diane.

# 17

In late October, 1937 the medium sized freighter, the Emilio Star, had sailed into Rivemouth harbor and tied up to one of the commercial docks. She was on a regular run from the Caribbean loaded with molasses, sugar and fruit. The crew, which consisted of 21 Italians, was a happy go—lucky group, who enjoyed their stay in port as long as their money lasted and they were anxious to sail when the fun ran out. Their stay in Rivemouth usually lasted less than a week and during that time they unloaded the ship, move to a new dock and loaded with lumber.

They had just started taking on their new cargo when a fire broke out in the engine room. By the time the Rivemouth fire department had brought the fire under control the damage was so extensive that major repair was required before the Emilio Star could sail again.

An agreement was reached between the ship's owners and the Canadian government whereby the ship could remain tied up at an unused dock until a resolution of the ship's future was reached. The agreement included the provision that one crew member could remain to watch over the ship. This duty was assigned to Vinnie Lacosta, the ship's first mate.

He went about providing himself with comfortable living quarters by sealing off the crews dining area from the rest of the ship except for a small part of the galley that contained a sink. He bought a used kitchen stove and installed it in a corner of the modified dining area where it provided heat and cooking facilities.

The captain's bedroom became his own. His only problem was how to live on a sailor's pay while permanently docked. The ship's owner had given him an extra allowance for food and fuel but the supplement had no surplus for entertainment. He wasn't allowed to work in Canada so finding legal employment was not an option.

The duties of the Emilio Star had been assigned to another ship owned by the same company. Named the Santa Clara she was captained by Gino Pastori and Vinnie had established ties with him on his first landing in Rivemouth. He knew several members of the new ships crew and took advantage of this to relieve any feelings he had about being isolated from his country.

Vinnie had found one place in town where the crowd, although all male, offered some enjoyment that was within his budget, Charlie's pool hall. Playing pool was cheap if you were a good shooter as the looser had to pay for the game and Vinnie was close to being a pro. It wasn't long before the regulars at Charlie's knew Vinnie was looking for a way to increase his income. There were always individuals in the hall who passed on bits of what they heard at Charlie's and in due time the knowledge of his needs was heard by the right person.

# 18

Vinnie was on his way back to the ship from a night of pool when he became aware of footsteps approaching from his rear. He glanced back and saw a tall man walking briskly towards him. He slowed down and as soon as they were abreast the man slowed to keep even. He addressed Vinnie in a pleasant voice and asked if they could enjoy a drink together. "I have a business deal I'd like to discuss that could turn out to be very profitable for you. Let's go to your ship and see if you're interested." Vinnie thought that he should proceed with caution but not having anything to hide decided to take a chance. After all, he needed more funds. "I can't make any promises but I'm willing to listen to what you have to say." He told the stranger.

A small light lit the gangplank that spanned the distance from the dock to the ship. Vinnie went to the hatch that opened into his living quarters and went inside switching on the light as he entered. The stranger made a comment about his door being unlocked. "I haven't got any thing to protect, so why bother?" He asked. "If you agree with my proposal, you will have." Was the response he received.

The stranger introduced himself as Elliot Johns, a tall, medium built man with blond hair, green eyes, a sharp nose with a thin mustache above his small mouth. He extended his hand to Vinnie and they shook. "I know about your situation from the official records that have been filed in the customs office. You must be aware that the government is watching you closely and that any wrong move you make could get both you and your company in trouble. On the other hand by co-operating with the right people you could become freer to do as you please."

Vinnie was plagued by the idea that he had met Elliot before. He searched through his memory and suddenly he remembered. Elliot was the RCMP Constable who had accompanied the fire department when the ship was burning.

"I mentioned a drink while we were walking, would you like one now?" Elliot asked. Vinnie produced two glasses and set them on the table while Elliot pulled out a pint of rum from his jacket pocket. He passed the bottle to Vinnie and said. "You open it." Vinnie had opened many liquor bottles during his career as a sailor and the cap on this bottle felt unusual. A quick glance told the story, there was no tax seal, and the cap was clean.

They sipped their rum in silence. Vinnie spoke first. Aren't you the policeman that came when we had our fire?" He asked. Elliot answered without hesitation. "Of course it's I. What took you so long to ask?" "I guess I was so preoccupied at the time I forgot some of the details." He replied.

"Now that you know that the law will be on your side if needed do you want to learn more about what the deal consists of?" Vinnie had never broken any laws except for an occasional fight and some vandalism when he was drunk so he decided to proceed with caution. Perhaps, he thought, this was what he needed, an increase in income if the risk was small. "O.K.," he said, "I'm willing to listen."

Elliot proceeded to tell Vinnie how his partner and he were giving the area bootleggers protection from police raids. For a fee the bootlegger would be warned in advance or be taken off the list of planed raids. Elliot was being transferred to Halifax and a new participant was needed. The only action required of Vinnie would be to collect the bootleggers' donations. "Would you be willing to take on that chore for 10 % of the fee?" Elliot asked. "It sounds simple enough but I haven't got any transportation." "My partner, or more correctly yours, will drive you to walking distance from each pickup. It is vital that he is never suspected of being involved."

"I'll tell you what I'll do," said Elliot, "I'll take you on a trial run and that way you'll know exactly what you have to do for your pay. If you want to stop after that trial all that'll be expected of you is to keep your mouth shut. How's that sound?" By now Vinnie was on the verge of accepting. He really wanted to have more to do than watch a disabled ship and this opportunity seemed to be the answers. There would be more money to spend and exciting things to do. "O.K., I'll give it a try."

The run was set for the next day. Elliot had explained that the period between 10:00 A.M. and 2:00 P.M. was the best time to collect because this would be the time when business was at a low level for their contributors.

Vinnie was picked up three blocks away from the ship the next morning and they began their route. "I never stop close to their place and always vary the place I stop at. By agreement I go to the back door and receive a plain white envelope from the occupant. I repeat this routine until all scheduled visits have been complete for the day."

They had arrived at Elliot's first pickup. After parking Elliot led Vinnie in a round about way to a small house located on a narrow street and knocked at the back door. A woman peeked out the door window and quickly disappeared. The door was opened by a man who handed Elliot an envelope and simultaneously asked. "Who is this?" And he pointed at Vinnie. "He's your new collector." Without another word being spoken the pair left taking a different route to their auto.

This routine was repeated 12 times without any unexpected action. "That's it for today." Elliot said. They had covered most of the town's outskirts and ventured to a few nearby villages. "I'll drop you off near you ship and visit you tonight for your decision."

At 7:00 P.M. Vinnie heard steps on his gangplank and knew his visitor had arrived. He had spent most of the time after leaving Elliot pondering the pros and cons of the offer that had been made. The risks seemed to be small and the rewards were yet to be determined. Once he was apprised of the amount of money he could expect he would decide. The hatch opened and Elliot entered.

There was still a bit of rum left in the bottle and Vinnie poured it into two glasses making sure it was evenly divided. Elliot handed him an envelope and said. "Go ahead and open it, it's your pay for what you did today." Vinnie hands shook slightly as he tore the end off the sealed envelope and out slid a $10 bill. "That's yours to keep no matter what you have decided." Elliot added.

The average day's pay for a skilled worker was $1.50 and in less than 4 hours of easy activity he had earned more than that worker would get in a week. He didn't ponder long before he gave Elliot his answer which was, "Yes, count me in."

"We've only gone through the first part of our operation. The second part involves supplying liquor to the vendors. As you probably already know, the sellers have their own methods of obtaining their stock. We are going to offer them a way too resupplies without any effort on their part except preparing a list of their needs. Your part will be to provide storage and delivery of the items that I'll bring to you and of course that will increase your pay." Vinnie's eyes widened as he listened. What had first appeared as a simple collection operation was beginning to look like a complicated conspiracy.

Elliot pulled a second envelope out of his pocket and handed it to Vinnie. His command of written English was limited but he was able to make out that the document was an order to expel both Vinnie and the Emilio Star from Canada. The order was unsigned but the intent was clear, Vinnie had better co-operate. Elliot assured him that the action was on file but would require some sort of violation on Vinnie's part to cause it to be implemented. "Remember, the people who need you are the same ones who can cause you problems. Now that you're a full member, I'll give you the remaining details."

Vinnie was aghast with the message he had just been given. He was caught in a trap from which there was no escape. He had to go along with Elliot or face ruination. If his company lost their ship his sailing career was over and seamanship was his sole means of making a living. With a look of dejection on his face he nodded his acceptance of the situation. Elliot slapped him on the back and said. "Don't look so lost, we're on the same side and your income is going to increase by a significant amount." He than explained that his transfer to Halifax placed him in a position where he would get untaxed liquor at wholesale prices, transports it to Rivemouth, store it on the Emilio and sell it to the bootleggers on demand. Vinnie would be provided with an auto to make the final deliveries. "I noticed a hatch the size of a door located on the port side of your ship just above water level. That would be an ideal place to bring the liquor on board from a small boat without being observed." Elliot said.

The last thing remaining was for Vinnie to meet his other partner or more correctly his boss. "There's not much time left," Elliot said, "my transfer is coming shortly so we'll meet here tomorrow night and you'll be introduced.

True to his word, Elliot came the next evening accompanied by a tall muscular man who appeared to be in his forties. There was no reason to tell Vinnie who Elliot's companion was, everyone knew him on sight, Sgt. Paul Naples. Introductions were gone through never-the-less and a form of comradely was soon formed between the three people

"Elliot and I have gone through the arrangements you have agreed to and we discovered a weak point in the plan. We have to avail you of a vehicle so that I can distance myself from all the overt operations." Naples said. "I'll take care of all undercover events and you'll do all the deliveries and collections." The meeting was short and only one additional thing was established, how Paul could be contacted and a code name [Josh] that Vinnie was to use when contact was necessary.

An old but dependable Ford was found and kept in an out-of—the way shed that was for business use only.

# 19

When Joel Batist met with his unfortunate accident, it left a void in the illicit supply of alcohol in an area of Rivemouth. With the economic situation that existed that void was soon filled by Jerry Conway. He had been one of Joel's customers and lived a few blocks away. His first task was to get the stock required to open up and he recruited a few of his closest buddies to buy from the liquor store in small quantities. The operation went well for a few weeks and Jerry was surprised at the rate his profits grew.

He was sitting alone in his kitchen when he was startled by a loud knock on the door. He was surprised as none of the people he knew bothered to announce their arrival, they just walked in. He went to the door and opened it. Standing in the entrance was a tall, muscular man with dark oily skin, curly black hair and dark piercing eyes. He extended his hand towards Jerry and said. "I'm new in town and heard I could get a drink around here." Jerry was so surprised that he automatically took the man's hand in his and shook it. He had only sold to people he knew up too now and he hesitated before answering. His decision made, he offered the man a seat at the table and said. "I do have a bottle of rum in the pantry and I can give you a glass of that if you want it." The man nodded in acceptance and Jerry took the bottle out of the pantry and poured a stiff drink into a glass. The man took a sip, swished it around in his mouth. He then tossed the glass to the floor with spitting out what little he had in his mouth directly in Jerry's face.

Jerry's reaction was swift. He reached across the table to grab the stranger by his shirt. His intention was to throw him out and be done with this entire affair but much to his surprise he found himself setting on the floor with his pants soaking up the rum.

The man looked down at Jerry and signaled him to stay where he was. "My name is Vinnie and I live on a ship in the harbor. I wish to say two words to let you know how important it is that you co-operate, Joel Batist." Jerry was aware of the implication of the mentioning of that name but couldn't see how this affected him. Although he was not cowardly, he understood that he was outclassed and his best chance of surviving without further harm was to be submissive.

When Vinnie saw that Jerry had given up he told him to get off the floor and sit in his chair. "I'm sure you realize that there's more to this than a bad drink. I'm going to make a proposal that will be profitable to both of us. I, personally have nothing to lose if you turn me down but your loss could be painful and complete. Do we understand each other?"

With no other choice but to listen Jerry nodded. He was beginning to feel a warm spot on his bottom and a glance told him he was bleeding. Vinnie was quick and to the point. "I'll supply you with the beverages you sell and you'll pay me a commission of 10 % of your profits. Joel thought that was too much but under the present conditions he had to go along. "Joel objected and think of where he is now. Of course he had an accident but accidents happen all the time." Vinnie said with a smirk. Jerry had no place to run to; he either had to accept this bad deal or he would get something worse.

With his mind slowly recovering from shock, he said. "How will you get the liquor to me and how will you collect your earnings?" He asked. "Just continue your operation and you will be contacted at a time of my choice. Don't forget about Joel." Vinnie said as walked out the door. Jerry changed his pants after applying a bandage on his cut that was only superficial and proceeded to clean up his kitchen. The implied threat had shaken him to the core and he had not even been given the choice of getting out.

Jerry's home was located on a narrow street that ran perpendicular to the shore line. The street behind him was barely more then a path. There was room for a motor vehicle to enter but not enough for a car to pass from the opposite direction. All the buildings that abutted that street faced with their backs to it. The building across from Jerry's was an old warehouse with a single wide door facing the street that had a padlock on its hasp. The area was ideal for underhanded operations.

With his operation continuing at a normal rate for several days, Jerry began to feel relieved. Maybe it had all been a practical joke and he had nothing to worry about. The longer he was left alone the better he felt. Then, about a week after Vinnie's visit while he was sleeping, he heard a bang on his rear door. He jumped out of bed and rushed to the rear kitchen window that faced the alley and saw the back end of a dark model T Ford turn onto Harbor Street which paralleled the harbor. He could also see footprints in the wet grass that went up to his back door and stacked neatly on the top step was a pile of three medium sized boxes.

He opened the door and looked up and down the alley and seeing nothing unusual he directed his attention to the items on the step. A message was scrawled on the top of the biggest box that said first delivery. Without further hesitation he brought the three boxes into his house and opened the marked box. On top of a variety of partly filled liquor bottles was a note that simply said. "These items are free because they were already paid for. I'm not greedy and can be a pleasure to work with." The other two boxes contained bottles that had never been opened but they had one significant difference from the liquor store stock, they didn't have a tax stamp over the caps. A neatly written price list accompanied the boxes which had the notation; a commission of 10%will be collected on your profits. There was no mention of when the money was to be collected.

A quick calculation by Jerry resulted in the knowledge that Vinnie was not charging more than liquor store prices and his only apparent gains were the 10% of Jerry's profits. It remained to be seen how much Jerry could raise his prices without losing his clientele.

It was business as usual for the following week. Most of Jerry's customers were ones who had bought from Joel and his demise was a frequent subject of discussion while the drinking progressed.

One customer, Stan Gray, who was an inquisitive person and he had noticed that Joel would draw a pencil line around each bottle about three inches from the bottom. He had asked Joel why he did that and Joel had replied. "I'm a little forgetful so I use the line as a reminder of when it's time to reorder that brand." Stan had forgotten that discussion as it had happened a while back when he had been feeling good. After he became a regular at Jerry's he soon adjusted to the minor differences between the two hosts and found this new environment was as pleasurable as the other had been.

He had noticed a sudden change in Jerry but hadn't given it much thought. One evening he decided to order a Crème De Mint, liquor he craved at times but had not had since Joel had died. Jerry mumbled about having to dig it out and came back with a half—full pint bottle which he placed in front of Stan and said." Help yourself." Stan picked up the bottle to pour some in his glass when he was startled to see a pencil line drawn the same way Joel did. He finished pouring his drink and slowly rotated the bottle in his hand as he examined the pencil mark. His heart jumped when he found what he had hoped wouldn't be there, a small part of the line had been rubbed out at the right side of the label. He remembered erasing that very line when he had visited Joel a few days before his death. How could Jerry have gotten hold of Joel's old stock? His curiosity was at a peak but his sense of self protection prevented him from revealing his discovery. Was it possible that Jerry was involved in some sinister action that involved Joel's death? The police had ruled the death accidental so how could that be? He suddenly recalled that nothing was said about Joel being involved in bootlegging and his liquor supply was never mentioned. Stan gulped down his drink, paid his bill and hastily left the premises.

# 20

My father had acquired an old Schwinn bicycle in need of repair in Halifax. He had tied it to the back of the automobile that brought him home. It was a one speed, coaster brake model which is all that was available at that time. It had a generator installed that, when engaged to the front wheel, provided light for night use. Working together with spare parts we soon had it in useable condition. To me this was a gift from the haven. It opened up an area that had been denied to me all my life, a way for me to independently travel long distances at a reasonable speed.

I found myself riding my bike to Diane's on Thursday morning and I felt like I was on top of the world. The weather was clear and warm; most of the harvesting was done and today was payday. I got off my bicycle at the back of the house and leaned it against the steps railing.

The door opened and Diane stepped out. "I saw you through the side window and couldn't resist coming out to see your bike. When did you get it?" She asked.

I explained without leaving out any details. "Now I can visit places that used to be too far to walk and I can take along a friend on the handle bar."

Diane asked if she could try a short ride and I was happy to let her try.

"Be careful getting on, it's not a girl's model." I said.

She giggled and without another word she was on the seat and going down the road. When she returned, she was out of breath but the look on her face showed she had enjoyed herself enormously. As she disembarked, she said. "I want you to hurry with your chores today. We have a lot of talking to do."

With my work done I entered the kitchen and made my way to my regular seat at the table. Diane had a pot of tea already on the table and she took her seat facing me.

"Danny," she said, "I'm tired of living a lie. I'm sure that you have a lot of questions about me and most of those will never be answered. The one thing I want to make clear is that you have been the best friend I've had since I lost my husband. You have always done what you were asked to do and have never made any demands. I wish all men were like you. If I was your age, I would certainly be trying to pull you into my web. I hope I haven't embarrassed you with my speech but I felt I owed you that much."

I had been wondering what Diane did for entertainment but had never asked. I was flattered by her compliments and I felt my face redden as she spoke.

"I'm going to the dance tomorrow night and I'll be curious about what kind of comment you hear said about me. I'm not asking you to violate your sense of good manners but at least tell me if the community seems willing to accept me as one who belongs."

I accepted the request without question and proceeded to tell Diane about the villagers being happy that they were about to have a long awaited good time. We continued talking until noon and as I was leaving left Diane said. "Be at the dance early, I want to have the first dance with you." I left feeling good about myself as I mounted my bike.

# 21

Friday was finally here and the village was more active than usual Although Belle Pointe had their own hall James Babin had negotiated with the Seal Lake councilors for the use of their larger hall that would accommodate the expected large group of fun loving people more comfortably.

The Seal Lake hall was two stories tall with a large kitchen on the lower floor. The entire upper level was laid out to be used as a theater of sorts and with some rearranging of chairs it became an immense dance floor.

There was an elevated stage where the traveling entertainers such as magicians, silent movie projectionists, etc. could display their talents for a small fee. This same stage was where the musicians sat to provide the music for the reels danced by the Acadians.

The musicians were all self-taught and consisted of fiddles, guitarists and an occasional accordion player. They donated their time with their only reward being the peoples' appreciation of their talent. Unlike the western reels there were no callers during the dance. The music and the knowledge of how the reel was performed were all the dancers needed.

The chairs normally arranged in front of the stage were lined up against the walls with the males sitting separately from the females. In order to get a dance partner one had to approach the opposite sexes' seating to ask. Even if refused by one's original choice it was unusual for the asker to leave the seating area without a partner.

For this particular event the women of the Parish had lit the kitchen stoves and were prepared to serve a few snacks to increase the school's coffer. The one thing that was not available through the hall's supply system was alcoholic beverages. This commodity, however, was not difficult to find. The local bootleggers were all there with their supplies within reach. They had no fear of being bothered as the RCMP had an unwritten rule of allowing the villagers to police their own dances and selling booze outside the hall was part of what they overlooked.

The hall opened for business at 7:00 p.m. The music wouldn't start until 8:30 but with people expected from other Parishes it gave the visitors time to renew acquaintances with people they hadn't seen for a long time before the real fun began.

I arrived early and started looking for Bob. After going through the hall and surrounding area I saw one of Bob's neighbors, Ruben, coming up the road. When Ruben came within hearing I asked him if he had seen Bob. According to Ruben Bob had to accompany his mother to her sisters home when the sister had suddenly become ill and would be gone for a few days. Thanking Ruben for his input, I wandered around observing the events one would expect to see on a night of frivolousness.

Leo had found someone with a pickup truck and with his stock arranged in a large wooden box in the back they had parked it at the far end of the hall yard. There were other vendors in the hall vicinity but they were less obvious than Leo, who was, after all in his home territory.

I had acquired a quart of home-brew that I had hidden in the nearby bushes. I wasn't a frequent drinker but on a dance night it was a must to act like a grownup. I had sacrificed part of my pay which meant I would have to skip the trip to town tomorrow. "I can't have every thing." I told myself as I made donation at the door and went inside.

The first fiddler, Peter Muise, was busy on the stage tuning his fiddle. Peter was one of the best fiddle players in the area. He was a full blooded Mi'kmaq Indian who lived on the shores of the mill pond and made baskets for a living. I had visited him a few times and had been impressed with Peter's talent at taking a tree trunk and converting it into a practical carrying tool or a beautiful work of art.

Setting next to Peter was Gerry Boudreau who was the guitar player. They had finished readying their instruments and played a short warm-up tune. It was time for the dance to begin.

There was a noticeable quieting in the hall that lasted a few seconds when Diane walked into the hall. She was dressed in a provocative red dress that complemented her dark hair. She glanced around the room and spotted Danny sitting in a far corner. Without any hesitation she made her way to his seat and took his hand in hers. "Let's get in place before all the positions are taken." She said as she led him out onto the dance floor. With a full complement of dancers gathered in readiness Peter began with the Saint Anne's Reel. By the time the reel was over Diane was radiant with a look of joy. "Where have I been all this time?" She thought as Danny led her to a chair where the other women were seated.

When I was returning to his seat, I noticed Jules Comeau looking at me in an inquisitive way and he motioned to me to come and sit by him. I accepted the invitation and was soon in earnest conversation with Jules.

"Was that Diane Le Have you just danced with?" Jules asked.

"Yes, that's she." I responded.

"I hadn't seen her for years and she hasn't changed a bit. I always thought she was the most beautiful woman alive. Do you think she would dance with me?"

I was taken by surprise to be asked for my opinion on such a matter but it also made me feel important. "Jules," I said, "I owe you for bringing the bike from Halifax so the least I can do is asked for you."

Jules was an excellent carpenter who had spent a good deal of time away. He had never married in spite of being good looking in a rugged sort of way and being in his early thirties. He was light complexioned with gray eyes and light brown hair. It was common knowledge that he was shy when he was with women, which was the main factor why he was still single.

The second reel had already begun and Diane was on the dance floor with an older man. She seemed to be having the time of her life.

I snuck out and took a swig of my beer and promptly returned in time to meet Diane as she returned to her seat. A brief discussion about Jules followed during which I pointed him out to Diane. She looked at me and said. "Why not, he's the best looking man in the hall, except for you of course, and he could be a lot of fun to get to know."

I was on my way back to tell Jules the good news when I felt a hand on my arm. I looked to see who had grabbed his arm and came face to face with a petite woman who seemed to be in her early twenties.

I waited for an input that was quick in coming. "Could you dance with me when the next reel starts?" She asked.

"I'd love to but I have a message to give to a friend first. I'll come back as soon as I'm able." I continued across the hall and told Jules the answer to his question was yes. "It's all up to you now."

I returned to the young lady who had asked me to dance. The music had already started for the next reel so I was forced to sit that one out with Julie. She introduced herself and told him she was the new Belle Pointe teacher.

"I noticed you dancing with that pretty woman and saw that you know the dance moves well. I've never danced a reel the way you do it here so I feel that I'd better start with an experienced man."

If my head had been a balloon, it would have filled the hall. To receive that kind of compliment from this attractive woman was beyond my expectations. I needed a sip of my beer so I excused myself with a promise I would be back before the next reel started.

The musicians were due for a break and this gave me time to see if anything exciting was in progress outside.

Having located my bottle I wandered around the hall grounds listening to the gossip being circulated. Diane was one of the main subject's talked about. Besides talking about her good looks there were also discussions about what had brought her out after the long time she had spent in near isolation. I noticed that the conversations about her were quick to die down whenever I approached.

There was also talk about the new Belle Pointe school teacher. After all, they had her to thank for the good time they were having. As I came close to Leo's supply truck some loud shouting broke out. A local rowdy had caused a customer to spill a fresh drink and tempers were at a peak. Before a blow could be struck, Leo was between the two combatants with his axe handle held over his head. "It's only a drink that's easy to replace," he said, "So calm down and you each get one on me."

With that confrontation settled I wandered back to the hall just in time to see James Babin climb the steps to the stage where he addressed the hall occupants. "I want to thank you for your support for Belle Pointe School. We have collected a grand total of $96.75 and after the $10 donation to the church and the $5 hall fee we have $81.75 left to apply towards the needed repairs. I estimate that the actual cost will be higher so if you feel generous we have set up a donation box by the exit."

He motioned to Julie to join him on the stage and when she reached his side he said. "The lady standing next to me is Miss Julie Leveque, our new teacher. Let's give her a big welcome." The applause was loud and long with some of the younger men letting out appreciative whistles. Julie curtsied and said. "Thank you." She left the stage with James.

A different fiddler, Arthur Saunier, was tuning his instrument. It wasn't long before the hall was consumed with the joyous sounds of a new reel.

I escorted Julie to the dance floor danced with the newfound confidence of an expert. She responded with enthusiasm and by the end of the reel she felt that she had found a new home amongst a wonderful assemblage of people.

The hall was closed at mid-night and the residents of the Parish and their visitors went back to their less than exciting routine, or at least some did, while others went on to do things that Father Frotten would hear about at confession.

# 22

My father was leaving next week to return to Halifax. One of the jobs that I wasn't self-sufficient in was the hauling of the 12 cords of wood needed for the following year. I discussed this with him and he told me that he had obtained a promise from Edward D'Entremont that he would use his ox to do the hauling. With that problem solved I felt at ease when my father left.

We had been raising a steer but it was too young to be of much use in doing work and it was destined to be converted into beef when it reached the right size anyway.

On the Thursday following the dance I noticed a different tire track in Diane's driveway. I also noticed that the pipe was installed in the trench I had dug and prior to going to the door I took a look at what had been done. Neatly run from the well wall to an entrance into the basement was a 1 ½ inch lead pipe. At the well the pipe had been bent and its end disappeared into the water.

Satisfied with what I saw I went to the door where Diane stood watching me through the window. She opened the door and as I stepped inside.

She threw her arms around me and exclaimed. "Danny, I want to thank you for helping me to meet Jules." as she released him.

"He's the most wonderful man I've ever met."

Something must have happened since my Monday visit because Diane had acted normally then, I thought.

"Look at my new pump." She said as she rushed to the sink and started to move its handle up and down. Water flowed out in a clear stream and continued down the drain.

"You won't have to carry all that water in any more. We'll put the barrels in the barn and I'll have more room in the entrance hall for wood."

The first thing that came to my mind was that I was going to loose some of my pay because of the reduced work. As if she had read my thoughts Diane said. "I'll still pay you the same amount but I might call on you for extra help when the cold weather comes."

With my work done we discussed the dance and Diane asked about the new teacher I had danced with? I told her that I only knew that she came from Ottawa and was interested in Acadian history. "She's was staying with the Babins during the school term." I concluded.

The conversation became centered on the new plumbing and Diane commented that Billy would probably miss the evasive action he had to take to avoid being hit by the water bucket. "I have to confess that Billy is my confidant. Whenever I feel like I need to talk I'll go to the well and pour my heart out to him. Remember that Billy knows me better than anyone else, fortunately, he's only a fish."

# 23

Sitting at the table, sipping her hot tea Diane's thoughts wandered over the series of events that had brought her to this point in her life. When Jacque was alive, life had been simple but also boring. As a fisherman he was frequently away and she was left to fend for herself.

Two things kept her from being accepted by the other women of the area, the fact that she was childless and her beauty. Both were unnatural for a married woman of her age and these oddities were not looked on with favor by the women in Acadian societies.

Her sudden loss of Jacque had left her in a vacuum with no place to turn. When the priest and boat owner came and told her the shocking news she would have welcomed any comfort offered. Father Frotten was the first and only person who showed her the sympathy she required.

Diane had abandoned the religion she was brought up in after her brutal treatment by Sister Greta. Her last official connection with the church was the day she buried Jacque. She had been approached by a few of the older members of the congregation but she had resisted all their efforts to bring her back. Father Frotten, for some strange reason, had not attempted to convince her that she had erred and acted like a close friend on his increasing frequent visits. She remembered her naivety in accepting his concern as sincere but gradually awakened to the fact that he had motives that were not those expected from a priest.

Whenever he mentioned God, it was in a way that showed how forgiving he was and how he understood the need of the creatures he had made to satisfy the desires he had implanted in them. His welcoming hugs became more intimate and being a young woman with more than her share of God's gifts she found herself responding.

Raymond Frotten was not what most women would place in the must have class. He was short, thin with gray hair that highlighted his late 40's age. His features were rather sharp and they adapted well to his oratory style. When required he could alter his demeanor to fit any circumstance. Now, as he found himself in the role of a sinner he had to justify to Diane and to himself that what he was proposing was acceptable to men and God.

His first overt effort to seduce her seemed comical as she looked back. Ray, as she came to call him, whispered in her ear as he hugged her in greeting, "I desire you more than I want to save my soul. Will you help me in my urgent need?" At that moment he released her and fell to his knees with the most wistful look she had ever seen. As she looked down at his pleading eyes, she felt pity for this poor man who had never made love to a woman and succumbed to his plea.

She remembered clearly her surprise when she realized that this man of God was certainly not a novice in the art of making love. He knew every place a woman wanted touched, how to touch it and the proper thing to touch it with. He gave her a trip of pleasure that she had not only never experienced but, until that moment, had no idea it could even exist. They had risen from bed after their lovemaking and dressed. He suddenly fell to his knees and broke into a torrent of gibberish that she couldn't understand but she was sure it was directed to the supernatural. His last two words as he got to his feet were "Forgive me."

When they returned to the kitchen, he had become Father Frotten again. "My child, we shall talk about this when I return but always keep in mind that God forgives sinners and I grant you absolution." They drank tea together and then he left. Diane wondered at the time what she had allowed herself to become involved in and how she should react to him in the future. As she cleaned the table, she found a $5 bill neatly folded under his cup.

The flood of emotions that passed through her when she saw the money was beyond comprehension. What had she done? Not only had she made love to a priest and enjoyed it but she had been paid for her participation. She came back to the present and marveled at how naive she had been then and how quickly she had become what she was today.

Continuing her recollections she remembered considering whether to return to being the pure, purposeless creature she had been or should she take advantage of this new opportunity and let it lead her into the future?

Her answer came a few days later when a cartload of stove wood was dropped off. Instead of having to delay payment she took the $5 bill, still lying on the table, and passed it to the deliverer. Her new career was now in play.

It wasn't long before Diane realized that her fall from the strait and narrow could be widened to include other participants. Ray had become a regular visitor and even though she never asked he always left a token of his appreciation on her table.

Her second benefactor came to her door for a completely differently reason. She remembered seeing a dark automobile pull up alongside her house a few weeks after Jacques' death. A tall middle age man wearing the uniform of the RCMP got out and made his way to her kitchen door. With his Stetson hat in hand he introduced himself as Sgt. Naples from the County detachment. "Are you Mrs. Diane Le Have?" He asked. Diane answered with a nod of her head. "I have to have you sign this report concerning Mr. Le Have's death." He said "Can I come in and explain the form to you?" She had mumbled her O.K. and led him to the kitchen table and offered him a chair. She had taken a chair on the opposite side but the sergeant suggested she move next to him so he could point out the more intricate details that required her verification.

It required several minutes to complete the operation and Diane signed her name on the appropriate line. They rose from the table and the Sgt.'s hands brushed against her breasts. He quickly apologized for his clumsiness, folded the paper and placed it into his jacket pocket. "Mrs. Le Have," he said, "please feel free to call on me if you experience any unwanted attention. Young widows are frequently preyed on by men who feel that their grief leaves them open to manipulation." He then turned and walked out the door.

Diane had been taken by surprise and had blindly co-operated with the Sgt. As she regained control of her rational thinking, she realized that some of what had just happened was contrary to what one expected from a protector of the people. His leg had come in contact with her thigh throughout the report review and he had frequently made sure she was reading the right portion by physically guiding her hand with his. "Could his final statement have been an invitation rather than a warning?" She asked herself. At that moment fear overwhelmed her. Later, she realized, it gave her an easy opportunity to gain her second source of income.

Her affair with Ray had reached the point of being routine. Even though his desire for her hadn't waned, his duties of keeping the St. Agnes parishioner on the proper path to God's kingdom interfered with his realm of pleasure. He had settled on a weekly visit every Wednesday afternoon

By the time Sgt. Naples returned in the guise of giving her a copy of the recorded form she had signed she was ready for him.

He had arrived late on Friday afternoon. Her helper, Tom, had finished his work and would not be back until the following week. Ray had visited Wednesday so there was no one to interrupt the action that was to follow. Instead of sitting away from him as he showed her the form she pulled her chair close to his and let her hand touch his thigh. She felt his leg stiffen and then shift to contact hers. "It's hard for someone like me to keep my bills paid with the small income I have available. What do you think I should do to keep food on the table?" She asked as she returned his pressure against her. His hand displayed a slight tremor as he reached over and caressed her bare arm. "There are ways to live comfortably if you have the right friends." He answered. By now both participants were in what seemed to be a state of sexual arousals. His was real and Diane's was faked.

Having accomplished her preliminary objective she led him into the bedroom where the expected happened. In her mind he could not compare with Ray's savior-faire but what he lacked in talent he made up in equipment. She was still uncomfortable with what she had been doing but the shame diminished as time passed. They got up and dressed. Sgt. Naples was in a jovial mood and he told a few off-color jokes. These amused Diane and she began to see how sheltered a life she had been living.

Paul Naples sat at the table and drank a refreshing cup of black tea. He reached in his pants pocket and pulled out a roll of bills. He took the top bill that happened to be $10 and handed it to her. "This will help with the food." He said. "I'll be back soon."

Diane abruptly realized with two lovers she risked having them bump into each other at the most inopportune time. Ray was coming every Wednesday afternoon but was not committed to only visiting on that day. "Paul, I would appreciate it if you restricted yourself to one visit a week. It wouldn't look good to the local residents if they knew a RCMP was visiting a young widow, especially when he's married. How about visiting me on Friday afternoons?" She asked. He agreed and left after giving her an affectionate hug.

Diane now stood up and for the moment returned to the present. She had neglected to keep her stove at its required temperature to cook her meal and now busied herself adding wood and opening the draft. By the time she finished peeling her potatoes and carrots the water had begun boiling in the pot. She returned to trying to sort out her present position to the one she wanted to attain.

# 24

Her fear of accidental encounters between her men had to be allayed but how could she eliminate that possibility? A subtle plan began to hatch in her mind and as it developed her gained confidence that it would insure that there would never be a face to face meeting at her house. She had her worker, Tom, rearranged the barn interior so that there was room enough to park a large auto inside. The entry door was in disrepair so she had a new one made that could be opened and closed with ease and securely locked with a padlock. She also had Tom place blinds on the two windows at the ground level which rendered the barn into a secure hiding place. Placing a visiting auto in the barn also kept the unexpected innocent visitor from knowing someone else was visiting her.

A vital part of her solution was how to prevent two persons from using the barn at the same time. She had solved this problem by obtaining five identical padlocks with one difference; they needed different keys to be unlocked. When she purchased them, the clerk jokingly asked if she was trying to lock the weasels out of her henhouse "No," she had replied, "I'm trying to keep them in." They both had a good laugh

Now that she had perfected her plan, she proceeded to put it into effect. Her first action was to make up a schedule book out of a diary. In the front of the book she wrote the names of each visitor she had already made appointments with and assigned each a separate number. In the beginning there were only two completed lines and beneath those first two she added three more lines with numbers but no names. She planned to add names later if she had acquired any new partners.

In the body of the diary she wrote the appointments by date and time but identified the visitor by his code number only. She then lined up her five locks on hooks in a spare cabinet with the keys belonging to each hung above it and marked each position one through five. She took lock number one outside and locked the barn.

The next visitor scheduled was code number one and when he arrived she would give him a key and ask him to lock his car in the barn to keep his presence secret. He was to keep the key and use it every time he came. For each separate person she would repeat these steps.

Her explanation for the need of secrecy was that in the event someone came unexpectedly he could remain hidden while she sent the intruder away. Her only effort in maintaining her deception was to make sure the correct lock was on the door when a visitor came. One pitfall in the plan was if one of her clients came at an unscheduled time and his key didn't fit the lock. To prevent this she would warn each one that the first time he broke the schedule would be his last visit to her door.

Her third companion was just waiting to be hooked. His name was Morris Cohen and he owned a clothing store in town. Once a month he would load his truck that had a walk-in enclosed back that was equipped with built-in drawers and rods for hangers. Now, with a fair sampling of his wares, he would travel to the outlying villages to sell what he could. He never failed to stop at Diane's even though she seldom bought from him.

His normal day for visiting the village was the last Monday of the month. He would arrive at Diane's in the middle of the afternoon and try to sell her some of the latest female fashions. He would get her to try on dresses and would comment on how attractive she looked. He had once asked her to work in his store on Saturday where all she would have to do was model clothing for the effluent women who came by.

Morris never made it a secret that he thought Diane was a very desirable woman. He was married to a wife who thought sex was a reward to be offered to her man on special occasions and those occasions had become fewer as time went by. They slept in separate rooms and lived like brother and sister.

Morris looked older than his age of 40. He walked in a stoop, slow, deliberate fashion with a slight limp. His features showed the image of a man who suffered from frustration even though his manner of speech was just the opposite. He expressed himself with a high degree of optimism.

On the day Diane had chosen to make her move Morris had arrived late. Diane had dressed in a dress that was in bad need of repair with the intention of offering to buy a new one. Her plan was to have him bring in several articles for her to try on and during this process she would reveal her body in such a way that the following negotiations would be predictable in their outcome.

The first actions taken after Diane had expressed her need for a dress to replace the one she had on was to determine the size of the new item. Morris said. "We must have a perfect fit. Let's go inside and I will measure to enable me to bring in the dresses that will most closely meet your needs." Diane knew full well she took a size six but the measuring fit into her plan. She had never been measured with such tender loving care. She could sense his unnecessary touching as he stretched his paper tape across her body parts and leaned forward at the right time to increase the contact. He reluctantly completed the operation and said. "You're a perfect size 6."

He went to his truck and returned with an armful of dresses and laid them on the table. Diane selected the one that best suited her purposes. It was long with a zipper that reached from her buttocks to the nape of her neck and was made of sheer material. After going into the bedroom and slipping it on she pretended to have problems with the zipper and came out of the bedroom with a large part of her body exposed. "Could you zip this up please?" She asked Morris.

By now Morris was going out of his mind. Had he not been such a gentle person he would have had Diane on the floor by now. He zipped up the dress without any difficulty thanking fate for another opportunity to touch Diane's bare skin. Satisfied that the dress fit, Diane went back into the bedroom to change. "I need your help again," she called, "could you come here and help. An unsuspecting Morris walked into the room and was faced with a naked Diane lying on the bed. "Take off your cloths and jump in." Diane said.

An hour later, thoroughly exhausted Morris sat with Diane at the kitchen table in an elated state. Diane complemented Morris on his lovemaking as she poured him a cup of tea. "I'd love to buy that dress," she said, "but when I noticed the price on the tag I realized that I can't afford it." Morris, still in heaven brought on by the hour of pleasure, said to Diane. "The dress is yours; it was made for your exquisite body." Diane then went into how difficult it was to make ends meet with the meager income she had and how she had thought of going to work. "The best I could do would be to move to Halifax and become a servant." She said.

Morris, who had just experienced the most exciting moments of his life, took on a look of concern. "Diane," he said, "maybe I can help ease the burden." He drew out his full wallet and handed her a bill. "This should help." The bill had a 20 inscribed on its face. They made plans for a rendezvous in the future. Morris' truck would not fit through the barn door so they agreed that social visits would have to be made by him using his car. She assigned him Sunday afternoons starting at 1:00. With his key in his pocket he left floating on a cloud.

She was brought out of her deep thoughts by the noise of her pot boiling over. She went to the stove and moved the pot to the cooler back surface and placed a cast iron frying pan on to warm it up for the fish she was planning to cook. She kept herself occupied and away from her reminiscing until her supper was finished and her dishes washed. With the unresolved situation still on her mind she retired to her parlor and sat down in an overstuffed chair which had been bought from her fourth conquest.

She remembered with vivid clarity how she had walked into Gray's Furniture store in town and had been greeted by a short man with a heavily muscled chest. He had the type of build that required him to frequently adjust his trousers to keep them from slipping down. His eyes were a pale blue and were set wide apart in a ruddy complexioned face. He had undressed her with his eyes before either had spoken a word. By now Diane's naiveté had been erased and she was able to read his actions as easily as reading a book.

They bargained on the price of the chair and once that was settled they talked about delivery. "I would like you to deliver this to me on Monday afternoon after 2:00p.m." She told him. "My driver is off on that day, how about Tuesday?" He asked. "I'm not asking for your driver to bring it, I want you to bring it on Monday. You'll be surprised at the bonus that comes with following instructions." He agreed to her terms and as soon as she left he began a search for someone to mind the store on Monday afternoon.

Sam Gray was a fairly aggressive man and he was not easily manipulated but on Monday he was quickly enticed into a relationship that, for the time it lasted, made him a pussy cat when he was with Diane. Her house decor improved as their affair progressed.

She now had all the clients she wanted and every thing went according to her plans. She returned to the present and noticed the sun had set. She lit her kerosene lamp and took a book from the mantel. She would return to her memories and possible paths open to her at a later time.

# 25

Several weeks prior to the dance Leo had been having an enjoyable summer day. Except for the periodic payments he had to make to keep him from being raided things had gone exceptionally well.

He was standing in his front yard on a Tuesday afternoon admiring how the insects pursued their ways of life. Some were gathering honey, others were landing on a dead mouse and a spider was making a net to capture his next meal. The wind was blowing gently and the sky was a deep blue with large white billowing clouds lazily floating by. As he scanned the area, he suddenly became aware of something that was out of place. Emerging from the path across the road was a woman and she was headed to the spot where he stood. He recognized her as the widow Le Have and wondered what she could want from him.

Diane reached Leo's nature observatory and stopped. She looked at the scenery and, like Leo, took in the movements of the multitude of life in the area, "I wonder if they are aware of the suffering of their fellow creatures or if they are solely preoccupied in their own needs for existence?" She asked, as if to herself. Leo felt that this profound question required an answer "Mrs. Le Have, all living things must have some awareness of the suffering of others, after all, they're the ones who cause it."

Diane continued. "I know we're not best friends but I have seen you in the village several times and have heard that you sell liquor. Forgive me if my information is inaccurate but if it's correct I have a favor to ask of you."

Leo wasn't sure what this pretty lady wanted but felt the answer was near at hand. "Whatever you want is yours if I have it." He said. Diane said. "I was setting at my kitchen table thinking about the past when all of a sudden I felt the need to do some drinking with a male companion. Jacque, my husband, and I used to sit at the kitchen table and get feeling good on a bottle of Rye Whiskey. We'd talk about every thing under the sun and usually we'd end up drunk. I was going to ask you to sell me a quart of Rye and help me drink it. If there's any left you can take it when you leave."

Leo, who had never served a drink to a woman, took his time coming up with an answer. Her request, although surprising, seemed to be genuine with no hidden meanings. If she could afford his price why not enjoy an afternoon of conversation and drinking with a beautiful woman? He said. "Wait here."

Leo went into his home and came out with a bottle inside a brown paper bag. At the front door he put up a sign that simply said, out. He never locked his doors and had yet to lose any thing significant. Customers could come and go, take what they wanted and leave payment in an empty tin can on his table.

The couple left following the path that led to the cutoff to Diane's house. The afternoon went by quickly and the level of liquid in the bottle went down. An agreement was reached during their talk that they would get together again but only when Diane went over to get him. They both had interesting things to discuss which included their separate childhoods, Leo's current business and the hard times the depression had caused. Nothing was mentioned about Diane's present state of affairs.

Leo left at about 4:00P.M. And found his way home where he already had three clients waiting his return.

# 26

Diane sat looking at her empty glass with a sense of satisfaction. She had spent the afternoon with an adult male with no mention of sex. They had spoken as equals and with the loosening affect of the whiskey a lot of humor surfaced. For her a load, however temporary, had been lifted. She now had six men in her life, four lovers, one worker and one conversationalist-drinking buddy.

Diane's plans were working like clockwork. By maintaining strict control of her scheduling she averted confrontations between her companions. In fact, none knew that any of the others existed in Diane's world.

A small glitch came up when Tom, her worker, had quit so he could start working in Halifax. She remembered how Danny had come to her door with a hopeful look asking if he could take Tom's place. She was glad now she had hired him as he had done a good job and had a subtle way of influencing people without being aware of it.

With her mind loosened up by her drinking she faced the fact that her life style had to eventually change. She had decided that at the proper moment she would leave and start life anew but first she had to acquire the means of carrying out her plans. She examined her appointment book that was now missing its first page. Her appointments were marked with the code numbers and the key to the code was securely hidden. It was understood by all that one could skip a meeting but could never visit outside of their scheduled time. She rose from her chair, cleaned the table and looked forward to repeating this pleasant episode soon.

# 27

The first violation of Diane's strict schedule happened during one of Leo's drinking visits. A car pulled up to the barn door and a man got out and tried to unlock the door. The key didn't fit. The man, Sgt. Naples, came to the door and briskly knocked. Diane had answered the knock and had carelessly left the inner hall door open. As she angrily spoke to the Sgt. Leo sat in full view. Although Naples didn't mention him Leo was certain that he had been observed. Naples left in a rage, spinning his car wheels in his haste.

Diane returned to the table and told Leo that the Sgt. was frustrated by his inability to catch a youngster whom had been letting cattle out of their pastures. He was checking the neighborhood to see if anyone had seen a kid acting in an odd fashion. Leo suspected that there was more to this than what Diane told him but the afternoon was just beginning and the company was pleasant so he didn't see any reason to cut his visit short. They continued their tête-à-tête until late in the afternoon. Leo rose and said. "I probably have people waiting for me. I'm looking forward to our next visit."

Arriving at his home he could see everything was not as he had left it. His sign was on the ground along with his front door that had been ripped off its hinges. Three of his regulars were standing in the yard with perplexed looks on their faces. One called out. "What happened?"

Leo ignored the question and went in. The inside looked like a wild bull had been set loose. Furniture was smashed and all the liquor bottles broken but the money he had left on the table was all over the floor. Leo's first thought was, "Who did this?"

With the promise of a few free drinks, Leo soon had his door back in place and while his clients cleaned up the mess and knocked the furniture back into usable condition he went to his secret catch and brought back enough stock to open shop.

One of his customers, Jake, indicated wordlessly that he wanted to talk to Leo privately. They went outside and Jake told how he had seen the entire destructive effort.

He had come through the shortcut but was still in the sheltered part when this black auto came racing down the road and stopped in front of Leo's, Sgt. Naples had jumped out and ran to the house where he tore off the door and entered. Jake could hear him swearing and the breaking of glass. Within a few seconds the Sgt. had completed his disruption and was back in his car and gone. Leo swore Jake into secrecy and they returned to house.

"What the hell's going on," Leo asked himself, "I pay those people for protection and look at the results. Does this have anything to do with me visiting Diane?" He made up his mind to find out the cause of the Sgt.'s anger.

# 28

The events that led to Joel's demise were preventable but the best path was not always followed by the participants. Greed, resistance to change and stupidities were all factors that contributed.

Joel had lived in a bootlegger environment all his life. His father was involved from the time of his first memories and he had inherited the operation from him. There wasn't a fortune to be made but the work was easy and the company pleasant at times.

During the winter of 37 he was visited for the first time by an RCMP constable named Elliot Johns. He had walked in by himself and ordered the customers out. Joel remembered his exact words. "I can break all your bottles, seize all that money on the table and put you in jail or we can make a deal where you can stay in business with no bothersome raids. The choice is yours."

Joel wasn't the brightest man in the world but he had enough sense to listen to a proposal he couldn't turn down.

He had the build of a lumberjack and had put it to good use in keeping his clients in line but here he found he was faced with a very powerful foe. "Tell me what you want," he said, "I'll do it if I'm able."

The constable laid out the plan in short but complete details. "Each month you will be visited by me or my representative and you will hand over 10 % of your profit in an envelope. It's either that or you'll be put out of business."

Joel started to object but before he could say a word the constable took a full bottle off the table and started pouring its contents on the floor.

Joel shouted out in anguish. "I agree."

So began Joel's path to a destruction that was partly of his own making.

Nothing changed for Joel except for the monthly visit and a 10 % decrease in his income. Rather than take a chance of losing customers, he accepted the monetary loss.

A significant event occurred in early spring. Instead of Elliot coming alone he was accompanied by another person that Joel had never seen before. Elliot introduced him as Vinnie and said that from now on Vinnie would be the collector.

"I will be gone from the area and he is my replacement."

Joel accepted the change without resistance but a plan developed in his mind on how to return things to their former fashion.

In its infancy the plan was to scare Vinnie into abandoning the collection. Joel reasoned that with the RCMP out of the picture Vinnie couldn't maintain his hold on the bootleggers of which he was only one of many.

He began a search through idle talk with his customers about who Vinnie was and where he lived. Bit by bit he uncovered the facts he needed to carry out his plan that would rid him of this pest

Vinnie was now living in much more comfortable fashion. With his increased income he could afford better clothing and food. He had even found a girl friend that spent time with him on his ship.

Her name was Yvette and he had met her at the house where he had his laundry washed. Although their relationship was intimate there was never any plan of marriage. Vinnie had a wife and three children in Italy and Yvette had a husband who was extremely jealous but was fishing at sea most of the time.

The fatal night arrived for Joel's plan to be carried out. He knew that Vinnie was on board the ship and his intention was to attract his attention so that he would come out through the hatch he normally used. What Joel didn't know was that Yvette was also on board.

He had a pick handle that was somewhat larger than a baseball bat and that combined with his superior strength was all he needed to do Vinnie in. The entire dock was unlit except for the small gangplank light so approaching the ship unseen was easy. Once at the gangplank he unscrewed the light which was accessible from the dock and now the area was in complete darkness except for the dim glow from the distant street lights. The ship's portholes were covered with blankets and it would appear that it was deserted.

Inside the captain's room Yvette and Vinnie were entwined in a lover embrace. Life had not been this good for a long time, Vinnie thought. The love tryst continued with the lovers completely unaware of the person sneaking up the gangplank.

Having reached the hatch undetected, Joel rapped on the hatch with the end of his handle and waited. After a few moments with no response he rapped again with a little more force. This time Yvette's passion was penetrated and she told Vinnie in a whisper that she had heard a noise. Not thinking that there was a problem Vinnie was returning to his lovemaking when the rap was repeated. This time he heard it and rose to dress. "What are you going to do?" Yvette asked. ""I'm going to see what's causing the noise, I'll be right back."

Yvette, who was deathly afraid of her husband grabbed Vinnie by the arm and said. "What if it's my husband, Marty?" She asked. "He's dangerous when he's mad." Vinnie, who had intended to use his normal exit to investigate, hesitated. Whatever he wanted to do did not include getting Yvette in trouble. He pondered the situation as a new rap came from the hatch.

With definite knowledge of where the noise maker was located Vinnie decided to surprise the visitor by sneaking up on him. He went out a hatch on the outboard side of the ship and soundlessly made his way around the stern and arrived at a secure place where he could see the entrance.

As he approached the inboard hatch he could make out a crouched figure with some sort of shaft in his hands. Knowing the person meant him harm Vinnie decided to ask no questions and use surprise as a tool.

He searched the area but all he found was a small wooden pulley which was useless as a weapon. He decided to use the pulley to distract his opponent and make an attempt to disarm him. He tossed the pulley so that it landed on the deck beyond the intruder's location and when the figure made a move in that direction he rushed him from the rear.

The figure swung around when he sensed the attack and barely missed Vinnie with a vicious swing of his handle. Joel was thrown off balance and Vinnie grabbed the pick handle and gave a push at the same time. Joel fell to the deck rolled over and leaped to his feet with the weapon now in Vinnie's hands. Without a weapon but blinded by rage he left Vinnie no choice but to defend himself. Vinnie swung the handle at Joel and it connected behind his left ear with a definite crunch. Joel stumbled to the railing and fell into the water between the ship and the dock

Vinnie looked over the side and in the dim light saw that the tide was taking the body toward the harbor entrance which led to the sea. He watched as Joel floated out beyond the stern and into open water. Returning to the cabin where he had so recently been making love to Yvette, he found her fully dressed. "It wasn't your husband," he said, "but I think it best if you leave so that no one knows you were here." Yvette kissed him on the mouth and without a word got off the ship.

The tide didn't carry the body out to sea but placed it in a position that created another of the many controversies between the two police forces.

# 29

I was anxious to see Bob after the dance night. I felt sorry for the fun my friend had missed and wanted to tell him about the new teacher at Belle Pointe. With free time available I rode my bike to Bob's hoping to find him home and I also wanted to see my sister Maggie. The bike was now the main way I traveled so I jumped on it and left for my visit. Upon arriving I went into the house and found Maggie washing clothes.

She had two big tubs full of water placed on a stand with a hand-operated wringer between them. She was scrubbing a shirt on a wash board when she saw me. Wiping her hands on her apron she embraced me and kissed my cheek.

"Hello Danny." She said. We chatted for a few minutes about things at home and I asked where Bob was.

"He's out by the clothes line clearing out the weeds that get in the way."

I went to the back of the house and found Bob swinging a scythe with determination. He was almost finished and after a few more swings leaned on the scythe and acknowledged I was there." Let's go to the barn and I'll put this away and we can talk."

Maggie came out as we were leaving with a basket full of wet clothes. You might think that two young men would volunteer to help her but tradition interfered. Men did men's work and women did women's work. Bob cleaned his scythe and placed it in its storage area. We sat down at the front barn door which had been slid wide open.

We spoke of their accomplishment since the last time met

I told Bob about my Dad's visit and how I was going to haul the logs home using Edward D'Entremont's ox.

Bob, who was a bit more daring, said. "I'll bet we could train your young ox to do the job."

"Dad didn't think so but if that's the only way I'll try."

Bob told me about his aunt's severe case of indigestion that had cleared up after the Doctor's visit. According to Bob he had given her an evil smelling liquid and told her to stay in bed for a day. "The medicine must have worked because she was up the next day, good as new."

I was impatient to get started on my story on the events that happened at the hall. As soon as Bob stopped talking, I broke in.

"You missed a good dance; there was a huge crowd, good music and not too much fighting. I even drank a bottle of beer."

Bob listened attentively. He had already heard about some of the dance activity from friends and had a few questions he wanted answered. "I heard you danced with Mrs. Le Have and the new Belle Pointe teacher. I'll bet that gave you ideas you shouldn't have."

I was amused by Bob's comments and replied. "Diane is only a friend and she wanted to use me as a tool to show she was there for a good time. The new teacher, being a stranger, surprised me by doing the asking. Anyway, I danced with the two most beautiful women in the hall."

"From what I heard the Belle Pointe teacher is pretty and young. Seeing that you danced with her I wonder what you thought of her? I wish I'd had that chance"

I felt like I was the hero of the moment. My best friend was envious of my experience and I was tempted to stretch the truth and to tell Bob she held me real close during parts of the dance. Instead I stuck to my normal honest self and said. "She's just as pretty as Diane but a few years younger. The best way for you to judge is to see her."

I then went on to tell about how good the beer was and how Leo controlled his clients behavior with his ax handle. I also mentioned that I had acted as go-between in getting Jules Comeau a dance with Diane and how they seemed to enjoy each other. "She thanked me for helping her meet him."

We came up with a plan to see Julie that to us seemed unobtrusive. We would bicycle past the school after it closed for the day and observe her as she departed for home.

"We might have to go past the school several times but we should get a good look at her." I said.

The plan was put aside until more important things were taken care of.

# 30

Diane found herself in a pensive mood. She was in the kitchen doing her dishes and her mind wandered back to the dance she had attended and its resulting effects on her life. Having settled on a maximum of four clients, she now found herself with a fifth lover, Jules who had healed and returned to work after having enjoyed several magnificent evenings with her. The significant difference between the first four and him was that she had fallen in love. As time passed, she acknowledged that she couldn't continue her charade. Her initial involvement had been for money and pleasure. The first four participants, although not aware of the complicated affair she had arranged, were getting what they paid for and she felt no moral obligations to them.

Falling in love presented a problem she hadn't anticipated. Her original plan had been to acquire sufficient funds and leave the village for Halifax where she could start life over. Fate, however, had intervened and now she was forced into following a different path or she would lose her newfound love.

What Diane forgot was that her feelings weren't the only ones involved. She had some advance warning when Leo had told her about Naples's reaction at having seen him in her kitchen but had chosen to ignore it.

After considering all the facts Diane made up her mind. She would break off with her four paying customers and convince Jules to live with her in Halifax. No matter what the outcome was, she had enough money saved to get by for a while. She took out her appointment book and reviewed her schedule. She would tell each one on their next visit that it was finished. Satisfied with her determination, she replaced the book in a drawer and resumed her cleaning.

# 31

After the vandalism on Leo's place of business he became more careful in how he operated. He placed locks on his doors and never left the house open when he was away. He was waiting for the collector to show up for his envelope to find out why he had been punished. He had always suspected that the protection was provided by someone at a higher level than Constable Johns but had never suspected Sgt. Naples was the one at the top.

As he thought back about the series of events since the raid by the Cpl. who was no longer in the Rivemouth detachment he recalled Constable Elliot Johns visiting him in the morning. He had assured Leo that it wasn't a raid but rather a friendly visit. "Let's sit and I'll explain the purpose of my visit. I'm sure you remember being raided by Cpl. Mason and how he warned you that the cost would go up if you were raided again. Well, there are factions in our office that feel that we should crack down hard on all bootleggers in our district and smaller groups that feel you provide a service that keeps a more peaceful environment. This latter group, of which I'm a member, has come up with a plan that will allow you to stay in business with minimum interference. There will be a small cost, 10 % of your profits, to insure your ability to stay open."

Leo knew when he was up against a situation he couldn't control so he readily agreed to the conditions. He was promised he would be forewarned of any planned raids and he would be visited periodically by a collector of the insurance payments. Elliot must have had a connection with someone in control because he was never bothered until Sgt. Naples nearly destroyed his place.

The only direct contact he had experienced with the Sgt. was when they had seen each other at Diane's. He reminded himself to ask Diane if she had any idea why the Sgt. had become so infuriated at their next meeting. Thinking back, he recalled seeing a man who could have been Naples at Diane's back door when he was on his way to the store to buy cigarettes. He had reached the point in the shortcut where her house was visible and saw a tall man dressed in the classical brown uniform of the RCMP holding a Stetson hat in his hand while he knocked at the door. With his back turned towards Leo, positive identification was impossible.

The day arrived for the payment to be made only this time there were two collectors, Elliot and a man introduced as Vinnie.

"There is going to be a change in the way we operate," Elliot said, "from now on Vinnie will be collecting the insurance money and he will also be delivering you your stock. I'm being relocated to Halifax but I may see you again in the future." Leo argued that he didn't need any help in obtaining supplies but was told if he wanted to stay in business he would have to follow instructions.

After collecting their payment the two men left a confused and angry Leo. He was determined to find out what was going on.

He recalled the last afternoon he spent with Diane with a degree of regret but also realized that the visits had to come to an end. He had knocked at her door carrying a new brand of whiskey that was the only kind his new suppliers provided. Diane opened the door and invited Leo to come in. They sat at their usual seats and without saying a word filled their glasses. Leo was aware that Diane's demeanor was altered from that of his past visits and his outlook had also changed since the Sgt.'s intrusion.

Leo was the first to speak. He told Diane about the things that had happened to him since his last visit. "What would cause Naples to go on such a rampage? Do you think that he did this because he saw me with you?"

Diane sat in deep thought. She started to speak but abruptly closed her mouth. She was desperately searching for the right words to use in reply to Leo's inquiry. She could pretend ignorance or tell him what she felt was the truth. Her decision had been made on her course of action concerning her clients but what to do about Leo hadn't even entered her mind. Of course when Jules became involved her need for Leo became greatly diminished. She reached a decision, she would tell Leo about her affair with the Sgt. while pretending he was the only one she was involved with.

"Leo, I have a confession to make and also an apology to offer. I have been seeing the Sgt. regularly since Jacque died. I knew he would react badly if he saw another man in the house but I never suspected he would become violent. Please forgive me for placing you in danger. You have been a lifesaver to me."

Leo absorbed her confession. Her apology was unnecessary and he told her so "Diane, you have given me a sort of pleasure that I had never expected to encounter in my lifetime. I enjoyed every minute of our conversations and the whiskey always seemed to taste better drinking with you."

They spent the remainder of the visit talking about meaningless things and finished half the bottle. Leo was the first one of her men that she told that there wouldn't be any more visits. He thanked her for her company and her contributions to his business and for the first time during their acquaintance he touched her gently on the hand.

Having calmed down from his earlier anger Leo pondered the new knowledge he had gained. Jealousy was obviously the motive for Naples's actions but he acted as if he knew what he would find when he went into Leo's home. Was he the boss of the extortion racket? The facts were beginning to point in that direction. A plan began to form in Leo's brain, one that would rid him of the drain on his income and, if properly implemented, place the Sgt. in a difficult situation.

# 32

Bob and I were now fully occupied in our new project. We had gathered the tools needed to cut our 24 cords of firewood. These consisted of two double bladed axes, a bucksaw, a two-man saw, one mallet with accompanying wedges and two pee-vees. We had started cutting on Bob's wood lot with the intention of spending as much time as needed to have all the wood ready to haul in December when the snow was deep enough to haul the wood on bobsleds.

We had cut 10 cords when we got the bad news. The ox we had planned on to haul our wood had broken a leg while logging. The owner was force to put it out of its misery and it ended up as meat for the table. After a fruitless effort to find a replacement for the dead ox we met in our private counseling area to ponder about a solution.

Bob came up with a suggestion. "Why can't we use your steer to help? I know he's small but he must have some strength."

I had to agree. "Even a small ox is strong but without any horns how could we harness him to a bob-sled?"

The oxen were always attached to their load by a head yoke that was connected by wrapping a leather strap around the horns so an ox without horns was useless.

"A horse doesn't have any horns and it still can be harnessed to do work. How about making a neck collar?" Bob asked.

Working on a neck harness taxed our inventive capabilities but in the end we came up with a workable device that had an iron chain core wrapped in old blankets and covered in burlap. The attachment point was provided by a rusty U bolt. We tested this on Dan, the ox, named as a joke after me, to find out if he could be made to follow directions.

With Bob on the right [gee] side and me on the left [haw] side we soon had Dan obeying four commands; gee, haw, whoa and go. Satisfied that Dan could be controlled the next step was to find a bob-sled to haul the wood on. All we could find was a discarded front end of a sled set up for a pair of oxen. Modifying the sled for a single ox was beyond our ability so an alternate solution was required.

I remembered having seen a red, white-faced steer the same size as Dan in a pasture in Belle Pointe. "Maybe we could borrow another ox to make a pair. I know where there's one the right size. Let's ask the owner if we can use him."

We mounted on my bike and went to see if the owner of the steer was home. We had to pass the Belle point school to reach Jeff Bourque's house and as they passed by Bob commented that he had yet to see Julie.

When we reached Mr. Bourque's home, we could see the steer lying in the pasture chewing its cud.

"At least he still has the animal, let's see if he'll let us use him." I said as we pulled into the yard.

Jeff was in his barn sharpening his ax on a foot-operated grindstone. He welcomed the pair with a statement, "You're just in time to help me get this ax ground to a peak."

He quickly converted his sharpener to a two—man mode and Bob grabbed the handle and started to turn the stone which was 30 inches in diameter and three inches thick. When it was rotated its lower edge passed through a trough of water. It was an ideal instrument for sharpening farm tools and in a few minutes the ax was ground to perfection.

"Now that we're finished doing my work how can I help you?" Jeff asked.

I explained what they needed and wondered if it was O.K. with him. "We'll take good care of him and feed him well. We won't need him for more than a couple of week of work and he'll be partly trained when he comes back."

Jesse thought for a moment and said. "I have a little hauling to do myself so I'll make a deal with you; I'll lend you Ace if you bring in my wood after you're finished with your work."

An agreement was reached and they all shook on it. "When can we have him?" Bob asked.

"Why not take him with you now and save yourselves a trip?"

I led the way walking my bike and Bob followed leading Ace with a rope tied around his neck.

As we approached the school, we met the older students heading for home. When they were passing a young woman suddenly burst out of the girls entrance and shouted. "Please wait a minute."

Taken by surprise we stopped and waited for the shouter to come up to us.

"Aren't you Danny, the young man I danced with?" She asked.

I recognized her and acknowledged I was one and the same. I introduced Julie and Bob and a discussion was begun.

"I was looking over some student reports and happened to glance outside and saw this strange procession coming down the road. You may find me nosey but I have an active imagination that needs to be satisfied. What are you going to do to this wonderful animal?"

I explained the predicament we were faced with and our proposed solution.

"I marvel at your ambition, if it was I, I would probably have thrown up my hands and given up. You Acadians don't know how to admit defeat." Julie said.

"Are you both finished with attending school?" She asked.

Bob answered. "Yes but we both finished the eight grades and that's pretty good for here."

Julie realized she was keeping them from their original intent and said. "I apologize for holding you up but I couldn't help myself. Perhaps I can repay you. Why don't you both stop by some day after school lets out and we'll talk about it?"

We both express thanks for her interest in us and with a brief farewell continued down the road.

We decided to keep Ace and Dan at Bob's and operate from that location in preparing the team to work together. With Dan already partly trained it didn't take long to get them to work as a team and obey the required commands. As an experiment we hooked them to a plow and were able to turn over the ground with ease. Now we had to complete the cutting and wait for enough snow for hauling.

# 33

Julie was sitting at her desk working on her project about the Acadians when she had spotted Bob and Danny leading Ace on the road. She had developed a system for gathering information about the Acadians. As a special assignment she had asked her class to bring in any old documents and bits of data that would help build a more complete and accurate history of their origin. A large part of the material was obviously tainted and some required additional research but there was also a surprising amount of interesting information that was based on fact.

One thing that began to materialize in her findings was that the Acadian way of life had not changed much through the years. If you took away the electric power, the telephone and the autos only a few people had you were back to living the way they did 100 years ago.

While talking to Mrs. Belle Muise she found out that not all residents were descendants from the original Acadians. Mrs. Muise said her grandfather had told her that in the early 1800's three men had landed on Isle a Joe in a rowboat. They never told where they came from and the names they went by were not French. These men had been accepted into the community and through the years their surnames became recognized as of Acadian origin. Also, the French had been very close to the Mi'kmaq natives and many of them carried native blood in their veins but in these cases their last names were always French.

As she sat at her desk, her thoughts turned to the two young men who had just gone by with their ox. She already had known that they were no longer going to school.

She had attended a meeting with the other teachers of the area and had been told that to finish the eight grades was considered a great accomplishment. She had specifically asked Mrs. Amy Vacon about what kind of a student Danny was and had been told that he had been the most promising student she had ever taught.

"Unfortunately he won't be attending school this year and for that matter his formal education is at an end. His friend Bob is not quite as smart as Danny but he also has a potential for higher education. I found that challenging them as a team always produced the best results." She told Julie.

Armed with this knowledge Julie pondered how she could ensnare the two into increasing their education. She felt certain that they would accept her invitation to visit after school hours so she proceeded to prepare a study plan to start them off. It was simply a modified version of her ninth grade instruction material with the simpler parts deleted. If Mrs. Vacon was correct in her analysis those parts would be wasted anyway.

With everything on schedule Bob and I met in the barn and talked about our accomplishment. Bob happened to mention that Julie was certainly a very pretty lady and we should accept her invitation. "Even if we don't agree with what she wants we'll still have a good time."

At shortly after 3:30 P.M. a few days later we arrived at Belle Point School and knocked at the boy's entrance door. Julie must have been on her way to meet us as she immediately opened the door and invited us in.

She led us to her desk and asked us to each get a chair from the student's area and sit facing her on her raised platform.

"How are you doing with the training of your oxen?" She asked.

Bob who hadn't taken his eyes off of her since their arrival remained silent.

I, who was also taken in by Julie, had retained enough presence of mind to respond. "We have them obeying our commands and we found out that they are stronger than we thought at first. When the snow comes we'll be ready to haul."

Julie said. "I have to complement you on your accomplishments, both at home and in school. I spoke to Mrs. Vacon about you and she was very disappointed that you were not continuing into the ninth grade. How do you feel about increasing your education?"

Bob, having returned to reality, answered. "Around here you don't need a lot of schooling to get by. If you can read, write, count, add and subtract you have all it takes to do any job that's available here. My father only went to school five years and he became a carpenter."

I added. "Even our teachers have only finished grade 10 and teaching is the work that requires the most education."

Julie realized that she was talking to two young men who had lived in a closed society all their lives and had no appreciation for what went on outside of their small circle. Even the Acadians who worked in the cities tended to gather in groups having the same background. She intended to try to break that barrier and make them aware of the possibilities open to them. Subjects such as History and Geography were supposed to bridge the gap between their isolated existence and the rest of the world, she knew, but to the student the knowledge of where and how other people lived was equivalent to fairy tales.

"The world you live in will change as you grow older. Wouldn't it be better to be ready for those changes? Even today your fathers have to leave to work in Halifax but the work they do is restricted to manual labor." She said.

Their response was not encouraging so she decided to change her approach by appealing to their sense of loyalty to their own kind. "During our meeting the teachers generally agreed that the English have better schools and the Acadians are being neglected by the government. From my point of view, being new to the area and having been exposed to several cultures, I have no choice but to believe that you are being treated as second class citizens. Would you agree to help me prove my point?"

This time she saw a glimmer of interest on both their faces. "How do you plan to do that?" I asked.

"I'd planned to write my own version of the Acadian's history up to and including the present since I was a young girl. That's the primary reason why I chose to teach here and observe first hand how you live. Your contribution would be to prove that given a chance you could and would keep learning. The choice is yours to prove me right or wrong."

"We can't go back to school so how will we help prove your idea?" Bob asked.

"With no ninth grade student at Belle Point I decided to formulate an abbreviated course that could be taught in one hour a week. When you consider that the time that I can devote to each class is less than four hours a week and much of that is spent bringing the less gifted students up to par, one hour may prove to be adequate. I've been assured that you're both fast learners so if you agree we'll give it a try."

We discussed the possible ways this plan could be implemented and despite some reluctance Julie finally got us to agree to try.

"You're not obligated to continue if it gets too hard. Some things start off with difficulty and ease up with time and the opposite is also true. We'll feel our way like a crawling child learning to walk."

Friday was the day they would meet when all the regular students were gone.

# 34

Vinnie had been an easy-going man all his life. Violence was only something to be used in self protection. Until Joel's unfortunate demise he had never caused an injury more severe than a black eye or a split lip. He was bothered by the action he had taken against Joel but justified this by the fact that he was the intended victim.

He had a long discussion with Sgt. Naples immediately after it happened and was assured that he was safe and the matter would be buried as an accident. "We must inspect Joel's place of business to make certain that he didn't leave any thing there that could point suspicion towards us." Naples had said and that is how Joel's liquor found its way into Vinnie's possession. The one thing that Vinnie had not told the Sgt. was about Yvette's involvement.

For the first time Sgt. Naples indicated to Vinnie that he was expected to use persuasion to keep the bootleggers in line. He felt that he was slowly but surely being dragged into a life he had previously abhorred but the rewards were such that he didn't resist. He was able to send money to his wife and also enjoy the pleasures denied him in the past. With mixed emotions he decided to continue playing the Sgt.'s game while seeking an acceptable and safe way out.

His affair with Yvette had resumed after she recovered from her fright. They were more careful and had abandoned the ship as their rendezvous site. Vinnie had located a cabin which he rented for the sole purpose of their lovemaking. It was accessible by auto but isolated in a lakeside area. An additional use soon occurred to him. The cabin was ideal as a hiding place for his money that had by now reached a significant amount. The episode on the ship had made him leery of it being a safe place when he was away so he had transferred his hoard into a tin box that was placed under the sink floorboards.

Another precaution that Yvette insisted on was that they drive past her home when returning from an evening of pleasure so she could be certain her husband had not unexpectedly returned. She had a ready excuse of having spent the night with her girlfriend.

After seeing that the house was empty, Vinnie would drop her off a few blocks away and wait until a light came on in her house before driving away.

The old Ford that was intended for work only was now used as Vinnie's private car although it was still kept in its remote garage.

Vinnie had continued to hang around the pool hall and had heard some of the customers talk about Joel and the unexpected way he had died. One of the frequent participants in these discussions was Stan Gray but he was careful to limit his knowledge of the incident to a small group of his close associates. Whenever Vinnie tried to listen in, the discussion was quickly changed to another subject.

Jules Green was another user of the pool hall who paid attention to the gossip that circulated amongst the pool players. In fact, he contributed his share of the information that kept the discussions in the place alive. He was the town constable who had released the news of Joel's death to the gang in the first place. He had managed to overhear the end of a conversation between Stan and his friends where Stan had indicated that Joel was murdered. When he tried to involve himself in the conversation, the group started talking about hunting.

# 35

Armed with information that cast suspicion on the original finding of accidental death, Jules Green wondered who he could consult about this rumor. He knew that it was fruitless to talk to the RCMP as they, particularly Sgt. Naples, had been insistent the death was not a criminal act. His own people, with the exception of Detective Sam Gleason, had seemed to be happy to go along with the RCMP and close the case. The obvious choice open to Jules was the Detective.

Jules and Sam met privately in Sam's office and Jules told him that he suspected that there was more to this incident then a person falling into the harbor and drowning. Sam had pulled out his file on the case and after writing what Jules had reported. He thanked Jules and the meeting ended with Sam asking Jules to keep the meeting secret

Sam sat at his desk for a long time and tried to construct a plan that would reveal the truth about how Joel had met his fate. He concluded that his only possible ally was Inspector John Connally. He knew, through office gossip, that the mayor had pressured his Chief to agree with Sgt. Naples so that way was closed. He decided to gather as much evidence as possible and present it to the inspector and ask for an unbiased opinion.

Two items had been left out of the initial investigation that intrigued Sam. When had the body entered the water and where? As the case was closed, Sam was obliged to spend his own time and money to pursue the answers. His first piece of information came from the closed file that had established that his last drinking customer had left at 10:30 P.M. on the night Joel died. He was seen by the fisherman at 11:00 A.M. so that was a span of close to one full tide cycle. He reasoned that Joel had probably not rushed to his doom as soon as his last customer had departed. He selected a start time of midnight as the first point in time for his experiment.

A little research showed that high tide was at 11:08 P.M. which meant the water was flowing towards the sea at his initial search point. His second consideration was that Joel had entered the water on the town side of the bay and probably some distance from the inlet or the body would have ended at sea. His experiment was simple and would be imprecise at the beginning but with repeated trials he felt he could get close to what he wanted.

Sam gathered 18 pint preserving jars complete with rubber seals that rendered the jars waterproof. He painted the interiors of the jars bright red and placed a sheet of paper in each one. He then added weight in each one to try and simulate the drift speed that would have been experienced by the body. He ended up with the bottles floating slightly above the water surface where they were very visible and compared favorably with a dead cat's movement in the flowing tide.

He now devised a schedule and location for releasing his bottles. Each paper stuffed inside would be marked with the time and location of release Sam had selected a day that had the same weather conditions and tide movements as those when the body was found. He released six bottles at equally spaced distances along the South shore of the harbor at midnight and repeated this twice at 2:00 hour intervals. He then went to his office to wait for the tide to do its thing. He would be out in late morning to look for bottles.

Sam sat at his desk and dozed for a few hours. He was awakened by a knock on his office door. "Hey Sam, you can't sleep all day. It's 9 o'clock and the boat's ready for your use. Did you have a tough night?" Sam answered the constable named Tim who had abruptly awakened him. "It was a long night but not that bad. The results of my work will determine whether it was wasted or not."

After eating breakfast he set out with Tim in the boat in search of bottles. He was primarily interested in any of them that were in the vicinity of where the body was seen and that appeared to be headed to the island. They found two bottles that fell close to that category but neither one would have landed on the island and in fact had floated past it. Both were from the second release interval of 2:00 A.M. and originated from adjacent release sites near the head of the harbor.

Sam prepared another group of bottles which he released that night. Again, he split the bottles in three lots and this time he narrowed the release area to the space that had been between the two recovered bottles. He took into account the high tide time change to adjust his release times. He released his first set one hour tide time earlier than the night before, which was actually 2:00A.M. real time, one set one half an hours later then that and the last group one hour after the first. Now all he had to do now was to wait for the tide to perform its work. This time he went home and slept till 10:00 A.M.

He joined Tim at the launch site at noon and they headed for the island. He was fairly certain of his time estimate and was more interested in where the man, dead or alive, had entered the water. As they approached the island, they spotted four bottles that were in the proper time zone to reach the island at the desired time. Only two of them were destined to hit the island with the others floating past on the left and right. They waited for contact and picked up all four bottles being careful to record the pickup point of each. Mission accomplished, they returned to shore and Sam took his recovered items and headed for his office for analysis. "Thanks for the help, Tim." He said as he left the dock.

Sam's conclusion was that Joel went into the water at 1:30 A.M. at a spot very near the disabled Emilio Star. This was a considerable distance from Joel's home but for now the reason for his being there was a mystery.

# 36

His next step was to talk to Stan Gray and try to find out what his suspicions were. Sam figured that a direct approach wouldn't work any better than it had for Jules. One of Stan's peculiarities was his habit of picking up his milk supply from the doorsteps of homes after the delivery was made. Numerous complaints to the milk company had initiated an attempt to catch the thief but the best the police had been able to do was suspect Stan based on his being sighted in areas where the milk went missing. On the pretext that he was seen taking milk by a home owner Sam had Stan brought in for questioning.

The plan was to place some fear in Stan's mind and then in a good—natured way lead up to Joel's death. After a lengthy discussion about the missing milk which Stan denied knowing anything about, Sam said.

. "You know, Stan, being convicted of stealing carries a stiff penalty and if it became known that you were the thief, everyone who has missed their milk would turn against you. I imagine the judge would be forced to give you the maximum penalty. It would certainly be helpful if you had some friends on your side." Stan sat in silence not knowing the extent of proof they had gathered against him. He knew what he had done was wrong but the money he saved was handy for buying the extra drink or two at the bootleggers.

Sam continued. "At present I'm the only one in the police force who has been told by the witness what you were seen doing. To me the taking of a few quarts of milk is not something a person should have to go to prison for. I could forget what I've been told and I'm sure my informant will go along with my decision. How's that sound to you?" Stan relaxed his face which had been showing signs of concern and said. "That sounds good to me. I don't want to serve time in jail. I guess you're the friend I need."

"Your right but my friendship comes with a price." Sam said. Stan's look of concern reappeared and he asked. "What do you want?" "All I want is information about a matter that you're familiar with, I want to know what you know about Joel's death."

Stan bolted out of his seat and took a step towards the door. "You're not going to stick me with that crime." He said. "Wait, Stan, I haven't the least suspicion that you were involved in any way with Joel's misfortune but am simply trying to find out if a crime was indeed committed. Your last statement implies that you believe it was."

Stan stood frozen in mid steps. He realized he had inadvertently told Sam that he suspected foul play and his mind was temporarily blank. He recovered his senses and realized he had been tricked. He returned to his seat and said. "I'll tell you all I know but you must keep my suspicions from reaching those who could harm me." Sam kept a serious look on his face as he told Stan that he would be protected and the milk affair was now buried.

Sam listened to what Stan had to tell. He explained his long association with Joel as a customer and the sudden shock of him being found in the bay. A new bootlegger had opened shop in the area and Stan, missing the companionship of having drinking buddies, decided to give the new places a try. He knew the owner from past drinking sessions at Joel's but had never formally met him. Jerry Conway, the new bootlegger, had introduced himself to Stan after a couple of his customers vouched for him. His first visit was uneventful and he had enjoyed the atmosphere and drinks.

Sam was writing as he continued to listen. "On one of my visits I had a sudden urge to have a glass of Crème de Mint. I asked Jerry if he had any and he told me he did but it wasn't in great demand. He left and returned with a partially filled bottle and placed it on the table in front of me."

He continued his story telling how he had poured his own drink and almost by accident noticed the line drawn near the bottom of the bottle. He was startled by the exact match of the line on the bottle at Joel's and this one. He had quickly concluded that things were not on the level and thought, "Jerry must have killed Joel to take over his business. How else could Joel's stock have found its way here?" Stan concluded. "I gulped down my drink, paid Jerry and left and I haven't been back since."

"Do you think you could go back once more and try to buy the entire bottle? I'll give you the money and all I want is the empty bottle." Stan was reluctant but the temptation of getting the contents overcame what he considered was good sense. He agreed to try. Sam handed him $2 and said. "Bring back the bottle or the money." The following morning the empty bottle of Crème de Mint was delivered to Sam's office.

Armed with the knowledge of approximately when and where Joel entered the harbor and the fact that at least part of his liquor supply had been salvaged, Sam pondered his next move. The answer to how the Crème de Mint had come into Jerry Conway's possession was his next quest. He concluded that a direct confrontation with Mr. Conway was the best way to get this information. He decided to go to Jerry's place of business in the morning when it would be empty of customers and use a friendly approach. He didn't share Stan's belief that Jerry was involved in Joel's death but he was certain that what he knew would lead to the real killer.

The sun was shining in a cloudless sky at 9:00A.M. When Sam knocked on Jerry's back door and pushed his way in without waiting for an answer. He was surprised to find a man sitting with Jerry with a drink in his hand. The man recognized Sam, gulped down his drink, stood up and hurriedly left.

Sam ignored the man and spoke to Jerry. "I'd like to talk to you if you can spare the time." Jerry shrugged his shoulders and said. "Do I have a choice? I guess I'm being raided." Sam absorbed this statement as he formulated a response that would lead to his real purpose for being there. "Mr. Conway, I have no desire to interfere with the neighborhood's entertainment. Bootlegging goes back before my time and it's only when it contributes to bigger problems that I become interested. Joel's death is an example of what I'm referring to. Could the sale of liquor be partly the reason he was killed?"

Jerry's mind went back to the time he was accosted by Vinnie and the anguish that had caused. He had his suspicions that Vinnie was involved in Joel's so called accident but except for the hint that harm could come to anyone and the pain that had been inflicted on him at their first encounter, he had no way of supporting that belief.

Desperate for a way out of the trap he felt had been sprung on him he gave a non committal answer. "Joel wasn't too bright so it's hard to guess what led him into the harbor."

Sam could tell that Jerry was sparring for a way to keep something to himself. He reached into a paper bag he had under his arm and brought out the empty Crème de Mint bottle. "Have you ever seen this bottle before?" He asked. Jerry picked up the bottle and examined it briefly. "I've seen a lot of this kind of bottle but I can't say that I've seen this one before." "Do you sell Crème de Mint as part of your menu?" Sam asked. "I did but I'm out of it right now. I sold my last partly empty bottle to a customer yesterday."

Realization of what Sam was doing began to dawn in Jerry's mind. He picked up the bottle and examined it again. This time he noticed the pencil line at the lower end and remembered how the previously opened bottles delivered by Vinnie had been similarly marked. All the other bottles had their contents sold and the empties discarded with the exception of the one he held in his hand. He now was aware that he had unknowingly inherited Joel's left over stock. How could he have been so blind? Could he be suspected of being involved in harming Joel?

Sam saw the look of consternation on Jerry's face and knowing he had aroused a sense of fear in his mind he kept quiet in hopes that Jerry would reveal something of importance. Jerry was going over the events that led him into the situation he now found himself in. Could he be charged with a serious crime? Had a serious crime even been committed? These and other questions raged through his mind as he sat there looking at Sam.

Sam saw that the right moment had arrived to ask Jerry a question. "Jerry, where did you get that bottle of Crème de Mint?" By now Jerry was almost in tears, he recalled the vicious first meeting with Vinnie and the implied consequences if he talked about what had transpired there. He knew his only mistake was to accept Vinnie's proposal but to lie to protect Vinnie would sink him deeper into a mess he wished he had never encountered. When his thoughts were interrupted by Sam abrupt question, he answered without thinking. "Vinnie brought it over." Then realizing what he had said he shut up. A long period of silence filled the room. Neither man made an effort to break the silence until Jerry said. "I'll tell you what I know including how I got the bottle." Sam responded with a quiet, "Go ahead."

"As an old customer of Joel's I used to admire his ability to keep his place running so smoothly. He only served people he knew or ones who were vouched for by his regular customers. He treated his clients with respect but he had seemed to become moody in the last days of his life. He hadn't confided his thoughts about this mood swing to me or to anyone else as far as I knew. When Joel was found in the water I saw a chance to take his place and that's how I got to where I'm at now. I never realized that Joel was paying someone to keep his place open until I was accosted by Vinnie shortly after I opened." Jerry paused and using his shirt sleeve wiped a line of sweat that had formed on his brow. He took a drink directly out of a whiskey bottle and continued by giving all the details of Vinnie's actions and implied threats. "I was forced to agree or go out of business."

Satisfied that Jerry had told him all he knew Sam thanked him, took his Crème de Mint bottle and left. By now he had no doubt that Vinnie Lacosta was involved in Joel's demise although he had no positive proof to back up his belief.

Armed with the evidence he had gathered he contacted Inspector John Connally and arranged to meet with him. He had made up his mind that it would be useless to consult with Sgt. Naples because of the position the Sgt. had already taken on the death.

The meeting took place in the Inspector's office and John was impressed with the results of the investigative efforts Sam had gone through. "I personally feel that we should reopen the case. I'll consult with Sgt. Naples and let you know what his opinion is."

Sam had his doubts about any positive outcome from the meeting between the two top RCMP officers but he was wise enough to keep those thoughts to himself.

# 37

Leo had decided on how he would expose the Sgt. The next time a collector came he was going to refuse to pay the 10% and wait for the expected retaliation. If his suspicions were correct Sgt. Naples would come to try and convince him to pay. He would be ready with a counter offer, his ax handle.

He didn't have long to wait. A few days later Vinnie arrived in his old Ford and walked right in "I'm here again." He said in a good-natured voice.

Leo was seated in the back of the room within reach of his axe handle when Vinnie arrived and he didn't move from his seat. Instead, he stared at Vinnie and said. "My paying days are over. You had promised to keep me free to do business without interference and yet your leader ransacked my place. I need his assurance that it won't happen again or there'll be no more money from me." Vinnie told Leo that he was aware that his place had been ransacked but it had nothing to do with them. He had no way of knowing that the Sgt. was seen and Leo decided to keep his secret. Leo replied. "You're lying."

Vinnie's automatic reaction was to take a step towards Leo but before he could start his second one Leo was on his feet with his axe handle ready to strike. Vinnie had little desire to tackle a man equipped with a weapon and his encounter with Joel had greatly reduced his need to assert himself forcefully. He backed away and turned toward the door. Leo's words to the departing Vinnie were. "Tell your boss I know who he is and I expect to see him soon."

Vinnie drove towards town and wondered where his involvement in this racket was taking him. Twice he had been involved in violent action and if he hadn't walked away this would have been the third. His once peaceful life as a sailor was now complicated with danger from all sides. He admitted to himself that he had experienced pleasures that he hadn't expected when he agreed to take care of the ship but it was time for him to get out before it was too late. The question was, how?

Meanwhile Leo was reviewing his latest action in his mind. He knew that his rebellion couldn't go unchallenged and he would soon have to answer for his act, the only question was, when? There wasn't much he could do physically to defend himself if attacked but he hoped that the knowledge he had of the Sgt.'s misdeeds would protect him.

He reached for a cigarette and pulled out an empty pack. A frantic search of the house came up with a half—filled package he had absentmindedly placed on the window sill. He lit one and filled his lungs with the tranquilizing smoke.

# 38

Diane had now reduced her active paying lovers to two. She had no problem with either Morris Cohen or Sam Gray. Although both had enjoyed their relationship with Diane enormously neither had formed emotional bonds with her. When she told them on their scheduled day that it was over Morris' eyes were wet when he left but Sam had left without a word. She asked them to leave their keys in the garage door lock.

The next two rejected suitors acted in far different ways. Father Frotten arrived Wednesday afternoon with high anticipation of the action ahead. Diane greeted him with a cool, "Good afternoon." She said as she stepped aside to let him enter. He tried to take her in his arms but she slipped through his awkward attempt and said. "I'm sorry Ray but my days of having you as a lover are over." Ray's face turned an ashen white and he gasped for air. "But its God's will that we continue the way we have!" He exclaimed. He fell to his knees and continued. "You have been my reward from him for all the good things I do for the Parish. You can't thwart the will of God or your soul will be damned to Hell forever."

He paused and his face was now a deep dark red. Diane was so surprised at his actions that she stood in mute awe. He sprang to his feet and made a lunge towards her. She regained control of herself in time to avoid him and ran behind the table. She now realized she was facing a madman and her survival depended on keeping him away from her. Maybe God spoke to Ray but, whatever the cause, his reason seemed to return. His face took on an angelic look and he said. "He has spoken to me and I now understand the punishment he has imposed on me. He has also told me what I must do to regain his acceptance." With those words he abruptly walked out the door and was gone. Diane didn't even have time to mention the key.

She sat at the table trembling like a leaf in a fall breeze. She had never expected such an angry confrontation and to make maters worse it was uttered in the name of God. Was Ray insane? She had no one to turn to so she suffered alone. At least she only had one customer left to rid herself of, the Sgt. As she thought of her recent encounter she came to realize that Ray never thought of himself as a client, as he said, he considered she was his gift from God.

On Thursday Danny showed up to do his weekly chores and he notice Diane was not her normal self. She had a cup of tea with him as usual but she didn't chat about their pet subjects with her usual enthusiasm. After an uneventful morning in which he spent most of his time banking the house he left for home after telling her he'd see her next week.

Friday afternoon had arrived and Diane was concerned about how her final lover would react to his being rejected. The Sgt. arrived on schedule with his Stetson in hand. She let him in and invited him to set at the table. "Paul," she said, "we have to talk. I've enjoyed your company all this time in spite of your fit of jealousy but I've reached a point in my life where I want to live normally. I hope you take this gracefully, Paul but we can't see each other anymore."

Paul reaction was hardly visible to the untrained eye. He stiffened slightly and replied. "Now Diane, let's not be too hasty. I don't think I could live without the knowledge that you're here for me. Isn't there a way we can work this out?"

Diane, with as firm a voice as she had ever used, replied. "My mind is made up and there's no going back. It's best if you leave now with no regrets. It's been fun." Paul began to display anger in his reddened face but his long years of police work took control. He convinced himself that he could renew their relationship if he was patient and did the right thing. With a shake of his head he seemed to accept the inevitable. "All right, Diane, I can see I have no choice, I guess its goodbye." When he rose to leave Diane added. "Please don't take this out on Leo; he has nothing to do with it."

Sgt. Naples left Diane's in an outwardly calm manner but inside he was a man in turmoil. He had lost the most precious person that had ever entered his life. In addition he was now placed in jeopardy by a worthless bootlegger who knew of his affair and could cause a great deal of trouble because of that knowledge. He drove straight to the office where there was a message for him to contact Josh. A message from Josh meant that Vinnie had some sort of difficulty.

# 39

The Sgt. met with Vinnie that evening. He was not concerned if anyone saw him aboard the ship as part of his duties was to keep an eye on the ship and its occupant. Vinnie invited him in and they sat at the table. The Sgt. was told about the event that occurred at Leo's and how Vinnie had walked away from the confrontation. "I believe that he knows you are the head of this operation and he is prepared to tell what he knows unless we leave him alone. I might have been able to overpower him but I've been involved in too much violence already. I'll continue to collect and deliver but I'll leave the enforcement to you." Vinnie said.

Naples wasn't used to his people telling him what they would or wouldn't do. He held all the high cards in this game and he wasn't afraid to play them. "Vinnie," he said with a harsh, cold voice, "You already know the price you will have to pay if you go against my wishes', I think you had better reconsider".

Vinnie had expected some sort of retort and was ready to respond. "Sgt. Naples, you can't make any charges against me without the world finding out that you're implicated in an illegal operation." Naples was on the edge of losing his self control but being a realist he was willing to pretend capitulation until he was ready to reverse the roles. With two major interruptions in his well-planned life of pleasure in one day he had to act fast before his entire world collapsed. "Vinnie, you've done an excellent job so far. Just keep doing what you feel comfortable with and leave Leo to me."

# 40

Inspector Connally called Sgt Naples into his office and showed him the report that Sam had prepared. The Sgt. took the same position he had expressed originally about the death being accidental. They discussed the evidence in detail but Naples wouldn't budge. "Inspector, Sam is trying to make us look like fools. I'll take time to check his suspicions but I think it's a waste of time." "Well, do the best you can and let me know your conclusion?" Connally said.

Sgt. Naples' mind was in turmoil as he left the meeting. With Vinnie now involved in Sam's investigation the need to silence him had become much more pressing than before. With Vinnie eliminated the only remaining people with personal knowledge of his wrongdoing were Leo and Diane.

Sitting in his office, the Inspector pondered over the Sgt.'s obvious reluctance to reinvestigate the cause of Joel's death. Did he have an ulterior motive in wanting to keep the case closed? A thought struck him like a bolt of lightning. What if the Sgt. was involved in some way? I'll call Inspector Levesque and ask his advice, he told himself. The call was placed by Alice White on the Inspector's private line and the two friends exchanged greetings after which John Connally explained to Maurice Levesque the problem he was faced with. "It may be nothing but my intuition tells me that there is something wrong." John said. "Give me some time to consider what the best path to follow is." Maurice answered.

"How's Julie doing in her new job?" He asked. John said. "She seems to be having a good time and both her teaching and learning goals are being met." Their conversation ended with Maurice's assurance that he'd call back soon.

Sgt. Naples had a plan in mind that would rid him of the threat Vinnie presented. His bootleg collection effort would be temporarily interrupted but his survival as a respected police officer was more important. His first task was to gather the raw material he needed to carry out the elimination of his imminent threat. He drove home and assembled the items on his workbench in a storage shed located at the rear of his property.

He then fashioned a crude bomb made up of sticks of dynamite that had been confiscated, an old alarm clock, a detonator, wires and a battery. He checked the alarm clock and verified it ran and that the alarm went off at the set time. He figured that this, accompanied by two cans of gasoline would be sufficient to destroy the ship and any occupants on board. The Emilio Star had a steel hull but most of her interior structure was wood.

That evening he watched the ship from a distance. Vinnie seldom spent the evening at home and tonight was no exception. At dusk Vinnie left the Star and made his way to the Santa Clara that had arrived several days earlier. After a short wait the Sgt. took his device and gas on board and set them on the main deck on the side facing the water. The bomb was set to go off at Midnight. He left the way he had come and was sure he had not been seen.

Constable Elliot Johns was on one of his unscheduled delivery trips to Rivemouth. He arrived at his parking spot located across the harbor from the Star, loaded the row boat with his liquor and rowed to the ship. According to their prearranged system Elliot could deliver without Vinnie being there and he did just that. The door on the outboard side was equipped with a lock that allowed it to be unlocked from either side and with a great deal of effort Elliot unloaded the boat. He decided to take a nap before starting the six—hour drive back and climbed the inside stairway to the living quarters. He stretched out on a chair with his feet propped up on a foot stool and went to sleep.

Vinnie, after a short visit with the crew of the Santa Clara, had picked up Yvette and they had driven to their rendezvous cabin where they had spent another evening of bliss. Time had flown by so fast that they over shot the usual departure time of 10:30. On the way out to the road a deer suddenly jumped out into their path and Vinnie, in a desperate effort to avoid it, veered into a ditch. By the time he got the vehicle back on the path it was approaching Midnight.

The remainder of the trip was uneventful and Vinnie was able to drop off Yvette without any problems. He was on his way to park the auto when he was startled by a loud noise and a brilliant flash that came from the waterfront. He drove to a vantage point where he could see the area and was astonished to see his ship enveloped in flames. He knew without a moment of hesitation the ship's destruction was meant to destroy him too. He left the area and headed back to the cabin. There he went inside and grabbed his cache of money and returned to town.

By now the waterfront was a scene of confusion. The ship was burning out of control and most of the people who would normally be in other areas were gathered as close to the Emilio Star as they dared. It wasn't often one could see such fireworks in the harbor. He abandoned his car a short distance from the Santa Clara and snuck on board.

Sgt. Naples watched the Star burn with a smile of self satisfaction. One of his enemies had been effectively eliminated, only Leo remained as a major threat.

# 41

It was Tuesday and the church cleaning lady had spent the morning tidying the main attendance area and had dusted all the reachable items suspended from the walls. She had accidently dislodged a large crucifix from its hanger and had propped it on a window sill until she could get a ladder to put it where it belonged. After completing her work she left for home having completely forgotten about the crucifix.

Father Frotten entered the church and verified he was alone. He knelt at the altar and pleaded with God to return things back to normal. "Your rewards were so generous and they gave me added zeal in protecting my parishioners from falling into the clutches of Satan. As you had sanctioned the arrangement that was as pure as your relationship with the Virgin Mary it is cruel of you, a just God, to terminate it. Please give me an answer or a sign to tell me how to regain your approval!" The church remained silent.

The cleaning lady had suddenly remembered the crucifix had been left on the window sill and fearing that Father Frotten would be mad if he found it out of place she returned to hang it where it belonged. When she opened a main entry door to the church a gust of wind blew into the church and the crucifix crashed to the floor with a loud bang. The pious priest's attention was drawn to the noise and he failed to see the women close the door and head for home." I hope he didn't see me." She thought as she almost ran in panic.

Father Frotten examined the crucifix and its hanger on the wall. There was no way that it could have fallen accidently, he surmised. A sudden thought passed through his mind, this was God's answer to his plea. He seized the cross and returned to the Altar. He knelt and thanked God for his answer. "I wish you could have been kinder in your decision but I will obey your direction." He prepared to carry out his order.

Sgt. Naples was at a loss on what he could do to bring his pleasurable lifestyle back. As he sorted out the details, he identified the areas that needed to be brought under control for his own protection. Only two people presented a real threat to his being able to remain a respected police officer. These were Leo and Diane. The first was expendable but Diane was not. He would attempt to convince her that she should return to their relationship as his first effort. The other, if left alone could be dealt with at his choosing.

# 42

It was early Tuesday afternoon when the Sgt. arrived at Diane's. He parked and walked to the door. His intention was to beg and plead for forgiveness but Diane wouldn't let him enter. She was curt and made it plain that she wanted him to leave and never come back.

He drove out of her driveway with a heavy heart. He had just cleared the entrance when he spotted a car approaching. As they passed the Sgt. recognized Father Frotten dressed in his fancy vestments and watched as he turned into Diane's driveway.

Curious about what the priest wanted with Diane, he turned around and parked where he could watch from a distance beyond the turn off to her house.

After receiving his message from God the priest prepared for his mission. He dressed in his most elaborate official clothes. He prepared the crucifix for its role in the coming event by lacing a cord through its hanging ring and tied the ends together leaving enough length so it could slip easily over his head. Satisfied that it hung at the proper height he was now ready to proceed. In his mind he felt that he had always done what was demanded of him by his maker. For the first time he was prepared to risk his soul and follow his own destiny but if it failed, he was ready to submit to God's will.

He drove to Diane's and saw an auto pull out of her place as he approached. As they passed, he saw that Sgt. Naples was the driver. He turned into Diane's driveway and parked in back of her house. Dressed in his finery he went to the door and knocked. Diane's first thought was to dismiss him with the same curtness she had used on the Sgt. As she glanced over what he was wearing she saw the crucifix hanging from a bright red cord and her resolve softened. He had obviously come to apologize for his past conduct.

"What do you want?" She asked. "I'm here as a servant of God and I want to make amends for my past actions. Please let me in." Diane opened the door and let him enter in spite of her original intent to ask him to leave.

Father Frotten exceeded any exhortation he had ever used in his lifetime. He pleaded with her to return to his arms as his lover. He spoke of the rewards she would ultimately gain if she agreed. Diane reacted with revulsion. "You think your God's gift to women but there are men that I found much more pleasurable than you."

By now Diane had lost all of her caution for maintaining secrecy and had only one goal. She was determined to hurt this demented priest in the worst way. "Sgt. Naples was much better in bed than you and he is not the only one." She went into the parlor and returned with a torn sheet of paper which she showed to the priest. "See who was sharing me with you." She said. "Now get out of my house, you're a vile creation from hell." She screamed as she turned to open the door.

That was the last conscious motion Diane ever made. Ray, as she had lovingly called him, took the crucifix from around his neck and tossed the looped cord over her head. Using the heavy cross as a lever he twisted it until it was tight around her neck. He maintained the pressure for a long time. The look on his face was one of adulation as he fell to his knees and said. "I have done your bidding, now I look forward to your reward."

Father Frotten was so engrossed with the after effects of his actions that his only conscious thought was to leave. He forgot about the cross he had used and the paper she had held in her hands. He left knowing he was protected from harm; he had done what God willed him to do. As he drove out, he headed strait for church.

# 43

There were no cigarettes in the house and Leo needed one desperately. He took off down the path to Mrs. Benoit's store to satisfy his urge. When he arrived, he realized that he had left in such a hurry that he had forgotten to bring money. Mrs. Benoit was prepared for such contingencies by allowing purchases on credit. Her account book had columns for the item bought, its price, the purchaser's signature, the date and time of purchase. Leo quickly filled out the required spaces, took his cigarettes and headed for home.

When he arrived at the place where Diane's house was visible he stopped to look. He reflected on the enjoyable times he had spent in the kitchen drinking and talking with Diane and he was sorry those times had come to an end. As he watched the back door suddenly burst open and a figure that looked like Father Frotten came out. He was out of sight for a short time and reappeared driving around the house and out the drive. Now what could that be about? He asked himself.

He paused in deep thought and lit his second cigarette. He was unaware of how long he had been standing there when his attention was drawn to a second car parking by the house and a man getting out. There was no doubt that the man was Sgt. Naples. He went directly to the door and without hesitating walked into the house. Leo, confused by all this action continued along the path to his home.

# 44

Naples watched the priest's auto disappear down the road and had a feeling that all was not well. Risking another refusal from Diane, he decided to go back. He arrived to find the back door wide open. He went in and saw Diane sprawled out on the kitchen floor and from all appearances she was dead. He quickly verified his suspicions and looked at the crime scene to establish what had happened.

His first observation of importance was that the murder weapon was still in place around her neck. There were no signs of a struggle and at first he concluded that except for the weapon there was no other evidence. As he pondered on what his next move would be he saw a sheet of paper lying on the floor close to the table

He picked it up and read it. He quickly absorbed its contents and a sudden look of understanding appeared on his face. He folded the paper and placed it in his breast pocket. He now realized that Diane was nothing more than a prostitute who had been able to keep her actions secret by her strict discipline.

She must have shown this paper to the priest to taunt him in retaliation for some action on his part. There's no doubt that Frotten now knows about my involvement with Diane. If faced with a situation where he had nothing to lose he would certainly tell all he knows particularly if I'm his accuser. I have to keep this murder from being solved or at least never have a perpetrator caught. He had lost one threat only to gain a new one. A plan began to develop as he organized his thoughts. The punishment for the murder need not necessarily come from a judge and jury; it could just as well be carried out by an individual. With this in mind he proceeded to reconstruct the crime scene.

The first thing he did was to remove the cord from around Diane's neck. He couldn't help thinking about the marvelous times they had spent together as he lowered her head to the floor. He then proceeded to disrupt the room by opening drawers and upsetting the furniture. It now looked like a struggle had occurred and the room had been searched. He then went from room to room and did the same to them as he had done to the kitchen. He wondered at the lack of any significant sums of money uncovered as he knew that he alone had given her a substantial amount. He took whatever a robber would have and placed it on the kitchen table. Not wanting to think of himself as a common criminal he decided to dispose of these items in a place where they would never be found.

His main concern was what to do with the weapon. He wanted it well—hidden but available if needed in his dealings with the priest. The answer was not long in coming; he tied it in a piece of wrapping paper and buried it in the fresh dug earth close to the house. No one would suspect a robber would dispose of any thing of value there. Having completed his path of deception, he drove his car to the road and stopped. He took a broken branch and swept away all tire tracks from the barn to the road. The discovery of the murder was left to the next visitor.

# 45

Thursday morning arrived and I was in high sprits. I biked along the road in the brisk clean air and thought of seeing Diane and enjoying our weekly chat. As I turned into her driveway, I noticed that there were no tire tracks, which was odd. I knew of at least five vehicles that came to her house on a regular basis although I didn't know who they belonged to.

I continued to the house and knocked. Receiving no acknowledgment I knocked again, only this time I applied more force. To my surprise the door swung open on its own and I was able to see into the kitchen. From my vantage point I saw that the kitchen furniture was strewn about but there was no sign of Diane.

Unsure of what my next move should be I hollered Diane's name and waited. There was no answered. Panic began to take over as I realized something was horribly wrong.

I cautiously entered the hall and pulled the hall door wide open. The scene that met my eyes was the most horrendous thing I had ever seen. Diane lay on the floor with a reddish blue mark around her neck.

I was sure she was dead so I didn't enter beyond the hall door. Tears rolled down my cheeks but I held back any verbal outburst.

I had seen dead people before as the Acadians taught their children about death at an early age and viewing the dead was a tradition with the bodies laid out in the parlor.

What I saw now was not the peaceful picture of a soul departed to heaven but was a scene of horror. It finally seeped into my brain that I had to take some sort of action.

My first thought was to find an adult who would surely know what to do. I left the house, my bicycle forgotten, and ran to the shortcut, turned and ran to Mrs. Benoit's store.

Mrs. Benoit was startled to see the young man burst into her house without any warning. He was out of breath and with a look of utter desperation on his face and he blurted out to her. "She's dead and it's horrible, what do we have to do?"

Mrs. Benoit was not easily excited and immediately tried to calm Danny down. "Take your time Danny and tell me the whole story. I can't help unless I know what you're talking about."

By now I had regained control of my breathing and the calming effect of Mrs. Benoit's presence brought me back to a semblance of sanity. I told her what I had seen and she came to a quick decision.

Diane needed the attention of a priest and the RCMP must be notified.

The Last Rites was an important Roman Catholic Sacrament that was administered by a priest, preferably prior to death but if that wasn't possible as soon as practical following a person's demise. In Mrs. Benoit's mind the religious requirement took precedence over the legal.

Not trusting Danny to be able to follow what she deemed was the right path she quickly wrote a note to the Bourque's who had the nearest phone. The note simply said Diane Le Have is dead. Call the priest and the RCMP. She signed it and handed the note to Danny with instructions to take it to Walter Bourque's house.

I seized the note and ran to my destination.

Mrs. Bourque was home and I handed her the note. Her face turned pale but without hesitation she called the two places indicated on the note. She then proceeded to notify the several households that had phones of the news.

She asked him to sit down and have some tea to help calm down. She wanted to find out more and hoped Danny would give her more details as he relaxed with his tea.

My first reaction was to say nothing but then reality began to sink in. I felt weak from the combined effects of the shock and the physical exertion I'd been through. I just sat in a kind of stupor as Mrs. Bourque made tea.

Several minutes passed and after a few sips of hot tea I began to lose my numb feeling. I told Mrs. Bourque about what I had seen and as I spoke she was drawn into the enormity of the event. Nothing of this nature had ever happened in St. Agnes Parish.

"Are we being punished by God for our sins?" She thought.

She was determined to keep Danny in her kitchen until she was certain he was calmed down enough to function normally but she had underestimated his recuperative powers. His mind was already trying to reconstruct the events that led up to this disaster. He thanked her for her kindness and left for Bob's home.

The news had already reached the Pottier home and when I arrived I was met by my friend, who led me to our meeting place in the barn.

This started our attempt to solve a murder that would be covered up by those who knew the truth.

# 46

The first person to arrive at Diane's was Father Frotten. He parked behind the house and made his way to the kitchen door. He was about to enter when his attention was drawn to another auto pulling up to the house.

Sgt. Naples and one of his corporals got out of the car and the Sgt. yelled to the priest. "Don't go in until I say it's O.K.

The newcomers walked past the priest and viewed the scene inside. The Sgt. told his Cpl. to rope off the driveway to keep the curious out.

With the Cpl. gone the two who remained behind glared at each other but no words were exchanged. By the time the Cpl. had erected his barrier a crowd of villagers had begun to collect. He asked one of the men to keep the others from crossing the rope that was strung across the entrance.

Having accomplished that task, he returned to the house where he found the priest performing the Last Rites for Diane.

The two policemen stood in silence until Father Frotten was finished. The Sgt. spoke to the priest. "You have done your duty, now please leave and let us do ours."

Father Frotten left without replying. The Cpl. said. "He's a queer duck; there was no emotion on his face as he performed his ritual."

The Sgt. almost said, "With good reason" but caught himself in time.

The investigation was short. Sgt. Naples had already made up his mind on what the results would be and he guided the Cpl.'s thinking along the path that would cause him to come to the same conclusion.

They went through the house and saw all the disheveled rooms. Without any clues pointing to a specific person Naples said that she had been strangled by an unknown individual and the motive was robbery.

The Corporal nodded in agreement.

# 47

We sat in our private meeting place and talked in awe about the death of my employer.

Curious about what was going on at the crime scene we walked to Diane's house driveway where a crowd was gathered. The rope across the entrance was guarded by a local farmer and no one seemed to be aware of what was happening inside.

A voice from the crowd called out. "Danny. The RCMP Sgt. wants to talk to you."

The man guarding the entrance motioned to me to go through. I reluctantly went through the barrier and approached the house.

As I walked toward the house, I noticed a tire track that I recognized as one of the five I had committed to my memory and as I passed the RCMP vehicle I saw that its tires matched another set of those marks. When I arrived at the door the Sgt. spotted me and told him to go set in the auto and wait.

Several minutes passed before Naples got in besides me and introduced himself. "So you're the young man who discovered the body." He said as he looked me over from head to foot.

This was my first encounter with a police officer and coupled with my earlier shock I was uncertain about how to react.

The Sgt. asked me a series of questions to establish why I had gone to Diane's home was and what I knew about Diane's affairs.

I answered as truthfully as I could but left out any reference to the tire marks.

The Sgt. seemed to be satisfied with my answers and said. "We think this is a case of robbery and the murder was committed to cover the robber's identity or to give him time to escape. We may be talking to you again but I'm done with you for now."

I left for the road, remembered to take my bicycle and signaled Bob to follow me as I walked the bike back the way we had come. A few voices called out to me trying to find out what had gone on but I ignored them and continued on my way with Bob close behind.

Having returned to Bob's barn, we talked about who could have killed Diane and why?

"Surely the RCMP will solve this case quickly." Bob said.

I had my doubts about what Bob had just said and proceeded to tell him some of what I knew.

I repeated what the Sgt. said about it being motivated by a robbery. "In all my dealings with her I never saw anything that would cause someone to kill for what she had but I did notice that there was activity that I can't explain."

I then told Bob about the tire tracks I had seen in her driveway while going to work and how there were none when I went to work this morning.

"The peculiar thing is that two of those tracks were in the driveway when we went back. The one track came from the police car but I don't know where the other came from."

"The priest had come and gone before we got there, one of the people in the crowd told me, and it must be his tire track you saw. I guess he did his Last Rites thing for Diane."

"What reason could the RCMP and the priest have for having regular visits with Diane?" I asked in a voice so low Bob had to make me repeat it. "And why were there never any of their visits while I was there?" I added.

We came to the conclusion that we would have to wait for answers to our questions and parted with a promise that Diane's death would be avenged.

"Don't forget that tomorrow is Friday and we meet Julie for lessons." Bob said as I left.

# 48

The village was in turmoil. No one could recall a murder having been committed in the Parish and the residents were questioning each other in an attempt to help find the guilty one. During this frenzy of information gathering an old woman named Doris Surette who lived by the railroad claimed she had seen a person jump off a stopped freight train on Tuesday morning. The man was shabbily dressed and had left the area immediately.

This information quickly found its way to Sgt. Naples and on Friday morning he spoke to Doris. Upon verifying that she indeed claimed to have seen what she now called a hobo exit the train he had found the core on which to build his cover-up.

The word quickly spread throughout the village that the RCMP had established that a stranger had killed Diane and was probably far away by now.

The investigation was terminated after a complete search of the area on that premise and the Sgt. felt that at least that part of his vulnerability was covered.

# 49

We had skipped the school session scheduled for the Friday because of Diane's murder but showed up at the school a little after 3:30 P.M. a week later.

Julie was pleased to see that she hadn't been abandoned by us, her erstwhile students and expressed her understanding of the need for me to recover from my shocking experience.

She felt her experiment with continuing their education under these unusual conditions would be successful. Julie was confident that if her afterhour's students didn't desert her they would at least obtain an education equal to that of any ninth grade student in the area.

Our first half-hour was spent going over the material Julie had prepared and she gave us a short test to evaluate our absorbency. With the formalities out of the way we became involved in a discussion on the tragedy that had happened in the area.

I was quick to state my doubts that a stranger had killed Diane but when Julie questioned me, I was unable to substantiate my belief.

"I know a lot of things that seem wrong but I need to find out more before I can make sense out of this. Bob and I are going to spend time finding out the truth about what has been said by the police."

Julie became alert as her investigative side was awakened. "Don't leave me out of your pursuit; I have some knowledge of how to track down criminals."

Bob, who had some misgivings in getting deeply involved in what could turn out to be a hazardous task, spoke. "Julie, I'm glad to have an adult on our side. Let's hope we all come out of this whole."

The ship burning in Rivemouth Harbor was talked about briefly and except for the report that a person living on the ship had been killed we treated it as a curiosity.

We parted with the hope that our next meeting would shed some light on the questionable conclusion reached by the RCMP concerning Diane's death and that our experiment in education would show some progress.

The two of us had returned to our barn rendezvous and we went through the facts that were available to us.

I was the most knowledgeable but I was pleased to have Bob as a devil's advocate. We sacrificed one of the writing tablets Julie had provided for school work to record what we knew and what remained to be found out.

I started to go over what I remembered that might help and Bob wrote what I said in the book. The list we ended up with was a haphazard one with information that for the most part seemed meaningless.

Two things stood out as being significant, the sighting of the hobo and the visitors Diane had received that was evident by the tire tracks in her driveway.

I told Bob about what I knew about Diane's visitors. "There were definitely four automobiles that came into her driveway regularly over a long period of time and towards the end a fifth one had joined in. The funny thing is that on the day I discovered her dead there were no tracks when I went in. It seemed like someone had erased them."

I paused and with my memory refreshed continued. "Remember that when we went back later there were two tracks that belonged to the RCMP Sgt. and Father Frotten? I'm positive that those tire tracks match some of those I saw before but what would cause either of them to rob and kill Diane? I think we have to look elsewhere for the guilty party."

Bob interrupted his writing and asked. "Danny, isn't it strange that you never saw any of these visitors while you were at work?"

"Diane had very strict rules about when I could be at her home. Do you suppose she controlled her guests visiting times in the same way?"

I didn't have an answer and suggested that we concentrate on the hobo sighting as our primary path of discovery. "By the way, I think the fifth set of tracks came from Jules Comeau's car. I noticed it didn't show up until after the dance and stopped after Jules went back to work. Well, back to the hobo's pursuit."

Bob completed his recording and closed the tablet.

I was too busy with work around the house to do any sleuthing before four P.M. on Tuesday.

Bob had come over and had given me a hand with some odds and ends. He told him of his idea of talking to Doris Surette about the hobo sighting.

I agreed it was a good idea and we set forth after convincing Betty to milk the cow, Molly, if we were late getting back.

We had timed the visit to be there when the daily train arrived in order to get a realistic picture of what could be observed from Doris' home. The train wasn't due for another ten minutes when I knocked at the door.

Doris, with a cane in her hand, opened the door after unlocking it. "I hope you'll forgive me but its time for the train to pull in and I have to see if it's on time. Come in and join me and after the train leaves we can chat."

A loud whistle blew announcing the train's arrival. It pulled in slowly and two passengers disembarked. The mail man, who was a large portly gentleman, stood on the station platform and took the mail pouch from the conductor and joined the two passengers by the station house.

Bob winked at me and said to Doris. "That's strange, that doesn't look like the mail man picking up the mail."

Alma seemed surprised at Bob's comment and said. "He's always there, someone must have taken his place"

As the train pulled away the three figures on the station platform proceeded to a truck partly obscured from Alma's window. "Aha", she said, "there he is now going to where he parks his truck with two women. They must have talked him into dropping them off."

We could plainly see that the two women were really a mother and her ten-year-old son.

We talked to Alma about the old days and how tough life must have been. She told us stories we had heard before and after a brief stay we left.

"She may have seen a hobo but my common sense tells me her story was influenced by imagination." I said to Bob.

"Her report to the police was never questioned and if it had been the Sgt. would have found out what we did, that she couldn't have seen anyone at that distance and been able to describe them." Bob replied.

"Let's start an inquiry amongst our village friends and see what they can find out concerning the hobo."

It had long been a tradition that the young males of the village, actually of the parish, had a sort of underground communications network. How else could they learn about the things their parents hid from them? Sex was the main topic and it was a subject riddled with misinformation. In the case of the hobo, however, any information that was gathered through this source could be depended on. Intentional deception was not tolerated and liars were soon barred from participation.

The word spread that we were looking for anyone with knowledge of the hobo's actions while he was in Seal Lake. At first we hit a blank wall but within a few days a glimmer of hope broke through.

A young man named John had been fishing in a small pond on the opposite side of the track on the day Doris saw the hobo. He came from an adjacent village and had no friends in the immediate area. After crossing the track he had followed a foot-path to the pond, soon determined that the fish weren't biting and retraced his steps to the track.

During his trip to the pond and back a freight train had stopped at the station and blocked his exit. Rather than walk around the train he simply jumped up on the cars' elevated hookups and from there he had jumped to the ground. He stood around to watch the train depart and left. No one else except the train crew was in the area but he thought he caught a glimpse of an old lady watching from a window of a nearby house.

To us the hobo was now a thing of the past. By having eliminated him it only made our task more difficult. Now we knew that the killer wasn't a stranger to Diane but someone she knew.

Also the question of why the police had done such an inept job of investigating popped to the forefront.

# 50

Bob and I arrived at Leo's on a bright Saturday afternoon. He had a few customers seated around his table in heated discussion.

"Lets go outside were we can talk freely." Leo said, as he led us to the far side of his wood pile.

We all sat on unsplit blocks and Leo continued. "I know your snooping around for information about Diane's death and I don't want you to get into any danger because of what I told you. To me bygones are to be forgotten and laid to rest but some thing has come up to change my mind, Sgt. Naples has done me a wrong."

"His messengers, first Constable Johns and then a guy named Vinnie had assured me I would be warned prior to being raided so that my main stock would be stashed away but this time the warning didn't come. Actually it was more of an act of vandalism then a raid. I know the Sgt. was the one who disrupted my place and he is aware that I know it was him. I think the visit was a warning of things to come if I don't remain quiet."

Without having spoken we waited in anticipation of what would follow.

"You might have thought that I killed that pretty lady and I don't blame you if you did. Well I know I didn't and I have a good idea who did. I went to the store for cigarettes a few days before you found her dead and, as I always did, I stopped at the clearing and looked at Diane's home. I'll admit that I wished she would welcome me with open arms as a lover if I went to the house but that's as far as I ever went with that idea, wishful thinking."

Leo continued, "On my way back I noticed a car parked close to the rear door that looked like Father Frotten's car. He must be saving a soul or losing his own I thought as I stood there watching."

Bob interrupted. "What does that have to do with the Sgt.?"

Leo raised his right arm and said. "Wait till I finish. My curiosity was aroused so instead of continuing on I stayed and watched. The priest came out in a hurry, dressed in his official garments and left without looking back."

"This is where the Sgt. comes in. As I watched Sgt. Naples car came down the driveway, he parked and entered the house. He wasn't there long before coming out and he was out of sight for a few minutes. When he reappeared, he glanced in my direction and I believe he saw me. He got his into the car, raced the engine and took off with spinning tires." Leo shook his head and looked at his two listeners and continued. "I hope you don't get into any trouble because of what I've told you."

A customer shouted to Leo to come in and that ended the conversation.

In a short period we had lost one suspect and gained another. It seemed obvious that Father Frotten hadn't committed the crime as he had left before the Sgt. and surely Naples would not have covered up for him. Was it possible that neither of them was guilty?

"Do you think that what Leo saw has any bearing on the crime?" Bob asked

"The Sgt. certainly displayed anger the way he drove off. He must know something that he's not letting out that concern's Diane's death."

I thought about his contacts with Diane prior to her death and tried to make sense out of the whole affair. She had never given me reasons to expect this disaster and always handled herself in a self-assured way. She had treated me the way an older sister would have but I suspected she had a good idea of what I thought of her. I remembered how she casually told me about the diary she kept and I wondered if the police had found it. If they had, it was never mentioned during the investigation. Maybe if I could find this book its contents would unlock the secrets she took to her grave.

We returned to our respective homes with the understanding that we would meet the next day.

As we had planned we met and devised a way on how to search Diane's home without being discovered. We took my brother, Dick, with us to be our look-out.

Upon arrival at the house we checked for an easy point of entry. The only possible way in without causing obvious damage was through the rock foundation where a stone was loose and could be moved. Dick was small enough to crawl into the cellar through the opening we made so he could unlock the back door using a key that was hung in the porch.

With access established; Dick would stand guard at the driveway entrance and warn us by blowing a loud whistle

That would give us all the time we needed to lock the door and hide. The only stumbling block was to get Dick to do his part. It cost me a candy bar and a lot of persuasion but I finally got Dick to agree to assist.

Dick had a little difficulty squeezing in but was soon at the back door which he opened and stepped out on the small porch. With his whistle in his hand he then went to the road and took up his guard station. We entered the kitchen through the hall and were faced with a very ordinary room. The furniture was still strewn about as had been reported by the police.

In spite of the destruction Bob made a comment that Diane had been living in a world of plenty. "This lady knew how to live", Bob said, as he looked around.

"It's going to be hard to find anything to help us in here."

I mentioned that she had told him a dairy she kept hidden and Bob got excited." That could contain the answer to most of our questions." He said.

We searched the house thoroughly but couldn't find it. "Maybe someone else had already gotten it." I thought.

We left the house after rigging the door so that it could be opened from the outside with a pocket knife. We walked to the road only to find Dick gone.

"It's a good thing no one came or we would have been caught." Bob said.

"My little brother can't always be trusted but I'll get even with him. We'll have to continue when we have more free time and hopefully more clues."

# 51

Sgt. Naples was in an angry state of mind. He had lost the most pleasurable sex partner he had ever had and he was also at risk of being exposed for some of his career ending activities. There were now two people who endangered his future, the priest and Leo. He reasoned that the priest had more to lose then him so a solution involving the father could wait. Leo, on the other hand, was very dangerous to his well being and immediate action was required.

The Sgt. sat in his office and arrived at the same conclusion that he had reached about Vinnie, Leo had to be eliminated.

He carried out his plan early the next morning. He arrived at Leo's house at seven a.m. and drove his car a short way into a muddy wood road until it was invisible from the main road. He made his way to the back of Leo's house and entered through the back door. He surprised Leo in the act of attaching his wooden leg. Leo tried to grab his axe handle but was handicapped by his leg not being attached. He lost his balance and fell to the floor. Without saying a word Naples hit Leo on the back of his head with a wood pole he had picked up outside.

Leo began to recover from the blow but then fell forward and lay face down with his detached leg by his side. Naples had no desire to hit him again as he wanted to make the crime look like an accident. There was a kerosene lamp on the table in the back of the room which the Sgt. seized and smashed on the floor. The fuel spread rapidly and without a second thought Naples tossed a lit match into the mess he had created. He had to repeat his efforts twice before he had a blazing fire at the back door.

He absentmindedly picked up the pole he had used on Leo and ran for the front door. He almost panicked when it refused to budge. In his haste he had failed to notice that the door opened inward and realizing his error he was out of harms way in a few seconds. As he proceeded to his vehicle, he tossed the pole aside. While he drove back towards town, he reviewed his actions and reasoned that even if the blow hadn't killed Leo the fire would finish the job.

Smoke was seen rising from the area of Leo's dilapidated home. The village men and the older boys ran to the fire equipped with buckets. They formed a line from a pond behind Leo's home, which was burning furiously, and managed to extinguish the blaze before the house was completely consumed.

As one of the bucket brigade, I was close-by when the front door was pried open. It was jammed shut by what appeared to be debris but as the door opened inward the exact cause was revealed.

Lying on the floor with his head nearest the door was Leo's body. He seemed to have made an effort to reach the door but didn't make it. The back of the house, which is where the fire had started, was collapsed so there would have been no escape through there. There was a faint smell of kerosene mingled in with the smoke. Although Leo clothing and hair were singed, his body hadn't been badly damaged by the fire.

As I watched in horror one of the men said. "There's a great deal of blood around Leo's head but it looks like he started bleeding before he reached his present position." A trail of blood was visible that started from towards the back of the house.

With the fire quelled most of the men returned to their previous pursuits with a few men remaining to make sure the fire stayed out. I stayed to learn as much as possible about the cause of this disaster. It suddenly occurred to me that my friend Bob hadn't been there to assist.

The RCMP arrived a half hour later. By now the remnants of the building had cooled enough to allow closure scrutiny to proceed.

The RCMP constable who showed up was a young man in his mid twenties. He was tall, muscular, had blond hair and deep blue eyes. The name tag on his chest identified him as Constable Fred LaPiere. He looked over the scene and told those present to stay clear of the house. With great caution he went close to Leo and looked him over carefully.

I heard him mutter that Leo had suffered from a severe blow to the head. "He must have fallen, injured himself, upset the lamp, dragged himself to the door and finally succumbed to the smoke or the head injury." LaPiere said in a loud voice.

As I listened in awe, my thoughts went back to the warning Leo had given Bob and me. "Could this be part of an effort to keep things hidden?" I knew that Leo was privy to information that would have helped find the truth about Diane's misfortune and if his death was not accidental, could that knowledge have been the reason for his death?

I wandered over to the woodpile and sat on a block of wood. I had sat here with Leo before but now it would never happen again.

As I glanced towards the house my eyes caught a glimmer of something sticking out of the ground. I wandered over slowly, not wanting to attract any attention, and examined the spot. I found that I was looking at part of a tin container with its top taped on and buried in earth that was disturbed during the fire fight.

By now I didn't trust anyone except Bob in the matter of my investigation so I decided to checkout the tin when no one was around.

The constable had finished gathering his information and told his audience not to touch any thing until the Sgt. came and the body was removed. They departed one by one with sadness in their hearts. The biggest sorrow was probably that with Leo gone there would be no place for the drinkers to meet socially.

I biked over to Bob's house where I knew he was busy shingling the back of their barn. The answer to why he hadn't shown up at the fire was obvious, his ladder had fallen and he was stuck on top of the roof. I put the ladder back in place and Bob came down.

I told Bob about what happened and asked him if he was afraid that we could be caught up in the mayhem that had struck our village?

Bob was shaken by the news of Leo's demise but felt it had nothing to do with the Diane.

When I told him about the metal container buried in the ground, he said. "What could Leo have hidden in there? It's probably just trash."

"I don't know but I'm going to find out. We're going to go there after dark and get it." We decided to go as soon as it was dusk.

To avoid any unwanted attention we walked through the path that led from the store to Leo's. The trip there was uneventful but upon coming within sight of the burned house a car was pulling away. "It looked like the priest's car." I said. Bob didn't answer.

We waited in the bushes until we were sure no one else was there and quickly made our way past the pile of wood to the container.

We dug into the earth and with a little prying the container was soon free. After retrieving it without any problem we quickly retraced our way to the path and returned to Bob's barn.

Because of the darkness and the fact that we didn't want to attract any attention by lighting a lantern we hid the container in the hay and agreed to check its contents the following day.

It was Thursday morning and I hurried to finish my chores. I was anxious to look at the contents of Leo's container.

Upon arriving at Bob's and after greeting the family, Bob and I went into the barn and took out the container.

The container was made of unpainted tin and was untarnished. "It mustn't have been hidden in the dirt for long." Bob said.

It was sealed shut by a narrow band of gauze tape that was used to hold bandages in place. Danny pulled the gauze strip off and pried the lid open.

The box contained a small roll of money that added up to $153. To us this represented a large sum but in itself contributed nothing to our search.

"This must be Leo's cache of restart money" I said. "There are probably other things hidden on his property. We'll have to go back and see what we can find."

The next morning we retraced our steps of the previous day ending up where we had found the container. The searching we wanted to do was such that we would have to risk being seen. If someone came by, we decided to say we were looking for a lost cat.

Bob made a comment about the high stump that Leo had left on a tree that had been uprooted by the wind. Apparently the roots and stump had sprung back into place when the trunk was cut. The outline of where the roots had been pulled out was visible.

I asked Bob to look around the house while I checked the adjacent area. In the act of wandering without any real purpose in mind I came to the wood road where someone had parked. The tracks in the soft ground were the same as those from the Sgt's car.

Further checking revealed a few broken twigs that indicted someone had gone through the bushes to Leo's. I followed the trail and just as the reached the opening that was Leo's property I saw a stick with dark brown stains on one end.

I had seen plenty of dried blood in my lifetime and without a doubt that was what was on the stick. I picked it up and continued to rejoin Bob. I placed the stick I had found on top of an old barrel and looked to see what Bob was doing.

Bob was studying the stump when I arrived and said. "I think that if we pulled on the stump we could cause it to rotate and expose the ground underneath."

I agreed with Bob but wondered out loud why we should bother.

"This would be a perfect place to hide something."

"All right," I answered' "but how will we do it?"

"Maybe if we tied a rope around the top and pulled from a distance it would go back to its uprooted position." Bob interjected.

"That's a great idea." I said as I glanced around for a rope. We searched the area and found a neatly coiled rope behind a bush, tied it to the top of the stump and pulled in the direction the tree had fallen. As expected, the roots, covered with loam, rose out of the ground as the stump was pulled. After tying the rope to a small tree they circled around the roots to see if they had uncovered any thing besides dirt and rocks.

The first thing we noticed was a group of bottles neatly placed in a depression that had been dug out under the raised stump. They were marked with labels of various brands of alcoholic liquids and none of them had tax stamps on their tops. At first glance, there didn't seem to be anything else hidden in the cache.

Bob said. "We've found Leo's backup supply of drinks. I wonder why the liquor store stamps are missing."

I walked over to the bottles and picked one up for closer inspection and immediately spotted a cellophane container that had been hidden from view. I replaced the bottle after obtaining the container and walked back to where Bob was standing.

"Let's put the tree stump back in place and hide the rope before someone sees it raised and then we can look at what we found." Danny said.

We released the rope and the stump roots sprang back to their original position. With the rope back in the place we found it we proceeded with our finds to a spot that hid us from the road.

I proceeded to tell Bob about the tracks and the stick I had found.

Bob examined the stick and agreed that it was dried blood on one end. "However," he said, "It could have come from an animal."

I took the stick and examined it more closely. "I see some dark hair stuck in the blood that wouldn't belong to any animal I know."

Bob scanned the stain and had to admit Danny was right.

"The tracks you found sure make it appear that the Sgt. hid his car there for some reason." Bob said." You don't suppose that he killed Leo?"

"It seems possible based on the things we've found out."

"Bob lets open the container and see what it has inside." As I spoke, I pulled the top off the container and looked inside. There was a single sheet of aged paper with some scrawled pencil writing. It wasn't easy to read but after some effort, we were able to come up with the intended message.

"I think I'm in danger. Whoever reads this is forewarned to not go to the RCMP with the information I'm telling you because some of them may be the involved in the act that made it possible for you to read this. For the past several months I've been paying a fee to a constable Johns and then to a guy named Vinnie to keep from being raided. As time passed I was forced to buy my supplies from them. When I rebelled against them, I placed myself in danger by telling Vinnie that I knew who his leader is. My belief is that man is Sgt. Naples My only request to you is to give my remaining liquor to my drinking buddies."

Bob's face paled as we absorbed the information and he asked. "What are we going to do?"

I pondered for a while and came up with an answer. "We'll keep gathering whatever clues we can and wait for the right time to act. At present I don't know when that will be but there's one thing I do know, we can't tell anyone what we've discovered."

Before leaving we hid the bloody pole under a portion of Leo's partially burned house.

# 52

At my mother's insistence I was required to go to confession on special days and at least once a month. This wasn't a pleasant thing for me but believing my soul could be endangered I had no choice.

The confessional was an enclosure that consisted of three cubicles. The priest would set in the center cubicle and the person who was confessing would enter into one of the side enclosures and close the door. There was a place to kneel facing a wall with a one foot square opening to the priest's location. This opening could be shut by a sliding panel while the priest heard a confession from the other side. The enclosures were dimly lit so the priest and the person confessing could see each other.

Father Frotten was not one to accept a young man's admittances of sins without a great deal of prying. He would ask how many times you masturbated, did you touch girls between the legs, and did you have evil thoughts and all sorts of other embarrassing questions.

Not long after Diane's murder the priest seemed to have discovered a new sin. He asked if I knew of any women in the village that had loose morals.

I didn't understand his question and the priest explained. "Women who like to sleep with men other than their husbands."

I denied knowing any and Father Frotten stated.

"It's a sin to withhold this sort of information at confession.

I said my act of contrition; the priest granted me absolution and assigned my penance. The real penance for me was the need to confess.

This new sin that had been introduced bothered me. All of the sins that one could commit were covered by the Ten

Commandments and the rules of the church and that was not one of them.

At the risk of tarnishing my soul I asked Bob if he had any idea where this came from.

"I have the same question. Father Frotten said the same thing to me and I don't have an answer."

"We could ask our parents but I'd be afraid of the consequences. To question a priest's utterance would invoke an angry reply."

Once a year the parish was visited by priests of the Jesuit Order.

My mother insisted that I go to confession when they were there. Her reason for this was unclear to me but I imagined that maybe their absolution was of a higher order.

Following my mother's orders I found myself in the familiar enclosure and went through the normal routine.

As I confessed all my real and imaginary sins I remembered the instructions about immoral women from Father Frotten and said. "I haven't become aware of any bad women in the parish."

The Jesuit priest lifted his head from a downward looking position and stared at him. "Son, could you repeat the last thing you said?"

I repeated my statement except I substituted the word immoral for the word bad.

The priest shook his head and said. "My son, knowing the actions of others, however sinful they are, is not a sin on your part."

I finished my confession, said the number of Hail Mary's assigned as penance and left the church.

The Jesuit's reaction to my input about sinful women was puzzling. It did however agree with belief that knowing women who were less than pure was not in itself a sin.

"Father Frotten must be wrong." By the time I reached home I had decided that I would keep this subject in the background until I had a better understanding of the subject.

# 53

I was on my way to see Bob about what had to be done to complete our wood cutting. As I passed Mrs. Benoit's store a sudden thought popped into my head.

Leo had said he saw some action at Diane's house on his way back from getting cigarettes and it was possible that Mrs. Benoit might remember the time and day he had been there.

I felt in my pockets as I retraced my steps and made sure a five cent coin I had been saving to buy a candy bar was still there.

Mrs. Benoit was usually too busy to drop what she was doing for such a small sale and allowed the purchaser to help himself.

I didn't want her to know what I was up to so I planned to nonchalantly mentioned Leo's death with the hope she would say something about his last visit.

With a little luck he'd find out when he had use the path.

Mrs. Benoit was busy scrubbing her kitchen floor and nodded at I when I entered. "What can I do for you today, Danny?" She asked.

My answer was short. "I'd like to buy a chocolate bar."

Before I could say any thing about Leo she responded. "Just go in and take what you want and leave the money in the change jar."

I entered the room and under the guise of having trouble picking the best bar I scanned the credit list. I found an entry on Leo for a pack of cigarettes recorded the Tuesday prior to me finding Diane murdered.

Mrs. Benoit must have sensed that I was taking a long time choosing a candy and I had just closed the ledger when she showed up at the door.

"My floor is finished and it's time for a rest. Why don't you join me in a cup of tea while you eat your candy bar.?"

Tea in those days was made in a large pot and left to steep all day. By afternoon it was at its strongest and laced with canned milk and sugar was a potent drink indeed.

Not wanting to miss out on any useful gossip I accepted the invitation and sat at the kitchen table with Mrs. Benoit who was a plump short lady with rosy cheeks. She was congenial and as honest as they come. She started the conversation by saying what a shock Diane's death had been to the community. "I hope they catch that hobo and hang him in a tree."

For some strange reason she didn't mention Leo's death. "Have you heard of any suspects other than the hobo?" I asked.

"No," she said, "but the talk in town is that Sgt. Naples is certain that's who did it."

With this information stored in my head and I gracefully bid Mrs. Benoit goodbye and continued on my way to Bob's

On my way, I concluded that Diane must have been killed on Tuesday based on Leo's previous input and the records in the credit ledger. Things were beginning to fall into place but even if we identified the killer we had no way of safely bringing him to justice.

When I arrived, I was told that Bob had to run an errand for his mother and wouldn't be back for a while. I jumped on my bike and returned home.

It was Friday afternoon and Bob and I were looking forward to going to Belle Point to see what Julie had in mind for us.

School had let out before we arrived and we were met by Julie at the door.

She had two side by side desks prepared with books, pencils and paper.

"In the next hour I'm going to run you through the subject's ninth grade students would have in a week. Just listen and remember what you can. The papers on your desks contain abbreviated but comprehensive information on these subjects that I hope you will have time to review before next Friday."

The hour went by quickly and Julie didn't waste any time with extraneous material. When she finished, she explained to us the importance she placed on education.

"It's the key to unlocking the door to success." She said.

We were preparing to leave but she indicated she wasn't finished. "We spoke briefly about the murder that happened in Seal Lake and now there's been another violent death. I'm curious if you have given any serious thought to the official conclusions reported in the Rivemouth News?"

I was surprised by her question and hesitated before answering. I was certain that Diane's murderer was not the hobo. Leo's death was probably not accidental and with the information we had acquired it was almost certain he had been murdered. What should we tell Julie and what was her interest in these affairs?

Sensing their hesitation, she continued. "My father is a member of the RCMP and he takes great pride in their ability to solve complicated crimes. One of his favorite games was to give me crime facts, real or fictional, and have me come up with logical solutions. I guess if I had been born a boy I would have followed in his footsteps. Given the facts reported in the newspaper I have doubts about the conclusions reached in both cases. Do you agree with me?"

Bob would sometimes react without thinking and this happened to be one of those times.

"We know the hobo didn't do it, he doesn't even exist."

I gave Bob a look that he had no trouble interpreting to mean, shut up.

Unfortunately Julie saw it too but she had the smarts to play the game. "Maybe you'll explain how you know that sometime but for now let's call it a day and meet again next Friday. We left with Bob carrying the study material while I pedaled us home.

It was still daylight when we arrived at Bob's so we sat in the barn to deal with the new developments.

The schooling we were being offered took second place to the fact that Julie not only didn't believe the crime reports but also had some knowledge in the methods used to unravel the mysteries.

Could they trust her enough to tell her all they knew or should they pretend to be as confounded as everyone else? It would be very comforting to have an adult on our side.

We discussed this in great detail. Bob made the observation that Julie was the first adult to express a desire to find the real answers. "She would be an enormous help if we could trust her to keep the information between the three of us until we reach a safe way to proceed" Bob said.

"What do you propose we do to find out how trustworthy she is?"

Bob could see the futility of their quest up to now more clearly than Danny. He said. "We're not risking anything by starting with your experience with Diane. You can tell her that you worked for her and that she was friendly. The way she reacts to this information will tell us if we should go further."

I agreed with Bob. "O.K., we'll do that but let's agree on a code to signal a stop if either of us feels we are out of bounds."

We decided a right clenched fist would be the signal to back off.

As I pedaled my bike home I felt a small load had been lifted from my shoulders. We needed help and I have a strong feeling that Julie will turn out to be the one to give it."

The week before the next lesson seemed to last forever. I was involved in cutting wood and had little time during the day to look at my homework.

I did the best I could by lamplight and found the diversion from the hard physical work to be soothing. I had neglected to tell my mother of the arrangement with Julie and when she saw me studying she asked. "Danny, I thought you were finished with school work, what're you doing?"

I had never lied to my mother on important things but felt that the truth at this point would only complicate matters. "Ma," He said, "Bob and I are competing for a chance to win a prize from the Farmers Journal. It involves a lot of writing so I thought I should get an early start."

That satisfied her and she said, "Don't stay up too late." on her way to bed.

The work was, for the most part, a review of the end of grade eight materials. I spent an hour on the material and after washing my hands and face in the kitchen using the small amount of warm water left in the stove tank I went to bed.

# 54

Morning arrived all too soon. The windup alarm clock was set to go off at six thirty and the first chore was to light the wood stove to provide heat and cooking capabilities.

We were equipped with a hand pump that eased the burden of obtaining water. Most families had to carry their water in from the well by bucket.

With the fire lit and the water heating he gently reminded his mother that her turn had come to take over the kitchen as she sleepily came out of her bedroom.

With the milking bucket in hand I went to the barn where I fed Molly. The cow was a good producer that kept us supplied with milk and butter. Cream was a delicacy reserved for special occasions but most of it went into making butter.

I returned to the house, placed the milk bucket on a shelf near the pump and washed my hands. The oatmeal was boiling on the stove and my mother had set the table. A pot of strong tea sat on the edge of the stove ready to be poured

Betty and Dick were up and busy dressing. Our mother announced that the oatmeal was cooked and we all gathered at the table where ourr mother said grace.

A usual breakfast consisted of a bowl of cereal, usually oatmeal, covered with skim milk and sweetened with sugar. The younger children drank milk, also skimmed, and the older children and adults drank tea to their liking. I preferred my tea with milk and sugar

After eating preparations were made for the day's events. Lunches were made for Betty and Dick to take to school. One mile was too far for them to come home for lunch.

Mary busied herself with preparations for her scheduled house work after the kids were on their way. The schedule she followed never varied, Mondays and Thursdays were her clothes washing days, Tuesdays and Fridays were her floor scrubbing days and Wednesdays were for butter churning. Of course those were only the main chores with cooking and bed making being some of the many additional things requiring attention.

My day cutting wood was active but boring. It consisted of choosing the right trees to cut and felling them in a position where they could be accessed easily for trimming the branches. The method of harvesting the forest was simple; I selected some of the smaller trees for burning and left the larger one to mature into usable lumber logs

Our wood lot was thus destined to be an efficient producer for years to come.

It rained a few days during the week and that curtailed outside activities and gave me a chance to study my school material.

I had never been an avid studier but rather a quick browser of the material at hand. Part of my present lessons involved geometry and this made me realize that one must know the rules or the problems remained unsolved. This alone was enough to start me on the path I eventually followed.

I compared our search for the murderers to a geometry problem and saw that without the appropriate facts in both cases the solutions were elusive.

As I lay in bed that night, I went over the facts Bob and I had gathered. Based on that information I came to the conclusion that one of two people was most likely to have done the killings.

They were Sgt. Naples and Father Frotten with the Sgt. at the forefront. But the motives of either one were not apparent. With that thought I drifted off to sleep. My dreams were unpleasant with Father Frotten chasing me and yelling. "Confess! Confess!"

Friday, which had become an important day for me, had arrived. I spent the morning in the forest making paths to wood I had already cut and hurried home for my noon meal.

My mother was never one to control except in religious matters so I was free to wander as pleased as long as I did my chores on time.

I went to Bob's and found him busy cleaning the stalls in the barn. He finished quickly and we sat down to chat about our lessons and the mystery we hoped to solve.

Bob felt that the schooling was worth pursuing for now but he was more concerned with the other subject. "If we quit our snooping now, we will never have to be concerned about being in danger. We could return the money to where we found it and let someone else find it. What do you say about that?"

I acknowledged that no one except Julie and a few of the local boys had any idea of our involvement and he was correct in his assumption that the safest path to follow was to leave things as they were.

"We would be safe from harm but would our consciences remain clear? I, for one, didn't want to spend the rest of my life running away from the priest in my dreams." I continued, "Bob, you're right for our sake but what about some other person meeting Leo's fate because of us being frightened."

Bob digested this input and with a brave smile on his face said. "Danny, I have to agree. What do we do next?"

"Let's follow our plan to include Julie if we find we can trust her."

We had just enough time left to start off for school. We arrived at the school late but Julie was still there waiting for us.

We followed the same procedure as the preceding week. Julie had prepared a package for each of us and she went over the new material. When she finished, she asked if the first lessons were too difficult.

Bob answered. "I had to really concentrate but I believe I learned what was expected of me." I agreed with Bob's comment.

Julie pulled out a new folder from her desk and brought it over to us. The folder contained newspaper clippings about the two deaths in Seal Lake. She read the one that described Diane's murder and said. "If the hobo didn't kill her who do you think did?

Bob said last week the hobo didn't exist but how could you know that when the police believe the opposite?"

Bob squirmed in his seat and was at a loss for words.

We had neglected to discuss how much they would tell Julie and we were now caught in a position of uncertainty.

I, being the instigator in getting involved, took the lead. "We have done a lot of research in who killed Julie and we definitely eliminated the hobo."

I went on to explain how we questioned and tricked Doris Surette into unknowingly revealing that what she believed to be true was highly questionable.

I continued with the information we gathered from our search for the person Doris saw and had concluded that she had seen John, a fisherman, who admitted being at the train when it was stopped and had not seen any other person except the crew and an old lady looking out her window at the train.

Julie digested this information and with a perplexed look asked. "How could you have found out all this and the RCMP didn't?"

I had wondered about the same thing and the only answer was that the police wanted this case closed quickly. I explained this to Julie and she didn't respond. Rather, she asked another question.

"Why would two young men like you have such a great interest in this?"

I saw Bob close his right hand and hesitated to gather my thoughts.

We had to give out some information or be forever stuck in a rut. I reasoned that the daughter of a high ranking RCMP official could be trusted in spite of the probability that the local RCMP were involved in what might be a cover-up.

Having reached what I thought was a reasonable conclusion I gave Bob a look that was meant to reassure him and Bob opened his hand.

My way of finding out what I needed to know was meant to be subtle but Julie must have seen what I was trying to do.

"Have you ever known of an RCMP who was dishonest?" I asked.

She smiled in a knowing way and said. "Danny, I have even known some personally. My father is in charge of the unit that seeks out the ones that are corrupt and brings them to justice. From your question I gather that you suspect the involvement of some of our local police. If so you're not the only one who thinks that way. I'm convinced someone in the force is not on the up and up."

Both of us were relieved to hear Julie's views on that matter.

I was about to speak when she continued. "My information has all come from the reported facts in the paper and the little that you've told me but I think you know far more then that. Can you tell me what else you've found out?"

I finally convinced myself that Julie was a person we could trust completely. With that belief in mind I proceeded to tell her about my association with Diane and continued through the entire effort Bob and I had gone through..

Bob commented on the fear Leo had expressed in the danger that could be encountered and his warning to us.

Julie now had in her in possession all we knew about the deaths and whom we suspected. She didn't disagree with any thing they told her and said they should keep this between the three of them until she could pull a few strings.

The session ended on that note and we headed for the door. As we left Julie called out. "You forgot your study papers."

With papers in hand they were on their way home.

"I hope we haven't made a mistake by trusting Julie." Bob said as I peddled the bike.

"I'm sure we're safe with her on our side."

Bob was dropped off at his home and I continued on. I arrived just in time to milk Molly.

My mother fed me in silence and when I asked if anything was wrong she said. "I received a letter from Dad and he won't be home for at least a month. The job is behind schedule and the boss wants to catch up."

I had been looking forward to having him help with his wood cutting but with Bob's help things should be all right.

Most of our farm harvesting was over with the exception of picking the winter apples. That was a family affair where we all pitched in when the individual varieties reached their optimum stage. Apples were the favorite snack in the winter and my mother made pies that were equal to the best.

Every chance I got I studied the material Julie had given me and occasionally Bob and I would review the material together. It may seem surprising but I enjoyed this way of learning better than going to school full time.

With only one teacher covering eight grades there were long periods of working alone without teacher participation. My way of coping was to listen to her as she addressed the higher classes. By the time I reached grade eight that luxury was gone.

The villagers had all but forgotten the deaths. Living in the demanding world of the thirties didn't give them time to waste on items they had no control over. Funerals in those days had a way of closing an issue.

What made these items less important was that both victims were not significant members of the community in the eyes of the elite.

I was sure that there was at least one person who was happy about the residents' attitude. Undaunted Bob and I, assisted by Julie, were following a different approach which we hoped that individual wasn't aware of.

# 55

Bob and I had reached a point where uncertainty was replaced with determination to solve the murders. Julie had given us the courage to continue looking for the truth.

Our chores had become routine; our studies tolerable so we had plenty of time to devoted to the investigation.

Recalling that Diane had mentioned that she kept a diary and up to now no one had admitted to having seen it I tried to reason on what could have happened to it

"Could it have been found and destroyed or was it still hidden?" We will have to search Diane's home again."

In order to ease our search I went through my dealings with Diane that might include a clue about its location. She had told me about the diary's existence and that it was hidden but that was the extent of our conversation on the subject.

I reviewed the tasks I had done for her that might contain a clue. They consisted of maintaining her wood supply that was delivered ready to use, cleaning her yard, helping her to keep her flower garden weed free and fetching water from the well.

Maybe it was buried in the garden but that was unlikely because of the constant changes and digging that went on there. As I reviewed my conversations with her nothing seemed relevant. We had searched the house but that had proved futile.

The time had come to consult with Bob.

When we met Bob suggested that we give the house another inspection.

"It can't hurt to try but I have my doubts we'll find anything." I said.

"Let's go over now and at least try to find places we overlooked the first time." Bob said.

Not wanting to be hampered by having his bike at the house we went to Leo's place and hid the bike in the bushes. The remains of Leo's home had been flattened as a safety move. We were surprised to see his wood pile was gone. Someone had taken advantage of poor Leo's departure.

We followed the path to Diane's and cautiously examined the house from a distance before going to the back door. Our tampering with the lock hadn't been disturbed and they went right in.

After spending a half-hour looking in every conceivable hiding place we abandoned our search.

I showed Bob the cabinet where the locks were hung. They were still in place, hanging on pegs, with their keys.

As we left the house, I happened to glance towards the well which was covered by a wooden structure and had a crank used to hoist the water bucket.

"Diane had once told me she had a big trout in there to eat the bugs that fell in." I told Bob.

"Let's see if Diane's trout is still in the well."

We looked down at the dimly lit water surface but couldn't see in enough detail to tell if it was still there.

An insect fell in as we looked and a sudden swirl on the surface told them that the trout was there.

"We'll have to come back with a fishing line and see if we can catch it." Bob said, as they walked back to Leo's.

"We can't hurt him, let's think of a way to catch it safely and release it in the Mill pond.

Before leaving the area we looked over Leo's lot. The bloody pole they had hidden was still where they had put it. Except for the wood being gone and the structure having been flattened the place was undisturbed since the fire. We mounted the bike and pedaled to Bob's home.

Sitting at our table in the barn, we talked about the trout in the well. Our intention was to return the fish to its native environment without causing it any harm. Hooking it was out of the question so they decided to net it in a dip net. We would have to lengthen the handle to reach the bottom of the well and Bob came up with a solution.

"We can take an eel spear which had a fifteen-foot handle and attached the net to it."

The eel spear is a device that was used to spear eels through the ice. The spear end was made of steel with a stiff center and a side by side set of prongs on each side. The prongs had hooked ends that were extremely sharp. To catch an eel a hole would be cut in the ice and the spear would be used to probe the mud bottom. The prongs were forced apart and if an eel happened to be caught between two adjacent prongs it was squeezed and held when the spear was withdrawn.

Our main problem was to get this unwieldy contraption to the well unseen. Bob suggested that they take it to Leo's after dark and hide it at the end of the path, then in daylight we could follow the path to the house without being seen. Once the plan was conceived, we acted.

The following morning found us at the well trying to capture our prize. The trout proved to be harder to catch than we had anticipated. Finally I passed the net across the bottom in a quick sweep and felt the fish wiggling in the net. As I raised the net, I could see the fish and another object.

We had brought a galvanized bucket to keep the fish alive and we transferred it into the filled pail.

I took a quick look at the other object and my heart felt like it would jump into my throat. It was a two quart pickling jar with its top latched on tightly with a rubber seal between the lid and the body. The bottom was full of sand to make it sink and stuffed inside was a soft-covered note book.

"This must be Diane's diary." I said, with great excitement. Bob was just as excited.

Attached to the wire lid closer was a short piece of string that must have broken to let the bottle sink to the well's bottom.

We had to hurry to keep the trout alive until it was released in the nearby pond so we took the bottle along in its original state.

After completing our mission of mercy we returned to Bob's barn and examined the bottle without opening it. By now we had become more cautious and decided if this was Diane's memoir it would be better to have an adult with us when it was examined. We added note to our list and hid the bottle with the tin box.

Thursday a student from Belle Point School came to Danny's home with a message. He had come into the kitchen without knocking as was the custom and although they lived in adjoining villages Danny only knew him slightly.

He handed me the message and said the teacher had told him to give it to me personally.

Betty overheard him and started to ask a question.

I led the boy, Tom Muise, outside and away from inquisitive ears. With the pretense of admiring Tom's bicycle he asked if Julie was all right and he assured me she was.

"She took off yesterday and we had Mrs. Piere taking her place. Nobody liked that very much."

Having done what he was asked to do Tom was soon on his way.

"I wish I had a new bike like that." I though, as Tom left.

The note was short and to the point. Be sure to be here tomorrow. I have enlisted a new ally.

My first reaction was to feel a sense of betrayal. We had promised to keep this between the three of us and now there would be four.

"Our knowledge in the wrong hands could be disastrous." As I pondered the situation I became less paranoid and decided that I had no choice but to let her explain.

I biked over to Bob's and told him about the note. Like me, he was edgy at first but soon calmed down. Tomorrow would reveal which way our quest had veered.

I spent the morning in the usual routine. I made the fire in the stove, woke my mother, milked the cow, ate breakfast and resumed cutting on the wood lot. My mind was wandering over what future events could pop up in the investigation. I felt proud of what Bob and I had found out so far but I realized that until Julie became involved we wouldn't have been able to use it anyway. "It is difficult for two teenagers like us to fight authority no matter how just the cause" I thought.

I had doubts that even Julie's involvement could influence the outcome. Occupied as I was in my analysis I automatically went through my wood harvesting and at noon was surprised at the volume of wood I had cut. Upon returning home for dinner I ate with relish the meal of potatoes, salt herring and carrots topped off with a delicious blueberry pudding and a cup of strong tea.

Following my meal my attention turned to the impending meeting with Julie and the potential new partner. Unable to convince myself to return to wood chopping I left to see if Bob was free.

Bob was involved in gathering material to bank the house foundation for the winter.

Because the houses were built on top of stone foundations without the use of mortar, the wind could blow through the numerous holes this type of construction left. It was a desirable condition for all the seasons except winter when the unheated cellar had to be kept above freezing. This was accomplished t by sealing the foundation with a barrier of sawdust or dried seaweed held in place by boards. In the spring this was dismantled to be repeated in the fall. The heat from the dirt floor was sufficient to keep the fruits and vegetables at a safe temperature. The only threat to the stored food was rats.

I joined Bob in his efforts and we soon finished what he needed done for the day.

We entered the barn and sat at what had become our strategy table.

I opened the conversation by asking Bob if we should delay showing Julie the new material until we were satisfied that the ally she had acquired was acceptable to us.

. "Let's bring the items with us but we'll leave them with the bike until we are satisfied she made the correct choice."

With this in mind we searched the barn for a container to put the jar and tin container in. We found an old burlap potato bag and wrapped both items in it. With the bag tied securely to the back carrier rack we left for Belle Point.

# 56

They arrived at the school on time and leaned the bicycle against the building. After entering they took their regular seats and Julie came over and welcomed them. She must have detected their chagrin as she immediately began to speak.

"I know I have broken my promise to keep things quiet but an opportunity arose and I couldn't afford to let it get away. You're not committed to anything you won't like and the person who has agreed to join forces with us has strong reasons to want these crimes solved. In fact, his livelihood could depend on it.

Danny has had some contact with him but only in a cursory way. His name is Fred La Piere and he is a constable in the RCMP detachment. He was the first policeman at the scene of Leo's death and the author of the report issued on the matter. I didn't tell him who my informants are and the only reason I know you saw him was because he was impressed with your interest in the fire disaster."

Julie continued. "We now come to the crucial decision making point in this discussion. Will you both accept the constable as our ally as I already have?"

I was now more in doubt then ever about the proposed arrangement. "How can we trust someone who put out the unbelievable report about what happened to Leo?"

Julie had her answer ready. "The constable is a recent addition to the detachment and when he suggested an in-depth investigation his boss, Sgt. Naples told him there were more important things to spend money on than a bootlegger's death. In fact he wrote the report and told Fred to sign it."

"Let me tell you about my visit to the RCMP office in town. I took a day off from teaching and went to town with the intent of finding out what kind of conditions existed in their office.

I went there without any specific plan in mind. The only person present was Fred LaPiere and he let me in when I knocked. I have to admit that I found him very attractive, especially his blue eyes which seemed to absorb my entire being as we looked at each other. At the mention of my being Inspector Levesque daughter he invited me in and escorted me to his office.

The sparely furnished office held two chairs and a desk whose top was uncovered except for a telephone, a large ink blotter pad and an in-out basket. The office was constructed so that a private conversation could be held without being overheard from the outside. We sat down facing each other and he asked how he could help me."

Julie paused, glanced at a sheet of paper in front of her and then continued. "You have to realize that I had to be careful in my response. I told him I'd like to know some of the local members of the police force personally as it gave me a comfortable feeling of having increased protection. Especially, I added, in an area where two unsolved deaths have recently occurred.

This brought an immediate response from Constable LaPiere. He told me I should be aware that the cases were closed as one was an accident and the other was committed by someone who was probably in British Columbia by now.

"His response gave me the opening I had hoped for and still pretending to be frightened I remarked on the circumstances of Leo's death."

She paused again and instead of continuing about her meeting with Fred she said. "I need your approval for my next move." We were in agreement with her suggestion so she continued.

"Fred seemed to hesitate at my mention of fear and proceeded to reassure me that nothing was left unanswered in the cause of Leo's demise. Unwilling to accept his feeble defense I got braver and after making him aware of my unofficial training in crime solving I proceeded to poke holes in the newspaper's report that originated with him about the death."

"Faced with the inconsistencies between the report and my rendition of what I knew, he became defensive. However, I detected a definite weakening in his arguments as he continued to try and reassure me. Finally he broke away from his protective defense of his report and admitted that it was not up to the RCMP standards and was probably incorrect in its conclusion. He confided in me that he had been intimidated into backing the report produced by his superior, Sgt. Naples."

"In justifying his action to me he said he feared that going against the Sgt. would put his career in jeopardy. It appears that the Sgt. rules the detachment with an iron fist and nothing left their office without his corrections applied. Having wrung this bit of information out of him I then asked his opinion of the hobo solution applied to Diane's murder. By now he had loosened up and realizing he was talking to someone who had connections to higher levels, even if only a relative, he proceeded to answer."

"I didn't get involved in that investigation but I was consulted unofficially by the constable who was. According to him he was told to assume the hobo was the perpetrator and concentrate on finding him. Now that I feel free to express myself, I'm convinced both cases should be reopened. The only question is how?"

Julie had a satisfied look on her face as she continued. "I had succeeded in finding out what I needed to know and now, with confidence, I answered his uncertainty in this way. I have some informants who know significant details about both deaths. If I can gain their approval and you agree we will conduct our own detective work and at the right time we will have all the help we need. He agreed so now it's your turn to decide."

We both sat silently and digested what we had been told.

I was beginning to think that Julie was in the wrong profession but I had never heard of a female policeman.

My belief in the ability of women to reason was rapidly changing. Julie had managed to convince the constable to risk his future based on her logic and I was convinced to go along.

Bob was still in deep thought when I said. "Julie, I'm in agreement. What's the next step?"

Bob spoke up with a look of doubt on his face. "I'm outnumbered so I'm with you."

Julie said. "We now have a team and we will have to be honest with each other if we expect to learn the truth. Do you have any thing to add?"

Without a word between us Bob went outside and returned with our burlap bag.

Now came a period of complete revelation. After going through everything we had held back we counted the money in the tin container. It added up to the $153.00 we had previously counted.

Julie read the note we had found in Leo's hiding place and had placed in the tin from lack of a better place to keep it. A look of grave concern appeared on her face as she read about the probable involvement of the Sgt.

The next thing we did was open the glass jar. The book inside was filled with written entries that were explicit except for the names of the people talked about and was missing its front page. Most of the information consisted of coded names, dates and money paid.

It was getting late so we called the session over until the following day. The subject of where to hide the material we had brought was discussed. The school had a high ceiling with an access hole to the attic. The hole was sealed shut by a cover that opened upwards into the above space. We opted to use this as a hiding place as it was never used and was difficult to reach. It took a balancing act to reach the opening but we managed to do it with the aid of the teacher's desk and a chair.

School was out for today but I could hardly wait when Bob and I would meet our new partner.

# 57

I started on Friday morning with my usual tasks but I was faced with an additional one that would take up part of my afternoon.

My mother had gone to town to stock up on groceries and to buy wool she needed to knit stockings and mittens for the coming winter. That meant a short day in the woods as I had to prepare food for my noon meal and then meet the bus where it dropped off my mother with her load of supplies.

Every thing that was used often was bought in bulk and stored in the pantry. Flour, sugar and cornmeal came in fifty-pound bags, oatmeal in twenty pound boxes and molasses in gallon jugs with the buyer providing the jug.

The bus arrived on time and after helping my mother put the heavy items away found him with a little free time.

With the thoughts of the deaths and my involvement always ready to pop to the surface in my mind I set off to meet with Bob and prepare for our school meeting.

Bob was splitting wood that was left over from last years harvest and had somehow been overlooked. He set his ax on the chopping block, wiped his brow and greeted me with a slap on the back. Without any overt signs of agreement they both headed for their private meting place in the barn.

Bob opened up the conversation. "Danny, I'm worried. This thing is getting too big for my liking. When there were only the two of us we were safe from detection about what we were doing but now I'm afraid the killer will become aware of us and then watch out."

This wasn't the first time that thought had come to my attention. Leo had warned us and my own analysis had sent up red flags.

"We can't change what we have already done Bob and without help we were sure to be found out if we continued. I feel that we'll prevail now that we have two allies who are experienced in these matters unless our new partner is not what Julie thinks he is. Let's be cautious in what we tell him until we assure ourselves that he can be trusted."

Having neglected our studies for a full week we spent time reviewing the material we had and, that done, we switched over to how we should react to the new partner.

"Let's allow the two of them to do the talking while we listen for clues about Constable La Pierre's real intentions." I said.

"Seeing that one of the people we suspect is his supervisor it's difficult for me to believe he will be loyal to our cause and take the chance of losing his hard earned position." Bob replied.

I saw a spider weaving a web in one corner of the empty cow stall and wondered if we were the web weavers or the flies about to be caught in it? "We are committed to finding the truth and we can't back out now. Let's hope for a fast solution without being dragged into any difficulties."

We arrived at the school house at four p.m. and were surprised to see that the Constable wasn't there. We went inside and there sat Julie pretty as a picture. She must have wanted to give a good impression because she had her hair neatly arranged; a touch of lipstick on her lips and her dress was much nicer than the drab one she usually wore at school.

"Our studies are going to suffer if we continue the way we're going so I'm suggesting that we meet on Wednesdays for class work and reserve Fridays for detective work. Is that O.K. with you?" She asked.

"It'll be hard to take two early afternoons off a week but it shouldn't be for long or will it?" I asked.

"I suggest we ask Fred that question when he gets here. He should be here soon and he assured me that he had some interesting things to tell us. Let's go through some lesson material while we wait."

We had just completed our review when a model T Ford pulled up in front of the school and a man debarked from the passenger side. The auto turned around and left the way it had come. The man, dressed in civilian clothes, walked up to the boys' entrance and knocked. Julie hurried to the entry hall and opened the door.

Julie and the visitor were not visible from where we sat but we could hear her welcome Fred and there was a short discussion between them before they entered the schoolroom.

I recognized the Constable as the one that was at Leo's. He had an authoritative look in spite of not being in uniform and as they walked towards us I couldn't help but notice what an attractive couple they were.

Constable La Pierre gave us a broad smile as Julie introduced us.

"I remember seeing you at the fire scene where Leo Petite died." He told me. "But I haven't seen you before, Bob." When he concluded as he shook hands with both of us.

His shake was firm and not overly strong but one could sense the power that could have been applied. To me this was a sign of sincerity but that alone wasn't enough to gain my complete confidence.

Julie gave Fred a nod that must have been a prearranged signal and the constable started to speak. "In case you're wondering why I came in civilian clothes and had a friend drop me off I'll explain. I'm acting in a role that is unofficial and also one of secrecy. If I used RCMP equipment or wore my uniform I would, in my mind, be violating my oath of office. Even now I'm probably subject to disciplinary action for working with you. What Julie has told me, strengthened by my own observations, has led me to believe that the causes of both deaths remain unsolved. Now, I imagine you wonder why I'm willing to go along this route instead of working out in the open with my fellow officers. The answer is that I have already tried and failed. I believe that most of our officers are honest but we may have one that isn't."

He paused and observed his audience, was satisfied with the apparent effect and continued." Julie gave me the confidence I needed when she told me about her father's role in keeping our organization clean."

He had been standing as he spoke and when he finished he sat down next to Julie.

I sat in awe of the power and commitment that Fred had placed in his statement. All doubts about whose side he was on evaporated from my thoughts.

"He is on the side of justice and so am I"

Overcome with emotion I stood up and shook Fred's hand with all the strength I could apply and Fred returned the pressure I applied with one of equal force. To me that meant he accepted me as an equal.

Bob observed Danny's actions and thought. "If Danny is convinced, I have no choice but to go along with him." He then stood up and shook the Constable's hand. The team was now ready for the next step.

Our first step was to tell Fred the entire story in chronological order leaving nothing to imagination and ending with our finding the trashed rooms inside Diane's home and Leo's stash in his back yard. Fred expressed amazement at how two unassisted teenagers had uncovered such an abundance of information.

We recovered the items we had hidden in the attic and reviewed their contents. Fred studied Diane's diary with great interest. The group concluded that the entries were meant to help her keep track of what had been a busy and hectic life. With the front page missing only part of the story was revealed.

There were five numbers and three names. The names were Tom, Danny and Leo and the numbers were one through five. By taking Danny's name entries and comparing the days he worked with the dates recorded it was obvious that the diary was a record of when someone had visited her.

The money entries were recorded with a plus or minus sign in front of the amount. All three named individuals had minus signs where money entries were made. Numbers one through four had plus entries and number five had none.

"I wonder where all the money Diane seems to have collected is?" Fred asked.

Julie replied, "That is a good question, maybe it will show up."

My brain did a flip-flop as I grasped the meaning of what was revealed by the diary.

"This answers a lot of questions that have been bothering me. Tom, Leo and I were paid for services we performed for Diane. The amounts next to my name agree with what she paid me and I would bet the same is true for Leo and Tom. The other amounts would seem to be money she took in but what for?"

A quick knowing look was exchanged between Julie and Fred as I continued.

"Although I can't prove it the five other visitors must have been the ones that left the tire tracks."

Bob interrupted with a sudden input. "We know who owns two of the cars that left tracks; Sgt. Naples and Father Frotten and we think that one of the other tracks belongs to Jules Comeau. That leaves two that are unknown."

While we studied the diary in more detail, Fred noted that the entries had stopped several days before Diane's death and he also observed that there was no overlap in any of the times the assumed visits had occurred. He expressed his opinion that one of the five numbered visitors was the one who had killed her. "We don't even have any idea who two of them are. That will have to be one of the first things we must find out. Once everyone is identified, we will be able to eliminate the obviously innocent ones and concentrate on the ones left." He said.

I said we can eliminate Jules on the basis that he was in Halifax when Diane died. The others agreed with my reasoning and Julie spoke up.

"I believe there are only two viable suspects in this case and they are the Sgt. and the priest. With the information Danny and Bob received from Leo it is difficult to see how anyone else could be involved."

Julie seemed to have had a sudden thought as she made her last statement. She looked at Fred and with an apologetic voice asked if Danny and Bob would excuse them for a few seconds?

She led Fred into the boys' entrance and posed a question to Fred. "Do you think it's all right if we make them aware of what we both suspect, that Diane was selling her body?"

Fred's thought wandered through his own youth where, at their age, a lot of information about sex was unknown or incorrectly believed. The solution of Diane's murder could depend on not keeping their partners in the dark and if they weren't aware of this possibility, telling them shouldn't hurt them. They agreed to reveal their thoughts and returned to the school room.

Fred started the conversation with carefully chosen words. "Julie and I have come up with a possible explanation of what Diane's numbered visitors were paying her for. I'm sure you have heard of women who are not the best examples of whom you would want for a wife, women who would do almost anything for the right price." He hesitated to observe the reaction of his audience and seeing no sign of resentment he continued. "Julie and I feel that Diane was a prostitute." He ended his statement abruptly.

Bob blurted out. "What about the priest, was he trying to save her soul."

"That must be what he was doing. He was searching for women like that. Now I know why he asked me about them at confession." I said with a quavering voice.

No one spoke immediately and the two adults had looks of puzzlement on their face.

Julie was the first to recover from this unexpected input and asked me to explain.

I told her about the new sin the priest had introduced during my confession. I also told them about the Jesuit priest telling me I was not a sinner if I knew such a person.

Fred said. "This will take additional thought but it could be an important part of our investigation."

Julie looked out the window and saw that Fred's transportation had arrived. We agreed to meet on the following Wednesday and returned the material to its hiding place.

Fred had kept notes of our meeting and before he left he asked me one question.

"I want to make sure that I know one thing for certain, was Leo a bootlegger?"

"Of course he was but he never sold us any thing."

# 58

Julie stayed behind when the three others left. She wanted to think about what had happened without any interruptions. One thing that made her uncomfortable was that she had involved Fred into an unofficial investigation which could result in punitive action by his superiors.

She decided to call her father and tell him about their involvement in the investigation and ask his advice. She would have to find a secure phone as the ones in the village were all party lines and anyone could listen in on her conversation.

The only secure line she was aware of was the one in Inspector Connolly's office but she thought that it wouldn't be easy to use that phone undetected so she searched her mind for a solution and the answer soon popped up. She would go to the phone company's office in Rivemouth and ask for a private line.

With that problem solved, she picked up her belongings and went home. On her way she pondered on when she would be able to make the call. "Tomorrow is Saturday and that would be an ideal time for me. I'll ride the bus to town and get this done." She told herself

When she arrived in town the following morning she went directly to the telephone company office and made her request. She gave the operator her parents' phone number and asked how she would pay for the call. "You can pay here in cash or I can process it as a collect call." The operator said.

Julie opted for a collect call and gave the operator her name. A few minutes later she was seated in an enclosed booth and was talking to her mother. With the greetings over Julie asked to speak to her father. He came on the line immediately and expressed his pleasure in hearing from her.

Julie than proceeded to tell him about the situation she was involved in and her concern about Fred's vulnerability if he was found out.

Maurice refreshed his memory about the call he owed Inspector Connolly and quickly came up with a plan that would serve all requests.

"Julie," he said, "give me Fred's full name and I will call Inspector Connally and set up a plan that will protect your Sherlock Holmes." He said with a twinkle in his voice.

"I also want you to see Fred and warn him not to mention his involvement with you or the closed cases. Can you do that soon?"

Julie assured her father that she would carry out his instructions as soon as they finished their call.

"Don't worry, Julie, the wheels of justice will turn in your favor. Now go meet your fellow conspirator and tell him what I said."

Armed with her father's optimistic input Julie walked on Main Street toward the RCMP building to find Fred.

She knocked on the door and a constable she had never seen greeted her.

"Could I speak to Constable LaPiere?" She asked.

The constable told her he was off duty but was in his private room. "I'll go get him for you. Please wait in here." He said as he motioned for her to enter into the foyer.

Fred was at her side in a few moments and Julie said. "We have to talk."

Fred, with a puzzled look on his face asked. "What do you want to talk about?"

"We need a private place were we won't be overheard." She responded.

"Let's go in here." He said as he walked toward a closed door and led her into one of the offices.

Once inside Julie let out a big sigh of relief. "I'm glad I was able to find you this quick." She told him."

"I just got off the phone with my father and he told me to tell you not to acknowledge that you are involved in any of the closed cases that we have been looking into. He didn't give me any details of his plan but he assured me that you would be safe from any retribution."

Fred told Julie that he had been doing a lot of reviewing of their material and the picture was beginning to take form.

"I have even found out that some of the closed cases in town could be connected to what we're looking at. By Wednesday I'll be in a better position to tell you what that is." He concluded.

Julie suggested that they go out for a cup of coffee, Fred agreed and went to his room for a light jacket.

They wandered around town and looked at the activity in the harbor finally arriving at the Royal Store where they drank their coffee and ate a cookie. During their discussion Fred asked if she had noticed the small island in the harbor.

She acknowledged seeing an island with a post sticking out of the ground.

"That's the one I meant." He said. "Keep that in mind and I'll explain on Wednesday.

They parted company when they left the store, with Fred returning to his detachment building and Julie spending her remaining time browsing through the clothing stores.

The bus left town at three P.M. and Julie was on her way back to Belle Pointe.

# 59

After Maurice received his daughter's call, he reviewed the information she had given him.

Realizing that he owed, his friend, John advice on how to handle a possible problem within his detachment, he decided that he could combine the two requests into one.

The way his operation was constructed he was able to access RCMP personnel files in spite of it being a Saturday. The results of one phone call he made were all he needed to help establish his next move.

He called Inspector Connally at home and after a few personal exchanges he addressed the situation that was foremost in his mind. "John, I'm sorry I couldn't get back to you sooner on that problem you posed but things have been hectic here. I have to agree with you that there is something suspicious going on in your group. My first choice on how to proceed would be to send one of my investigators there to help. Unfortunately all of them are presently occupied in work that takes precedence over what you are faced with. My second choice on how to proceed is one that you can implement on your own and in the end might be the best. I reviewed the background of your personnel and came up with one constable who is relatively new to the force and had excellent grades in the investigative field. His name is Fred LaPiere and I believe he replaced Constable Johns who was transferred. What you must do to implement my plan is to form a secret relationship with LaPiere and have him try to find out what's going on."

John absorbed Maurice's input and reluctantly agreed that it was a possible way to proceed. "I'm not used to being secretive but I have to accept the fact that there's no easy way out. Let's hope your plan works and we find my suspicions are groundless. Whatever we do, the integrity of the RCMP must be protected."

With an agreement reached they hung up after assuring each other that they would keep in to keep in touch.

.

Inspector Connally relaxed in his favorite chair and thought through the actions he would have to take to implement Maurice's plan. He realized that any unusual dealings between Fred and him, if observed, would cause suspicion in the detachment. He needed an intermediary to pass information back and forth and arrange meetings. Whom could he trust to carry out this vital task?

No one in his work force could fill this roll. It had to be an outsider with a believable reason for seeing both of them frequently.

As he pondered this problem, his wife entered the room and asked if he had heard from Julie lately. He answered that he had not and that they should have her over soon.

The mention of Julie caused a train of ideas to rush through John's mind. Of course, what better messenger could he find? If he could convince both Fred and Julie to join him, they could fake a love affair and no one would suspect they had an ulterior motive.

Another thought came to the forefront which, if used would provide cover for his meetings with Fred, he could use him as his driver while they were on duty. All that remained now was to try and implement his plan.

His first move was to talk to his wife and get her O. K. to have Julie visit them the next day. With that accomplished, he proceeded to call the Babin home and he spoke to her

"Elizabeth and I were wondering how every thing is working out for you and we thought it would be pleasant if you could join us for lunch tomorrow."

Julie responded with an enthusiastic, "Yes, but how will I get to town?"

"I'll pick you up after church services if you agree?"

Julie agreed and another step in a complicated arrangement between several people with a common cause was complete.

John picked up Julie at the Babins shortly after noon on Sunday. He had been doing a lot of thinking about how to approach her with the suggestion of her being a go-between. He had arrived at the conclusion that appealing to her loyalty to her father would produce the best results and the best time to do so was on their way to town.

They started conversing about meaningless things. John then mentioned that her father had called and they had discussed a problem that could have a detrimental effect on the local law enforcement organization, specifically the RCMP detachment.

Julie was somewhat amused at John's apparent embarrassment at bringing up this subject but held her feelings in check as she listened.

"I know that you're aware of how your father has devoted his service to keeping our organization as clean and honest as possible. I also suspect that you would assist your father in his efforts if you could. Am I correct in my assumption?"

Julie nodded her head in agreement before she spoke. "Of course you're right, John. There is very little I wouldn't do if I was allowed to but, after all, I'm a woman and that places restrictions on the possibilities."

Her thoughts were mixed as she spoke. In a way she was matching wits with a person who was far superior in the subject being discussed but he had no way of knowing that the conversation they were having was motivated by her prior actions. She was determined to protect her involvement in the investigation and that meant keeping Fred from being found out.

John felt he was proceeding in the right direction and continued. "Julie, if I told you that you could be a great help in solving a puzzle that I'm faced with would you consent to do so? Of course this would all be kept quiet, you'd almost be an under cover agent."

By now Julie was trying to guess what John had in mind for her to do but whatever it was she knew she had to accept. "John, I'm honored to be offered a chance to help you. What do you want from me?"

"I intend to start an internal investigation of a certain individual in our group and with your father's help I have come up with a plan. It involves using on of my constables to do the investigative work and this creates a communication problem. If excessive familiarity between a constable and I is observed, the project would become difficult, if not impossible, to keep secret. I want to use you as my go-between. No one will suspect you of any underhanded activity if you work in the guise of being the constable's girlfriend. Can you give this a try?"

At this point Julie saw the implication of John's proposal and felt that if the Constable was Fred her efforts had been successful. "Can you tell me who my so-called boyfriend would be?" She asked.

John pondered her question momentarily and said. "The lucky man is Fred LaPiere and he is the person that your father suggested. He based his suggestion on the results of Fred's past studies and the fact that he was the least likely member to be influenced by the person we will check on."

Julie broke out in a big smile. "I know of Fred and the thought of him and me being friends is appealing. This could turn out to be exciting and fun. You've convinced me." In her mind she was already plotting on how she would now be able to influence an investigation that was far more complex than the Inspector imagined.

With the major obstacle out of the way, John was now ready to implement the next phase of his plan.

"Fred is the duty officer today and he will be alone in the office. I'd like you to approach him with my proposal and then let me know what his response was."

They had arrived at the Connally home and as they turned into the driveway John said. "Don't forget, this is to be kept quiet, I don't even want Elizabeth to know."

They disembarked from the car and entered the house where Julie was greeted with a big hug. Shortly after, they were seated at the dining room table and ate a delicious meal.

Julie was seated in the living room with John while Elizabeth attended to clearing the table and washing the dishes. John was anxious to complete his instructions for Julie and wasted no time in addressing her on this "As soon as Elizabeth has finished with the cleaning up I will mention that there is a big schooner in the harbor that you might like to see. This will give you an excuse to take a walk and go talk to Fred. Just make him aware of what I'd like him to do and. if he agrees, give him this note." He handed her a sealed envelope and that ended the conversation.

It wasn't long before Elizabeth had finished her chores and joined the others in the living room. They chatted about how Julie had adapted to the Belle Pointe environment and if she had any regrets about her decision to teach there.

Julie told them that she was realizing all the goals she had wanted to achieve and then some.

John casually mentioned the schooner in the harbor and Julie, on cue, said she would like to see it. John offered to accompany her but she said she would be fine on her on.

"I'll just be gone for a short time while you folks relax." Julie said. She put on her light jacket and made sure she had the envelope in her purse as she departed on her errand. The walk to the RCMP building was uneventful and she was soon knocking on the front door.

Fred opened the door and greeted her with a big smile. "You're the last person in the world I expected to see when I opened the door." He said. "Come on in."

Julie looked around and was pleased to note that Fred was alone. "I've come with good news. We are about to make our investigation official." She then went on to tell him about every thing that had transpired and what Connally had in mind.

Fred absorbed this information and asked Julie if she knew exactly what John wanted him to do?

"I don't know precisely but maybe this will explain." She handed him the envelope.

He tore open the envelope and read its contents. With a look of concern he said. "The Inspector's note only tells me that if I agree with the proposed action that you have passed on to me he will have me drive him to a made up meeting that will give us the opportunity to talk in private. He said that I must maintain absolute secrecy about all of this."

Julie added a bit of information to the exchange. "John told me that our relationship could be explained as a girlfriend-boyfriend thing. That won't be hard to accept." She smiled as she spoke.

They went on to plan how Fred could continue his meetings with their two junior partners and saw no problem in the way they already had. "You know what, without them this entire investigation would be dead." Fred said.

Julie left the building with her expectations at a very high pitch. Not only had she broken the barrier that kept women out of police work she had met a man that she felt attracted to. She returned to the Connally home and after more small talk the Inspector drove her home.

During their journey Julie told John that Fred had welcomed the chance to help uncover any abnormalities in their units' operation and she would continue to help in any way she could.

"The RCMP's reputation is of utmost importance to me; after all, I have been a part of it all my life."

John dropped her off at the Babins' and returned to town.

# 60

Monday morning the RCMP detachment was gathered in their headquarters preparing for a standard day of operations. Fred was sitting in one of the shared offices when their secretary came in and told him to get one of the automobiles ready to take the Inspector on a trip.

Fred asked were he was going and she replied. "John has to attend a meeting in Digby that concerns some question about Native rights on hunting. I'm not sure of the exact place." She left the room as Fred prepared to go outside.

Fred chose one of the Chevrolets and after making certain that it was fully gassed, he drove it to the front of the building and waited for the Inspector. Shortly after, John appeared in the doorway carrying a black leather brief case. Fred jumped out of the auto and opened the rear door for John to embark. John signified that he preferred to ride in the front and said. "Fred, get back in, I'll open the door for myself."

Seated next to each other the officers took the road north east towards Digby.

They had not gone far when John opened the conversation. "Fred." He said. "We are not going to Digby as you probably suspect. Drive a little further and you will see a small farm house painted red on the right side of the road. We'll turn into the driveway and park behind the building where we can't be observed from the road. The place belongs to my friend who only uses it in the summer when he visits from Boston. That will give us privacy while we talk about what could be a serious problem in our organization."

Fred followed the instructions he had been given and when they were secure in their chosen spot he killed the engine. The time to talk had arrived.

"I'm glad that you have chosen to help me establish the truth about some uncertainties that have come to my attention. You were highly recommended by chief Inspector Maurice Levesque, who is Julie's father, on the basis of your passed record in investigation studies."

Fred displayed a look of surprise at his supervisor's comment. Although he knew where the recommendation came from he did not expect the reason given for his selection. He said. "I am glad to be able to help."

John began his explanation of what had brought him to suspect that at least one of his team had veered off the acceptable path. "My suspicions were aroused by Detective Sam Gleason of the town police. As you know, we did a joint investigation with them on the death of Joel Batist and it was declared an accidental death by all concerned, including us. Sam has apparently continued a search and has come up with some convincing evidence that points a finger at our Sgt. Naples. Needless to say, if the facts support the suspicion we must find a way out. You are now charged with as heavy a burden as any RCMP officer should ever be asked to bear. Do you have any questions?"

Fred was slow in answering as he marveled at how three untrained individuals had drawn him into a web that included more than he had anticipated. Was there a connection between the Seal Lake deaths and the one in town? Undaunted, he looked at John straight in the eyes and said. "Inspector, I will do my best."

With the agreement reached they discussed the rules that applied. There was to be no obvious direct communication between them, every thing was to be channeled through Julie or by the same method used today. John then opened his briefcase and handed him a manila envelope and said. "This contains all the information I have that concerns our quest. I suggest you have a private meeting with Sam to hear the facts he uncovered first hand. Let's go back." Fred, with his brain working overtime drove them back to Rivemouth.

With the Chevrolet parked in its appropriate place Fred entered the building and took the envelope John had given him directly to his room. He felt the contents would be safe as the only person who entered an Officer's private quarters uninvited was the house keeper and she would never snoop in the occupants personal belongings. He placed the envelope in his bureau's top drawer and went down to the main office.

With no action required on his part, Fred sat at a desk and went over the things he was aware of and the items that remained to be found out.

What he felt he must do was make the Inspector aware of his involvement with Julie and also reveal what the two young investigators had uncovered. However, he reasoned, doing this too soon could have a severe repercussion if the Inspector felt he had been used. It would be better to reveal their manipulations when he had compiled enough evidence to justify the path he had followed. He decided that his next step was to speak to Detective Sam Gleason but only after he had reviewed the material John had given him.

That evening he reviewed the contents in the envelope and began to see a pattern develop. The connection between the town and Seal Lake deaths was the involvement of bootleggers although Diane's death did not fit the pattern exactly. She had dealings with Leo, a bootlegger, but her connection with him would not justify such harsh action. There was one item that was obvious, if even part of the information he had at his disposal was accurate, members of the RCMP were involved in actions that were inappropriate. In the morning Fred was going to try and arrange a meeting with the town detective.

In spite of their competitive dislike for each other the two organizations did tolerate joint operations when it was advantageous to both sides. Fred planed to use the obvious distaste that Sam had for Sgt. Naples, as was evidenced in his report to John, to get Sam on his side. A single phone call was all it took to arrange a meeting.

They met in a small restaurant located on the edge of town. Sitting in a corner of the small dining area they addressed the case of Joel's death and the extensive work Sam had done to establish the true circumstances that brought it about. There was no doubt in Fred's mind, after they had explored Sam's report, that Constable Johns and Vinnie were involved in the extortion of money from the bootleggers and the added crime of violating the Nova Scotia liquor laws. With Vinnie dead and Johns transferred the local law violators were out of reach and the trail was at a dead end. They both agreed that there must be more left to discover.

Fred made up his mind to tell Sam about his own knowledge of the deaths in Seal Lake. He first ensured himself that Sam would keep this information to himself so that their search was not jeopardized

"I believe that there are some important people involved and they could shut us down and end our careers if not our lives." Fred said.

Sam reviewed his statement and had to agree that the thought was probably valid.

"Sam, I'm breaking a promise by telling you this but the only way we are going to get the guilty person is through complete cooperation." He then proceeded to reveal all the things that he had learned from Danny and Bob.

Sam had listened intently to the entire discourse and a look of understanding slowly appeared on his face. "My God," He said. "We have a priest and an RCMP Sgt. involved in this. You're right about one thing, we have to tread carefully."

"I think I know how to bring this entire affair to a head." Fred said. "At least we should be able to have the higher ups make an honest decision. Can you be available Wednesday afternoon to join me and meet my collaborators?"

Sam asked where they had to go and Fred said. "To Seal Lake, I'll give you a brief tour of the crime scenes and then you will be introduced to a school teacher and two eight grade graduates. Will you come?"

"I most certainly will." Sam answered. "Where will you pick me up and at what time?"

"We can meet in front of this building, its remote enough to not have any prying eyes. Be here at two thirty and we'll be on our way."

Fred left and returned to his work place, confident that the answers were not too far away.

# 61

Fred felt like he was conducting an orchestra in the performance of a complicated classic piece. He had never been involved, much less in charge, of such a complicated affair. His main concern at present was to keep all the participants in a co-operative mood and there were two in particular that he was worried about, Danny and Bob.

He developed a strategy that he thought would be the best way to keep their minds at ease. Julie was the prime tool he would use to implement this.

That evening he called the Babin home and after identifying himself as Fred, asked to speak to Julie.

When she came on the phone, she sounded excited. "Hello Fred, how are you?" She knew of the possibilities that the Babins could listen in on their conversation and not being aware of what he wanted she let him do the talking.

"I'm fine, Julie and I hope you feel as good as you sound. Since we met in town Saturday, I've wanted to see you. I want to drop by tonight and visit with you for a while?"

Julie was instantly aware that something important must have happened and she went along with the charade. "Fred, this is so sudden. Of course you will be welcome. When can I expect you?"

"I will be there at seven thirty if that's all right with you" "See you then." She said and she hung up the phone.

Fred arrived at the Babin home at the appointed time. He parked the government-owned vehicle close to the house and went to the back door and knocked.

Mrs. Babin opened the door and Fred introduced himself as Julie's friend. She invited him into the kitchen and called out to Julie that her visitor was here and Julie quickly entered the room.

All three went into the living room and Julie told the Babin's that Fred was a member of the RCMP. She explained that they had met through Inspector Connally who was her father's friend.

. With the normal inconsequential talking over the Babin's excused themselves and went into the kitchen leaving the door between the two rooms open.

The custom at the time was to give courting couples privacy but only enough for them to converse quietly and perhaps steal a kiss but not enough to be able to do things they would have to confess to the Priest.

Seated on the living couch they entered into a discussion the subject of which the Babin's would have never suspected. Fred brought Julie up to date on his actions. When he told her about Detective Gleason's involvement including his coming to their Wednesday meeting, she expressed her concern about how their helpers or rather, the two primary contributors would react.

Fred had given this a lot of thought and had a ready answer. "I want you to talk to them before we arrive and tell them that the investigation has widened to include another killing. Tell them that without the Detective's help we might not be able to substantiate their discoveries."

Julie was about to respond when Mrs. Babin called from the kitchen. "Would you like a cup of tea?" The offer was a customary courtesy which was seldom refused for fear of insulting the host so they readily accepted.

With their fresh cups of tea setting in front of them on a small oak table, the pair continued to discuss the potential problem. While reaching for his cup Fred's leg brushed against Julies and she didn't pull away. At that instant a make-believe relationship began to change into the real thing.

For the moment however, the reality of what they were faced with took over.

"I think I can handle the situation but it might take me some time. Don't come in until I motion to you at the door."

"We have to keep Inspector Connolly in the dark for a while. By the time we let him know what we have done behind his back we should have such convincing evidence that he will not be too mad," Fred said.

Julie reminded Fred that they had her Dad on their side and that was a big plus.

They had completed what Fred had set out to do and the time seemed to have passed quickly in spite of the seriousness of their talk. "It's time for me to go. If I don't get this car back they'll think I stole it." He said with a grin.

They entered the kitchen and Fred bade good night to the Babins and as he went out the door Julie patted him on the arm.

# 62

Bob and I were busy cutting firewood on the Pottier lot. We had brought lunches to minimize the time lost by having to go home and it was also a pleasant way to set and talk. The lunch consisted of sandwiches made from home made bread liberally coated with butter and thick slices of bologna.

We sat on a log beside a small fire and toasted the sandwiches and heated water in tin cans for our tea.

Bob started the conversation with an expression of concern. "I wonder what new things will come up on Wednesday?" He asked.

"With Fred involve I wouldn't be surprised at any thing. This can't go on forever, let's hope that he will have all the answers needed to solve this. I sometimes think we should have let things as they were."

Bob, who had been uncertain of what path they should have followed, expressed his opinion. "If something like this can happen in a small place like Seal Lake can you imagine what must be happening in the rest of this world we live in? If no one tried to find out the truth we would all be in great trouble. I now believe that we have to keep on helping, no matter what." When he realized what he had said he was startled by his own words.

We went back to cutting and at three o'clock returned to their homes.

Julie had spent the day at her school teaching her pupils using French as was the custom on Tuesdays. She spent the small amount of free time available thinking about tomorrow's meeting. Her main concern was how she could quiet the fears of her young investigators. Without a doubt they would be reluctant to have another person involved at this stage but the decision to include

Gleason was not reversible. Only time would tell what resistance she would face

The school day ended and she made her way to the Babins with anxious thoughts about the next day.

# 63

Fred arrived at the restaurant at the agreed time and found Sam waiting. As soon as the vehicle came to a stop Sam jumped in and they were on their way.

Sam was not very familiar with the Acadian villages because he had no need to deal with the residents professionally or personally.

They visited Leo's place first and tried to verify as much as possible what Danny and Bob had reported. Fred reached under the rubble and found the blood stained pole in the spot where they had told him they had put it. Most of the evidence the youngsters had found had been erased by the weather and but the remaining features fit what Fred had been told. With the pole in the back seat they went to Diane's home.

The place appeared to be deserted with no sign of any activity having occurred for some time. As at Leo's place, any outside evidence had been eliminated by nature. Sam commented that it was unfortunate the crime scene wasn't properly investigated.

Fred was stung by that remark and sprang to his own defense. "Sam," He said. "I was hampered by the same person who interfered with your case and in my case he is my supervisor."

Sam nodded his head and agreed that Fred didn't have any choice in his actions.

Everything was as Danny had reported. They checked the well, the path to the short cut and the barn.

Fred commented on the complex story that Danny had told and added. "If he made this all up, he's a genius."

"The way I see this we are going to have very little provable evidence. There is no question in my mind that your Sgt. Naples is deeply involved in three known murders and maybe as many as two more."

"It's about time we go meet with our co-conspirators." Fred said. They got in the car and were on their way.

While the two policemen were looking over the crime scenes Julie was busy in her school trying to convince her partners that the addition of one more person to the group was essential.

Danny and Bob had arrived at three thirty and were warmly welcomed by Julie. She had arranged four chairs around her desk with the intention of having one of her after hour students ask why there was an extra chair. The young men were asked to join her, on her platform and take a seat. Bob was the first to comment on the fourth chair

"I thought we were meeting with Fred, why the extra seat?" Julie was prepared for the question and hoped that her answer would put their fears to rest. She began with the intension of relaxing their fears and making them comfortable with the new developments.

"Fred has uncovered new information that has increased the scope of our investigation. It seems like there could be more killings connected with the two we are investigating, killings that had been deemed accidental. Without your actions surrounding Diane and Leo's deaths, these other cases would certainly have never been revived. We have gained one new ally who will be a great asset in solving these horrible crimes. Are you still willing to continue with the new person on board?"

They had already agreed that the truth had to come out but that was before this new person became involved. Bob, who was the most cautious, answered with a question of his own. "Who is this person and how sure are you that we can trust him?"

"I can assure you that the person who will be joining us has as much interest in bringing out what has actually happened then any of us. He has been hurt professionally by our main suspect. Could you ask for more assurance than that?" Julie concluded.

Danny and Bob looked at each other for signs of agreement on what to do. Bob shrugged his shoulders in uncertainty and Danny made the decision for both. "We have no choice, we either join or give up, count us in."

Julie had noticed that the auto was parked outside and she motioned to Fred to come in. They entered through the boy's door and were soon seated with the other three.

Sam was introduced to Danny and Bob and they all turned their attention to the serious business at hand.

The five partners were soon involved in trying to reconstruct the series of events that led to them being in their present position. There had been four deaths, three of them ruled accidental that fit into the trail they were following. They had no one who could testify that they had witnessed the events that led to the deaths so everything had to be determined by circumstantial evidence.

Sam spoke of the unlikelihood that the general public would accept the word of two fourteen year's old males without more substantial physical proof. "There is no doubt in my mind that we are faced with two murders committed in Seal Lake and at least one in Rivemouth. Two of these have a definite connection to the bootlegger operations in the area but Diane's death does not fit into that pattern. The observations made by Danny, substantiated by the diary, indicated that Diane's murder was committed by one of her clients, but which one?"

Fred picked up the conversation. "Based on Leo's statement to Danny and Bob and the time element involved it must be one of two people, the priest or the Sgt., both people who should be above reproach. In any case they both know who did it. Now it's time for us to find out"

Julie, who had been setting quietly, suddenly came up with an idea. "I know one way we can find out more about the Priest." She said. "Remember Danny telling us about Father Frotten asking him about immoral women during confession? Well, all we have to do is provide him with a name and see what happens."

Fred said. "It's an interesting idea but who can we use as our bait?"

Julie said with a smile. "I volunteer but don't get any ideas, I'll only be acting."

"The next question, if we agree on using this ploy, is how do we implement it?" Fred asked.

"We will simply have Danny go to confession and confess that he knows that I'm a loose woman." Julie replied.

This created a look of amazement on the other participants' faces. "Would you risk putting yourself in that kind of danger?" Sam asked.

"The risk is not great if we do this in a sensible way. His first contact would have to be in a public place where he would try to make a date to meet me privately. We would then be prepared to allow him to commit himself while others are listening from a concealed location. Any attempt at violence could be quickly controlled by the hidden persons." Julie said.

Fred was reluctant to agree with Julie. "Don't forget that we would be dealing with a person who is looked up to by all the people in this parish and if we antagonize him without getting what we suspect it will hurt all of us. If we go forward, we must do it very carefully."

When all the objections were over come by Julie, they laid out their plan.

I consented do my part which was to go to confession on Friday and confess that the school teacher at Belle Pointe was suspected of being immoral. I was told not to elaborate on the subject and act normal to keep the priest from being suspicious. Then we would wait to see if the priest responded.

If the priest made contact with Julie she was to make a date to meet him at the school after the kids had departed. Her protectors would hide in the girls' entrance hall with the outside door locked so no one could enter.

There was no way to anticipate what would happen after the priest came in so it would be a matter of spontaneous reaction to his conduct. With this settled we went on to talk about the connection between the two locations.

Sam brought up the fact that he had no direct knowledge that the Sgt. was involved in the town crimes even though he was sure that he was. He mentioned that Vinnie must have been working with someone but none of his informants had mentioned anyone except Constable Johns.

I said. "I just remembered that Leo said a man named Vinnie was one of the money collectors. Does that help?"

"If we know that Vinnie was part of the operation in both places and Naples was involved in one place it's likely that they were partners in the entire operation." Sam said. "Where is Constable Johns now? It might be useful to find out what he's willing to tell about his involvement in all this." He added.

Fred said that he was told that the Constable he replaced, Johns had been transferred to the Halifax detachment but that's all he knew. "I'll take a look into that when I get back to my office."

We came to the conclusion that we had run out of useful things to discuss and parted after ascertaining that I would do my part in the confessional and that Julie would inform Fred if Father Frotten reacted to my ploy.

# 64

For me the time flew by too fast. I was torn between the sanctity of the church and the need to help solve a grave injustice, Diane's murder.

After considering all the things involved I came up with the answer that justified the action I had agreed to take. The Jesuit Priest had given me the clue that would save my soul if I was ever called on to pay for my transgression. If Father Frotten could make up a sin to serve a questionable motive then I should be able to confess falsely to discover what that motive was.

Confessions were heard by the priest in the evenings so the daily routine of the parish residents was not interfered with. I had finished all my chores and finished my supper prior to leaving for the church. Upon my arrival I entered the pew where the people waiting for their turn to relieve themselves of their burden of sin sat and took my place at the end of row.

Many of them could not have much to tell the priest considering that they were too old to have been in anything sinful.

My turn came and I entered the confessional reluctantly. As most young men, I had a dislike for disclosing things of a private nature to anyone, even a priest. I could hear the confessor in the other cubicle but only in the form of muffled sounds.

The panel between the priest and me was abruptly slid open and I was face to face with Father Frotten.

I went through the formalities required prior to confessing and then went through the standard sins I had committed that were expected from every teenager. I had now reached the point where I had to deviate from the standard and insert the words that set our trap.

"Father," I said. "There is a rumor that the Belle Point school teacher sleeps with different men."

The priest looked up suddenly and opened his mouth to speak but had a sudden change of mind.

I quickly inserted my last statement. "That's all the sins I have to confess Father."

Frotten granted me absolution and assigned an unusually light penance.

I went to a pew to say my penance and added a few extra Hail Mary's to cover my veering from the absolute truth.

Having fulfilled my part in the plan, I went home with mixed emotions bouncing in my mind.

# 65

On Monday morning Julie prepared for her departure for school. She was looking forward to do what she enjoyed doing, preparing her pupils for the future. With every thing in order she walked to the school and was pleased to see all her students were present.

She usually ate her lunch at her desk and during this time she was joined by some of her female student and this gave her the chance to instill in them knowledge that was not part of the school curriculum.

Maybe it would help some of them rise above the normally expected position of being a wife and child rearing but she knew that the chances of that were slim.

She had just released the children for their fifteen minute recesses when a car pulled up in front of the school. As she watched she saw Father Frotten exit and speak to the pupils. After a few words he continued to the boy's entrance and entered. He greeted Julie as if she was a long lost friend.

He looked intently at Julie and started to speak. "Good morning Miss Levesque, I'm Father Frotten, the priest of Saint Agnes Parish. I heard about you when James Babin asked for the church's permission to have a benefit dance for school repairs." He continued to look her over as if she was a cow in the marketplace.

Julie had believed she was prepared to confront any situation concerning the priest but she became very uncomfortable at his obvious crude appraisal.

"Father Frotten, I've heard about your generosity in allowing Mr. Babin to hold that dance and the out come was very beneficial."

He listened with a broad smile and said. "Julie, I hope you do not mind my using your first name, I have wanted to establish some new practices in the local schools that will increase the children's understanding of our catholic beliefs. You are the first teacher I have approached about this and I want your inputs to help perfect my plan."

Julie, who had been born into the catholic religion but she had not followed in the footsteps of the majority of catholic women and she had abandoned church.

She wondered if the priest would make note of not seeing her at any of his church functions and she decided to beat him to that subject.

"You have probably noticed that I don't attend Mass in the Saint Agnes church and it's not because I'm not religious, it's due to my commitment to a friend in town. She talked me into going there."

"I wondered about where you receive your holy sacraments but that is not of great concern to me." He said.

Julie expressed what she felt was a correct statement to keep the door open to whatever he had in mind. "I like your idea of increasing the religious content of our school curriculum. It would have to be approved by the school trustees, however, and they have been known to resist change."

Frotten smiled and said. "Leave that to me, they all owe me favors."

Recess was over and the students had returned to their seats. Julie felt that if Father Frotten was going to commit to some sort of proposal the time had arrived for him to do so. She suggested that they should pursue his idea at a latter date when she would have more available time.

"When do you think that will be?" He asked. "I'm anxious to get this started as soon as possible."

Julie took a gamble on being able to get her partners ready to meet her proposed schedule and said. "Why not meet me here after four tomorrow. The pupils will all have left and we will have plenty of time to talk about your idea."

Frotten agreed and after blessing the school and all its content, he left.

Julie realized the enormity of her commitment and felt weak. Not wanting her flock to notice how flustered she was, she excused herself and went to the girl's outhouse where she almost vomited. She recovered her wits and returned to her desk. The day passed slowly for her.

As soon as she returned to the Babin home she called the RCMP and asked for Fred. The word had spread about their affair and the constable that answered called out in a load voice. "Your girl friend wants to talk to you."

She could hear laughter and good natured teasing in the background while she waited for Fred to pick up the phone.

Because of the danger of someone listening on their conversation, she had to speak in a way that would not reveal the true purpose of her call. She told Fred she missed him and hoped he could drop by for a short visit that evening. Fred recognized the urgency of her message and agreed to see her around eight PM.

With that taken care of Julie began to relax from the strain she had been under for most of the day

Fred was able to borrow one of the Mounties autos with the understanding he would reimburse the detachment for the gas he used. Inspector Connally had made this arrangement with his subordinates to help ease the boredom that came with being assigned to a small community.

He arrived at the Babin house at the appointed time and went through the formalities of being greeted by them and then taken to the living room where Julie waited. The same procedure as the one on his first visit was followed and the two make-believe sweethearts were huddled together on the couch.

Julie went right into the occurrences of the day and asked. "Are you going to be able to do your part?"

Fred answered in the affirmative and added that he would try to bring Sam with him. "The more witnesses we have the better." He said. "But I'm certain I can guaranty your safety if he can't come."

"He will certainly be there at the agreed to time so your arrival must be in between school day end and four p.m. Also you can't leave any visual evidence that I'm not alone."

Fred told Julie that he had thought the entire operation through in detail and all she had to do was let him in through the backdoor at exactly three forty five. With their plan solidified they sat and enjoyed each other's company for another half hour.

Goodnights were exchange and as Fred was reaching for the door Julie kissed him on the cheek.

Fred returned home and tried to call the detective but he receives no answer. "I'll just have to try tomorrow." He told himself.

Another item that he was concerned about was the lack of communication between Connally and himself. They were embarked on an effort that, if bungled, would create dire consequences for his team. On the other side was the likelihood that even if they implicated the priest, it was going to be difficult to convince anyone to take action against him.

Better to not involve the Inspector for two reasons, he might stop them from carrying it out and he could honestly say he was not aware of it if it backfired.

Of course Sam and he would still be at risk. With this concern justified. He prepared for bed.

"Tomorrow would be a significant day in his life." He thought as he drifted off to sleep.

# 66

The first thing that Fred did when he entered his office the next morning was to call the Rivemouth police station. He asked to speak to Detective Gleason and was told he had to go to Halifax and would be back late in the evening.

He thanked the person and hung up. "I'll have to do this alone." He thought.

He had just settled down to catch up with some report writing when a call came in that there was a call from a hysterical woman. "Two boats have collided in the harbor and one of them is sinking." That's all she said and hung up.

Fred was next on the list to respond to emergency calls and was on his way to see if the collision involved the need for RCMP participation? On his way he shuddered to think that this might keep him from being in Belle Pointe on time.

The accident turned out to be minor and was out of their jurisdiction. He made sure that he wasn't needed and returned to the office. He had now rotated to the bottom of the call list and felt a sense of relief.

He reviewed his plan of action. He intended to take the Indian motorcycle to the school and hide it in a wood hauling road he had observe not far from the school. Then he was going to work his way through the tree-covered terrain ending up at the school back door. He had spent a considerable amount of time on whether he should wear his uniform or go in civilian clothes and had opted on the uniform. If the priest's actions required his intervention, the sight of an RCMP officer would have a more profound effect than that of a civilian.

Fred, now confidant that he had everything under control returned to his report writing.

# 67

The church interior was quiet when Father Frotten entered. A few candles were burning on a table near the altar and everything was in its proper place. He glanced at the empty space where the crucifix had hung and thought that what he had done to Diane was an act inspired by God.

He knelt at the altar and his mind became absorbed in the knowledge that he was soon to be rewarded for his good deed. Nothing could interfere with this because his mission was directed by the keeper of his soul. He had hoped for a sign but the interior of the church remained tranquil.

He spent the remainder of his time in church praying and when he rose to his feet one of the burning candles sputtered and went out. He made a sign of the cross. His prayers had been answered. He went into the rectory to prepare for his visit.

Dressed in his plain black suit with his black shirt and starched white collar he went to his car and departed for Belle Point.

Julie had released her students ten minutes early to make certain that they would all be gone before Fred arrived. Her apprehension was at a peak as she waited his arrival.

At precisely three forty five she heard the knock on the downstairs door. She descended the stairs to the lower level and avoiding contact with the firewood stored there she opened the door for Fred.

Her relief at seeing him overcame any inhibitions she had and she embraced him with a hug. "Thank God you made it." She said and led the way up the steps to the schoolroom.

With only a few minutes available they made certain of what they were to do.

Julie was to play along with Frotten and find out what he had in mind, while Fred would listen. He would not make his presence known unless called on to do so.

Fred took his place in the girl's entrance and they waited for the priest. The wait was short; Frotten had timed his arrival with precision.

He wasted no time getting out of his car and proceeding to the boy's entrance carrying a small briefcase. Without pausing he entered and was all smiles when he greeted Julie

"My child," He said. "You look so fresh and pure. God must have put in extra effort when he created you."

Julie was surprised at his complement and suspected there was more to follow. Undaunted, she appeared to accept it with pleasure and said. "That's very kind of you to say that Father and I think you look quite distinguished in your vestment."

They sat at her desk and started to talk about the priest's stated plan to increase the students' appreciation of the religion they had the good fortune of having been born into.

In the guise of wanting to be able to point out the items in detail Frotten pulled his chair close to Julie's. He opened his briefcase and when he pulled out its contents a Twenty-Dollar bill fluttered to the floor. When he leaned over to pick it up he purposely brushed against Julie's leg.

She automatically started to pull away but caught herself in time. Father Frotten placed the bill on the desk and commented on the added cost that his program could add onto her small school budget

He proceeded to explain to her that God was so benevolent and forgiving and he was proud that he was an instrument in the process.

Julie asked the priest if this was part of the instructions he intended to pass on to her pupils. "Not exactly, my child," He said. "But I want us to have a good understanding of each other before we start that."

Julie felt his leg come in contact with hers and keeping the role she was playing in mind she responded with equal pressure. The preliminaries were over as far as the priest was concerned. He fell to his knees and thanked the Lord for his generosity.

He rose to his feet and addressed Julie." My child, God has spoken to me and complemented me on my accomplishments in my church. He promised me a great reward but I never dreamed it would be a beautiful woman like you."

Julie had expected Frotten to make some kind of attempt to seduce her but this was an approach she could never have imagined. She maintained her composure and waited for his next move.

The priest, satisfied with Julie's reaction continued. "My dear, I had to renounce many pleasures to join the priesthood but, in spite of that, I have been pleasantly surprised through the years by God's willingness to allow certain transgressions. This is one of them."

With his statement he reached out to embrace Julie who, by now, had lost all her courage. A wave of rage swept through her mind and body. Without thinking of the consequences she screamed. "Is this the way you seduced and then killed Diane?"

The priest responded before he had time to think and said. "It was Gods will." His face turned as white as his collar when he realized what he had said and his action was automatic, he tried to grab Julie but by now she had run to the opposite side of the desk

She screamed. "Fred, save me."

Fred knew that immediate action was required and he burst out of his hiding place. He confronted the priest as he was in the act of trying to seize Julie and grabbed him by the shoulder.

Father Frotten seemed to loose all control over his being. He screamed "God, what did I do to be punished like this?" He seemed to recover some of his senses and wrested himself from Fred's hold and ran for the door. On this way he shouted. "You will pay for this."

Julie ran to Fred and the two embraced. She was crying like a terrified child and Fred did his best to console her. Time passed and Julie returned to some degree of normalcy.

Fred noticed that the priest had left his briefcase and its contents behind. He looked at the papers that were scattered on the desk and was surprised to find that only the first page had any writing on it. His plan to introduce additional religious material into the school was a farce. He picked up the material including the Twenty-Dollar bill and put them in the case.

With Julie almost completely recovered Fred jokingly said. "I think he was going to buy you with that money."

Julie frowned at the joke and said. "Fred, I'm sorry I lost my reason, did I ruin our chance to implicate him?"

"No, as a matter of fact he actually admitted his involvement in Diane's death with his impulsive statement; it couldn't have come out better if we had planned it that way. Unfortunately we still haven't got enough to make an arrest."

They hid the priest's case with the other items and went their separate ways.

# 68

Father Frotten left Belle Point in an extreme state of agitation. The driving conditions had become precarious due to a rain storm that had developed. This slowed down his trip to church where he knew he would find comfort in the presence of God.

He was not certain who he was the maddest at, the teacher and her RCMP partner or God. "I have devoted my life to saving all these sinning people and what have I received? Not a reward but humiliation. I will look for the answer at the church." He thought.

He entered the church through his private entrance and was greeted by two elderly women who were kneeling in front of the altar. In his present state of mind he felt he had no time to patronize them and abruptly told them to leave.

The two women left with looks of amazement engraved on their faces. As they hurried out the main entrance Frotten knelt in front of the life sized crucifix and lost himself in the turmoil that had invaded his mind. He remained in that position for an unknown length of time.

He was shocked out of his state of near insanity by a loud clap of thunder that literally shook the building. His mind, now clear, wandered in search of a solution of his problem. He knew that he had made a statement that was damming but there had to be a way to keep it from being use against him.

Julie's RCMP friend was the most significant obstacle to any solution, the teacher, by herself, would never be believed. He continued his analysis of the difficult situation he was involved in and realized that someone had steered him into a trap. He recalled the young person who had told him about Julie but he couldn't remember who he was. After listening to other peoples' sins for many years he had learned to erase their identity from his mind.

Another loud thunder clap resounded through the church. It must have hit close by because the chandelier that hung over the altar actually swung on its chain. At that very instant a thought popped up in Frotten's head.

"Of course, all I have to do to stop this insane effort against me is to contact Sgt. Naples and tell him what happened." He told himself. He reasoned that in spite of bad feelings between the two they had a mutual need to protect each other. With his mind made up on what he should do he thanked God for his guidance and left the church for the rectory.

The church had a private line so there was no danger of anyone listening in when he called the Sgt. later in the evening.

Naples wife answered the call and after identifying himself he asked to speak to the Sgt.

There was a long pause before Paul picked up and asked. "What do you want?" In a voice that was filled with contempt

Frotten told Naples that they had a common problem that was going to require action by him and soon."

The Sgt. was perplexed by what he was told. Whatever it was must be serious, the priest would never have contacted him if it wasn't. He asked. "Where can we meet to go over this matter?"

The priest suggested that the Sgt. meet him at the church and he would give him all the details there. Naples agreed and was soon on his way. During the drive, he went through all the events that had taken place up to the present and he had difficulty imagining what he had left out.

All the people who could have implicated him in the bootlegger operation had been eliminated with the exception of the priest. How could there be a problem unless it was created by Frotten?

He stopped in front of the church and went in. Father Frotten was waiting for him in a pew close to the confessional. He didn't move as the Sgt. approached and when Naples reached him, he simply said. "Sit."

Not being used to taking orders from anyone, the Sgt.'s initial reaction was to reply with an angry. "Why." But he controlled his temper and sat next to the priest. They looked at each other and the hatred that they shared was displayed in their faces.

"What do you want that's so important?" Naples asked.

The priest was still on edge and his answer was not well thought out. "They know about Diane." He said.

The Sgt. was surprised at his answer and realized that in the state Frotten was in he would have to be careful. "Who knows and exactly what do they know?" He asked.

The priest carefully explained what had happened at the school leaving out any of the details that would make him look like the instigator of the event. "One of your Constables accosted me in the school while I was visiting the teacher. We were discussing a school project when he suddenly burst in and accused me of killing Diane. I was able to escape from the school unharmed but the fact remains that he and the teacher know about my involvement with Diane."

Naples knew that the priest was not being completely honest but that was the least of his worries. He asked Frotten if he knew who the Constable was. "All I know is that the teacher called him Fred."

"What did he look like and how do you know he is an RCMP member?" Naples asked. The priest responded with an insulting tone. "He was in uniform. He's tall with light hair and blue eyes."

"Beyond any doubt he is talking about Constable LaPiere." The Sgt. told himself. "What could he be trying to do and is he working alone? This is going to take some private checking on my part to unravel this so I can come up with a solution."

He addressed the priest. "All you have to do is keep quiet and let me handle this and don't forget, if my ship sinks your going down with it." With those words, Sgt. Naples stood up and angrily strode out of the building.

# 69

Fred had returned to his quarters and wrote a report that he intended to give to the Inspector. The path the report followed was long and complicated. It contained all the information gathered by Danny and his partner, Julie's involvement, Sam's contributions and his conclusions based on all of this. He had then added the plan that Julie, Sam and he had devised to trap the priest and the unexpected way that had ended.

He decided to neglect the cautious way he was supposed to follow in dealing with Inspector Connally and speak to him in his office. It had been a long day and he felt pleased with his accomplishments. He went to bed and slept peacefully through the night.

In the morning he waited until the Sgt. was absent from the office and knocked on the Inspector's office door. Connally told him to come in and ask him what he needed.

Fred told him they had to have a long discussion about his assignment and Connally suggested that they use the same method they had used before.

When Fred came out of the office Sgt. Naples had just entered the building. He stared at Fred but didn't speak to him. A short time latter Fred was given an assignment that involved driving Connally to a meeting in Digby.

Fred concealed his report inside his jacket and went out to ready the car. Within a few minutes they were on their way to go over Fred's report. They arrived at the red farmhouse and began a long and through analysis of the reports contents. For Fred, some of the items required explaining on why he had taken such liberties on his own. In the end the inspector said. "In this instance the end justifies the means."

The Inspector took possession of the report so he could study it and they returned to their office.

Sitting at his desk, Connally went over the report with an intensity he seldom was called upon to use in this rural environment. He marveled at the volume of data the group had produced in spite of the handicap they worked under. He concluded that there was no doubt that Sgt. Naples was involved in the bootlegger racket and was at least knowledgeable, if not responsible, for some of the deaths.

Diane's murder, however, fell into another category. The unthinking utterance Father Frotten made when confronted by Julie clearly placed him as the main suspect in that crime. The question that remained was exactly why the Sgt., who obviously knew what happened, was covering up for the priest.

Having reached these conclusions, he set his mind on how to proceed. The evidence clearly supported him but he was not confidant that it would stand legal scrutiny because of the sources and methods used to gather it. He pondered on the possibility of turning the two suspects against each other and decided to consult Fred about how this could be done.

Naples was gone on an assignment and Connally took advantage of his absence to talk to Fred. After exploring many possibilities they reach an agreement on how to proceed.

They created a report that indicated that Father Frotten was suspected of Diane's murder and he would soon be questioned. The report indicated that the area bishop was to be consulted before this action was taken and Fred was to pursue the case pending the discussion with the bishop. No mention was made about the bootlegger part of the case.

The file was identified with two words, Diane's Murder, and Connally placed it in his in basket. Having finished with their initial step that was meant to mislead the Sgt., Fred returned to his regular duties.

Naples returned to the office late in the afternoon and was called into Connally's office on the guise of discussing an ongoing case. The in-basket was located in a position that was clearly visible from Naples seat and was completely ignored by Connally. Their talk came to an end and Naples left for his private office. Connally smiled as he thought of the deception he was involved in. Regardless of the serious nature of what he was doing he felt a degree of excitement in being involved. He placed a small hair on the file cover before he left for the day.

The office was empty except for the Constable on night duty when Naples came out of his office. He mumbled something about a file he had forgotten in Connally's office. He went in and closed the door. He noted the position of the file and picked it up. A brief look was all he needed to absorb the contents and he replaced the file in its previous position. As he came out of the office, he said. "The item wasn't there after all."

He left the office with a mind in turmoil.

# 70

Fred was in his room thinking about the events of the day when it occurred to him that Julie could be in jeopardy because of her knowledge of Frotten's deed. He called her at home and disregarding the risk of being heard by others, told her that she must never be alone until he told her it was safe.

Sgt. Naples had explored all the alternatives open to him and had arrived at what he thought was his route to survival. He knew that his career in the RCMP was about to come to an end but if he could avoid being accused of a crime he could retire on a lucrative pension. "There are other things to exploit even as a civilian." He thought.

The actions he committed himself to carry out were both for self-protection and vengeance. He had to eliminate the sole witness who could incriminate him and do it in such a way that it looked like a suicide. He planned to lay the ground work for his task starting in the morning.

The first thing he did was to the visit the Saint Agnes church and familiarized himself with its layout. He was not concerned about being seen as the church was always open to whoever wanted to admire its architecture. He examined the stairway and ladder that led to the bell tower and actually went up to see how the ringing mechanism worked. With this accomplished he returned to the ground floor and left.

Now that he knew where the action was to take place he had to set up the circumstances that would allow that action to be carried out. The priest had to be lured into the tower without being too cautious.

Naples had established how this could be done and all that remained was the timing. He found out that Frotten always went to the Rivemouth Parish to visit the resident priest on Thursdays where he said Mass in the morning and stayed to eat supper before returning late in the evening. He was now committed to carry out his plan.

He drove to Diane's house and found it empty. "It would likely stay that way for a long time." He muttered. He went to the place where he had buried the crucifix and with a small shovel uncovered it and after cleaning off the loose dirt placed it into the trunk of his vehicle. Everything was now in place for his next move.

Fred was on anxious as he waited for the unknown events that must take place. Connally had told him that the folder had been moved in his absence and that most certainly meant that Naples had read its contents. He would only be able to react to whatever the Sgt. did.

# 71

On Thursday morning Naples was ready for his move that he was convinced would remove any treat to his well-being. He followed his plan carefully, knowing that one mistake could unravel the entire plot.

At ten a.m. he left for Saint Agnes and went directly to the church. He took the crucifix with its cord still attached and placed it inside his jacket and entered the church. Without any hesitation he went up the stairs and climbed the ladder to the bell tower. On his way up he noticed that the ladder rungs were worn from years of use.

The one weak point in his plan was that he had to depend on was the reaction of the bell ringer. His knowledge of human nature gave him confidence that the risk was minimal. He took the crucifix and hung it on the wall in a position that would be out of sight when one entered the tower but could not be missed when preparing to descend. He wanted to be certain that the bell was rung at noon as it always was. If he had interpreted the reaction of the bell ringer correctly, the ringer would leave the crucifix in place and tell the house keeper what he had seen. Naples intended to observe what took place from a distance. If things went as planed he was ready for his next step.

At a few minutes before noon Edward Comeau, the official bell toiler, walked up the road and entered the church. At precisely twelve the bell rang once and there was a slight delay before Edward came out. He paused at the entrance, as if uncertain of what to do. He went around the church and knocked at the rectory door. A lady opened the door and the two entered into a brief conversation. Naples noted that nothing was exchanged. His plan was right on track.

Father Frotten returned to Saint Agnes Parish after a pleasant day with his counter part, Father Robichaud, in town. He was looking forward to a quiet night and was surprised to find a note on the kitchen table. It was short and simply said. "Edward found your missing crucifix. It's in the bell tower hanging on a red cord."

The priest gasped in anguish as he attempted to comprehend what was happening. The last time he had seen the cross was at Diane's when he had carried out God's order. Could this be a message from his Savior? He told himself that he must recover the Crucifix and hide it in a place where it would never be found.

He hurried to the church, switched on the tower light and began to climb the ladder. Little did he realize that a predator was waiting in the tower for its prey?

Naples had parked his auto in the cemetery area behind a clump of trees and with the equipment he would require he had climbed into the bell tower. He prepared the area according to his plan and sat down to wait. While he waited, he reviewed the piece of paper that he had found in Diane's home and wondered what kind of a reaction he was going to get when he taunted the priest.

Father Frotten emerged from the ladder entrance and found himself face to face with the Sgt.

"Good evening Father." Naples said. "I'm glad you accepted my invitation. How are you today?"

Frotten's face turned a chalk white as he realized he had fallen into a trap. His mind turned somersaults as he tried to find a means of escape.

In his panic he had failed to notice the cross held by Naples. "Don't you think this is an instrument that was intended to deliver justice?" He asked.

Frotten had finally regained enough composure to try and reason with Naples. "It has already been used by God to correct grave errors." He said. "It should now be hung in a place of honor; it has fulfilled its intended roll."

By the look on the Sgt.'s face he could see that his religious approach was wasted.

Naples reached into his pocket and produced the paper that he was certain would push Frotten over the edge into insanity. He asked the priest if he was proud of having shared Diane with the other men and he read off their names.

Frotten was in such a state of fury that he failed to notice Naples motion until it was too late. The red cord was in place around his neck and pressure was being applied.

Naples addressed the priest as he gradually twisted the crucifix "You're the most despicable person that the devil ever created. How does it feel to be treated the way you treated Diane?"

Not expecting an answer he continued to tighten the cord but allowed enough slack to prolong Frotten's suffering. The pleading in Frotten's eyes had no effect on his actions and the priest finally slumped to the floor. Naples maintained the pressure until he was certain Frotten had gone to his just reward.

His next planned task was to make the death look like a suicide. He had made considerable preparation to provide this effect. His first move was to place the body in a position so that the red cord could be tied to the bell rope at the correct knot to have the body suspended in mid air. This accomplished, he pulled the bell rope until the bell was almost in contact with its clapper and he secured it in that position using a long rope he had brought. The knot he used to tie this in place was a bow knot that would hold an item in place until it was released by pulling the end that formed the bow.

After placing the red rope around Frotten's neck he coiled his release rope in preparation for his climb down the ladder. If all went the way he planed, the bell would ring once and the Priest would be hanging just above the platform level. There was plenty of time to leave the scene before anyone arrived and he would be free. He looked the place over to make certain he didn't leave any evidence and saw the paper he must have dropped on the floor. He picked it up and placed it in his breast pocket.

He lowered the release rope gently to the floor and began his decent. The third rung he placed his weight on gave way. As he started to fall his foot tangled in the release rope and he went plunging head first unto the floor below. The release rope functioned the way it had been designed to do. The priest's body was jerked off the platform and the bell rang once. Unfortunately for Naples he never heard the gong, he was dead the moment he hit the floor.

# 72

The members of the Parish heard the bell toll and the few phones in the area were quickly put to use. There was no answer at the rectory phone. The bell had never rung at such an odd time unless there was some sort of emergency.

Unable to ascertain the reason several male members of the community including the official bell caretaker converged on the church steps wondering why the priest wasn't there to explain. Someone ran to the rectory and found the place empty.

Uncertain of how and why the bell had sounded Edward suggested they go up and see if the priest was in the tower. They reached the top of the stairs and that's as far as they went.

Sprawled out on the floor was the body of Sgt. Naples with a long rope by his side. Someone said. "We had better call the RCMP." And another said. "But they're already here." Panic set in as they ran out of the church.

Edward Comeau had taken charge and determined that the RCMP should be notified, especially since the victim was one of their own.

Constable Sears was on duty when the call from the rectory came. He made Edward repeat his message twice to make sure he had heard correctly. "There is a dead RCMP officer in the Saint Agnes church. It looks like your Sgt. Naples." He repeated and hung up.

Sears was overwhelmed by this unexpected message and was undecided on the correct action he should take. A normal response was to send one of the off duty Constables to check out the complaint but this was far from being ordinary. He made up his mind that the safest thing to do was call Inspector Connally.

When the Inspector received the message, he was shocked. Assuming that the information was accurate there could be only one answer, the Sgt. had confronted the priest and somehow Frotten had won? The setup he and Fred had concocted had given results, but not what they had expected.

He called Sears and told him to tell Constable LaPiere to pick him up at his home.

On their way to the church Connally and Fred discussed the possible impact on the force if the Sgt. was dead and his death was unnatural?

They both realized that their ploy to expose Naples and the priest could have ended in an unexpected way.

"Maybe when we talk to Father Frotten the situation will be clarified." John said.

"The best way to handle this is to keep the local residents away from the body until we have found out how he died."

Fred pulled up in front of the church and they both got out. The villagers were standing around the entrance and it was obvious that they were in a state of confusion.

Inspector Connally addressed the group in a calm voice. "May I speak to the person who called our office?"

Edward stepped forward and said. "I called."

Connally took him aside and motioned for Fred to join them. With the three away from the crowed Connally asked where Father Frotten was.

"We looked for him but he isn't here."

"Tell us what you saw that caused you to call us."

When he had revealed all that he had seen at the top of the stairs the inspector asked him to tell his associates to go home but for him to remain in the rectory. "We will take care of everything and will contact you if we need assistance."

The group slowly dispersed leaving the two RCMP officers alone. They went in and climbed the stairs to the foot of the tower ladder. "Well, they were right about one thing, that's Sgt. Naples and he certainly is dead." The Inspector said.

"It looks like he fell from the top of the ladder. I can see where the rung gave way. I wonder what he was doing up there?" Fred asked.

"We will have to climb up there and see." Connally said. "But how are we going to get up with the ladder broken?" He added.

"I'll go ask Comeau if he can get a substitute ladder." Fred said as he turned to descend the stairway.

He was back in a few minutes accompanied by Edward with a long ladder that they had found in the shed. Between the two of them they put the ladder in place and Edward was told to return to the Rectory.

Fred climbed to the tower and as soon as he entered he called down to the Inspector. "I think you had better come up here. We have another body."

Connally went up with some effort. He thought that his age was beginning to slow him down as he gained the top. What he saw when he emerged through the opening made him gasp.

There, dimly lit by the tower light was Father Frotten, hanging on the bell rope with a red cord around his neck. A crucifix attached to the cord hung down on his chest.

"What an awful way to kill oneself." He muttered. "Or did he?"

Fred, having had more time viewing the scene, expressed his opinion. "I can't figure out what happened. There are many possibilities but nothing obvious comes forward. There's one thing that keeps popping up in my head, the trap we set for the Sgt. has something to do with this."

Connally went over the area with the thoroughness of an experience investigator. His mind was darting in many directions, some of which did not include solving the mystery of what had happened.

It was clear in his mind that they were looking at a murder and an accidental death. If he was correct in his belief, justice had been served.

Exposing several people, both living and dead, to scrutiny by the public with no beneficial results would be foolhardy. In particular the reputation of his organization and that of the Catholic religion was important to all concerned.

"What good would come from washing all their dirty laundry in front of the public when all of the guilty parties were dead?" He asked himself. His main problem was to get certain key parties to play along with his scheme.

The first and most important convert he needed was standing next to him. He looked at Fred and expressed his belief of what had happened.

"The report we made up to push Naples into action certainly seems to have worked but I didn't expect the mess we are looking at. However, with Frotten and Naples dead the courts won't be required to get involved. The guilty have managed to punish each other." He paused to give Fred time to absorb his statement.

Fred had already allowed similar thoughts to wander through his mind and as he waited for the Inspector to continue, he nodded in agreement.

Connally continued. "We could convert the scene into one of two accidental deaths and no one would dispute our findings. There is only one person we would have to convince to approve our deception, Bishop Bonregard."

Fred was in a quandary, this went against all the teachings of the Academy but it presented a solution that would prevent many people from the anguish of having confessed their sins to a corrupt priest. Also, he acknowledged that he had already deviated from the RCMP's normal procedure and that could hurt his future with them. He made his decision and said. "I agree, but how?"

The first thing they did was detach Frotten from the rope being careful to not ring the bell. Fred noted that the strangulation marks were lower than they should have been if Frotten had hung himself. When they straitened out his white collar it covered the marks and made their cover up easier. There were no visible injuries for the curious to see. All that was left was to invent a cause of death and use only trusted individuals to handle the body.

"What do we do with this?" Fred asked, as he held up the crucifix. "No one will ever know what it was used for so why not place it in a corner for someone to find it later?" The Inspector said.

With their plan now in play they descended to the ground level. "I'm going to leave you here to keep people out while I drive back to town. I'll send Constable Smith to help you keep the place secure." Before he left, they told Edward about finding the priest's body and asked him to let the village know.

While he waited, Fred glanced over the area where the Sgt.'s body lay. He noticed a piece of paper sticking out of Naples' jacket. He removed it and glanced over its contents. It was Diane's diary first page. He put it in his pocket with the intention of destroying it if Connally agreed.

# 73

The word spread quickly through the Parish and finally trickled down to the Pottier home. When I heard the news, I asked my mother if it was all right for me to go see Bob for a little while. In spite of the shock she had just received, she said. "Go ahead but don't be long, we're going to have to pray for Father Frotten's soul."

It only took a few minutes to bike over to Bob's. It was obvious from the commotion in the house that the news had beaten him there. After a few exchanges of amazement about what had happened, Bob and I went to the barn to have a private chat.

"We had better not say any thing about what's been going on." I said. "We could be in big trouble if somebody found out."

Bob reminded me that we didn't know what had happened. "Maybe they both died without any connection with what we did. All that we can do is wait for more information."

"Tomorrow's Friday, maybe Julie will have heard more than we have." Danny said. "I have to get back, Mom's extremely upset." We walked to the bicycle and I left for home.

My mother was on her knees with her prayer beads in her hands. Tears were rolling down her cheeks as she prayed. Looking up at me she said. "What a shame, he was such a saintly man."

At that instant I knew my lips were sealed, I could never let my mother know how unsaintly the priest really was." I joined her in her prayers but my thoughts were far removed from any sympathy for Frotten.

As soon as Connally had arranged for Smith to join Fred he returned to his home. He greeted his wife with a quick kiss on her cheek and he told her that he was going to have a busy night. "Both Sgt. Naples and the priest at Saint Agnes church have been found dead in the church. I have to be in charge of the investigation because of the enormity of the situation."

His wife sighed and rendered a comment. "John, don't overdo it, you're not used to working this late."

He went into the living room were their phone was located. He wanted to call Bishop Bonregard in Halifax but he didn't have his number so he called Father Robichaud instead.

When Robichaud answered and the Inspector told him that Father Frotten was dead and it was urgent for him to speak to the bishop. Robichaud was startled by the news and said. "But he was here a little while ago and he seemed healthy then."

Connally was in a hurry but didn't want to aggravate the priest. "I can't explain what happened to him until I inform your Bishop. If you give me his number, I'll make sure you are told the details later.

He was not too concerned about being overheard in his call as both his and the Bishops were private lines. Only the operator could listen in and she would lose her job if she divulged any thing she heard. The phone rang several times before the Bishop answered.

The two were soon involved in a difficult conversation and the Bishop was uneasy with what Connally proposed. Without reaching any agreement Bonregard suggested that he would use Father Robichaud as his messenger.

"I know he is level headed and will give me sound advice. I will call him and tell him to contact you immediately."

Connally agreed and their conversations ended.

Fifteen minutes later Robichaud was on the phone with John who suggested they meet at the town church rectory.

When John arrived he was greeted at the door and ushered in. Without any hesitation he went into a long explanation of what had happened. He included all the information gathered by the entire group and his conclusions derived from it.

Robichaud absorbed the data and after a period of silence in which he seemed to be in deep thought he said. "There seems to be no doubt that these two people were involved in unacceptable conduct, what do you propose we do?"

Connally made sure that the priest appreciated the need to protect the reputation of both organizations and the only way to accomplish this was to fabricate a believable tale that accomplished just that.

Robichaud was beginning to show signs of stress. He was caught in a situation that was never supposed to happen to a man of the Church. Should he support a lie or should he expose the Church to the ravages of the public. The answer was not long in coming, he must protect his religion.

"I will tell the Bishop that it is in our best interest to accommodate your proposal."

He called Bonregard and the deal was finalized.

The Pope and the King had spoken and their orders were carried out.

# 74

When Danny and Bob showed up for their lessons, Fred was there with Julie. Fred had a somber look on his face when he spoke to them.

"It looks like our investigation has come to a sudden halt. We have no one left to probe, they're all dead." He paused for a moment and then continued. "I'm proud of how you pursued your goal, the results of which achieved justice where, without you, justice would have failed. No one will ever know the complete truth about these affairs and it is best to let the people believe that the two new deaths were the result of accidents. Do you agree?"

I had listened to Fred with mixed emotions but I saw that it was the only path we could follow without causing unnecessary grief. I nodded in agreement and looked at Bob.

He seemed glad that our project was over and said. "We only did what we thought was right. If that's what you want I'm with you."

I spoke with a small tremor in my voice. "The people of this Parish may be fooled but I will never forget the evil ways of Father Frotten."

Julie entered into the conversation with a brief statement. "I love you both but as your teacher I must warn you that I expect you to keep your studies up to date." That ended the session for the day.

There was a funeral at the Saint Agnes Church that would probably never be equaled. The officiating cleric was none other than Bishop Bonregard. The church was packed and there was an overflow of mourners that blocked the road. After the ceremony, there were many tearful women all praising the saintly priest that had just been laid to rest. The bishop was pleased with the outcome; the church had avoided a scandal that would have taxed the beliefs of its members.

Another funeral was held in Rivemouth, but in this case the crowd was meager, consisting mostly of his former underlings and a few of his town friends. Sgt Naples had been catered to but had never been liked.

# POSTLUDE

The members of Saint Agnes Parish, Acadians all, survived the trauma of having lost their beloved leader and soon adapted to a new, younger and more open-minded Priest.

There were major changes in the Rivemouth RCMP detachment. Inspector Connally retired and returned to his place of origin. Fred resigned from the force and he formed an investigative group in Toronto with his wife, Julie, who was now able to do the kind of work she loved.

Danny and Bob finished their equivalent ninth grade education but were unable to continue when they lost their teacher.

Bob remained in Seal Lake and followed in his father's footsteps.

Danny joined the Canadian army in 1941 and was decorated for bravery in action. He went on with many educational handicaps to become a graduate engineer.

Sam was elevated to Chief of Police when Chief Roland White died of a harth attack and improved the Rivemouth law enforcement.

Constable Elliot had disappeared from his Halifax office and was never found. Yvette had received a letter, through a mutual friend, from Vinnie so she knew that the body in the ship was not his.

Diane's money was never found.

One area that went on as usual was the bootlegger trade, it still exists today

# About the Author

Joe Le Blanc served during World War II and the Korean War. He obtained a bachelor's degree in mechanical engineering from the University of Nebraska and worked in the aerospace industry, including work with the lunar landing program.

Printed in the United States
By Bookmasters